ASSIGNMENT: RENO, NEVADA

BY

ELIZABETH JUNG

© 2003 by Elizabeth Jung. All rights reserved.

No part of this book may be reproduced, stored in a retrieval system, or transmitted by any means, electronic, mechanical, photocopying, recording, or otherwise, without written permission from the author.

ISBN: 1-4107-3339-4 (e-book)
ISBN: 1-4107-3338-6 (Paperback)
ISBN: 1-4107-3337-8 (Dust Jacket)

Library of Congress Control Number: 2003092269

This book is printed on acid free paper.

Printed in the United States of America
Bloomington, IN

1stBooks – rev. 05/05/03

OTHER NOVELS BY ELIZABETH JUNG

THE BUDAPEST CONNECTION

GAME BETWEEN SPIES

PROJECT EVE

FORTHCOMING: IOWA'S DOUBLE AGENT

This is a book of fiction. All the characters and incidents portrayed in this book are fictitious; any resemblance to real people or events is purely coincidental. All characters have no existence outside of the imagination of the author and have no relation whatsoever to anyone bearing the same name or names.

Copyright by Elizabeth J. Jung 2003
WEBSITE:www.elizabethjung.com

Reproduction of this work in whole or in part in any form by any means, electronic, mechanical or other, now known or hereafter invented is forbidden without the written permission of the author.

ACKNOWLEDGMENTS

This book is dedicated to all my friends in Reno, Nevada and across the fifty states who offer technical information and encouragement, especially to David Daniel, Debbie Kennedy, Carol Crane, Kathy Livierato, John and Rena Chedester, Jack Cui and Rose Marie Wolden. Also, to my great editors, Matt Jung, Constance Luedtke, Gene and Lois Vanderbur as well as those special friends around the world who have offered their advice and kindness. Finally, with much humility and sincerity, a special thanks to you, my readers, who take time out of your busy schedules to read my books.

ASSIGNMENT: RENO, NEVADA

CHAPTER ONE

The former model's long silky blonde hair had been perfectly arranged, adding the right touch of color as it fanned out across the satin blue pillows. She looked beautiful. Her long slender arms had been crossed and the palms of her hands rested flat against her perfect shaped breasts. The thin straps of her shocking pink nightgown rested on her smooth white shoulders.

A decorative bright floral bedspread had also been carefully arranged to cover the rest of her body as well as the entire bed. With just a casual glance, no one could see that it been placed to hide the puddles of her blood and her numerous stab wounds.

The rest of the master bedroom was undisturbed. Everything was in its proper place and neatly arranged.

Down the gray, plush carpeted hall, a three-month old baby boy laid on his back, lifeless in his blue expensive crib. His numerous brightly colored toys had been carefully arranged below his feet. His dark blue blanket had been placed over his multi-colored terry cloth sleeper. A large white teddy bear with a bright blue ribbon had been carefully propped against the bottom corner post.

Across the room, blood dripped from the diaper-changing table onto the soft blue carpet. A long, blood- soaked kitchen knife had been discarded into the empty diaper pail. A stack of disposable diapers was piled on a near-by white table. Blood spots dotted the top diaper and beads of blood glistened on the white tabletop.

Across the room, broken pieces of a home monitoring system lay on the windowsill. In front of the open hallway door, milk from a crushed plastic baby bottle soaked the bedroom carpet and formed a large white-crusted circle.

Further down the hallway, a six-year old girl lay motionless on the floor just outside of her bedroom. Her long blonde hair and blue pajamas were soaked with blood. She clutched a once white cordless telephone to her chest.

Several large bloody footsteps covered the hall carpet. They formed a trail from the master bedroom to the nursery and down the hall to the girl's bedroom. Then, the footsteps turned, went down the stairway to the first floor and eventually out the front door.

CHAPTER TWO

A sudden noise caused Joe Collins to jerk. He rubbed his gray hairy chin, blinked and shook his head several times to clear the horrible memories from his mind. He stretched his neck back and forth. Once again, he had fallen asleep at the kitchen table.

He bit his lip, sniffed, reached up and wiped a tear from his cheek. Even after twenty years the memories of his family's murders were painful to remember. They were as realistic as the pictures he had seen of the crime scene.

He still lived with the guilt. He would never forgive himself. In those days, he had trusted others. He had put his job before his family.

Then, he believed what his supervisors had preached, that an agent's family was "off limits". Unfortunately, he learned the hard way. No one and nothing was "off limits" to the enemy.

After his family's deaths, Joe, the Knife, threw himself into his work hoping to ease the pain. No assignment was ever too dangerous. But, still the years passed slowly.

ELIZABETH JUNG

Glancing up, he twisted in the straight back chair and caught his image in the cloudy glass cabinet door across the room. He was almost sixty-five. His body ached from the numerous broken bones and torn muscles.

He stood up, stretched and then walked around the small room. His stomach growled but he ignored it. These days food was not important.

Suddenly, he smiled. He walked over to his desk and sat down admiring his newly acquired Hans Meyer-Kassel painting leaning against the wall on the other side of the room. He fought back tears as he remembered bartering with Charlie. He leaned back in his desk chair and held his head in his hands.

Now, the untimely death of Charlie McGuire flashed in and out of his thoughts. Joe rubbed his hairy chin, and looked up, studying the small, cluttered, dilapidated shack that he called home. Tears ran down his face.

Suddenly, a heavy thud banged against the front door. The wood vibrated causing the hinges to groan. He jumped up, instinctively rubbed his hand against his right leg feeling for his knife. He jerked and stared at the door. His eyes froze on the worn glass doorknob. The years melted away as he stood alert, ready to spring into action.

Ever since Charlie's death, unexpected sounds spooked him. His dark piercing eyes darted back and forth across the inside wall. Dead silence filled the room. He sensed movement, probably that of an animal.

After listening for several seconds, he sighed, relaxed, and took a deep breath. He shrugged believing it was only a stray cat or raccoon. He knew they roamed freely outside of his house because the river was so near.

Settling back in the desk chair, he felt a slight chill. Shivering, he reached for one of the old wool blankets piled high in a basket beside his desk. After pulling the old Indian style blanket over his shoulders, he leaned across the top of the desk. A strange sense of darkness filled him.

He shook his head several times, trying to fend off his sudden depression. Recently, thoughts of retiring had flowed through his mind. But, tonight he shuddered at the thought of having nothing to do. Maybe, all he needed was to move out of this riverside tarpaper shack and back into a regular house with four solid walls and neighbors. Maybe, he would even leave Reno.

Joe, a short, thin, pale looking man, shivered again and pulled the worn Indian blanket tighter over his bony, narrow shoulders. He felt unusually cold and damp despite the blanket and his long sleeved denim shirt. He rubbed his hands together. They felt cold and clammy.

He looked around the room but his vision had grown blurry. With his cold hand, he touched his warm forehead, and then rubbed his throat. It felt swollen and scratchy. He wondered if he was getting sick?

With his arms tight across his chest, he glanced up toward the letter from the city of Reno on the kitchen table. He hadn't even bothered to open it.

From the size of the envelope and the return address, he knew it was just another offer from the city for his land. His eyes moved over to the stack of similar letters piled two inches high on the windowsill.

Pulling the blanket tighter, still he turned slightly and caught a glimpse of his reflection in the mirror. His eyes widened. He shivered. He could scarcely recognize the old man's face and the cold dark eyes that stared back at him.

Dumbfounded, he considered his own reflection. The man in the reflection had greasy, tangled, silvery shoulder-length hair. The man looked dark, dirty and aged. He gasped when he realized he was that old man.

Joe sniffed and dug through his dirty pocket for a handkerchief. He hated admitting, even to himself, how much he missed his long-time buddy, Charlie.

His eyes moved to the corner of the table. The deck of cards was still in the same place where Charlie had left them after their last card game.

His friend, police lieutenant Tom Clausen's words suddenly flashed into his mind. Clausen had casually commented that Charlie's death seemed suspicious and said that the police hadn't ruled out foul play.

Joe, the Knife, stiffened and started sniffing. He wished he'd been more attentive to Charlie and knew more about what Charlie had been doing those last days of his life. Now, he wished he'd questioned Charlie about the desk, chair and paintings. He would like to know their origin. But, maybe it was best that he didn't know.

Carefully, Joe rubbed the top of the desk with the tips of his fingers. His hands moved slowly feeling the grain, trying to pull its history out of the wood. The top felt smooth and warm. Joe knew, just from the appearance, that the desk was not only a very expensive one but also possessed a deep dark secret.

Joe reached around, ran his fingers up and down the wood of the chair, and smiled. In his mind, the items still were Charlie's and he was only watching them for his friend. Even though he knew Charlie would never be back to claim them.

Suddenly, Joe jerked as car lights swung into view and moved up the long lane. They reflected in the small round car mirror attached outside to Joe's window. Normally, car lights meant someone had gotten lost and was too close to the river. For several seconds, Joe sat motionless and listened and watched.

He turned his good ear toward the outside wall and leaned forward to listen for the sound of the car turning around, realizing its mistake.

The lights, however, kept creeping up the narrow gravel driveway. Then, the lights finally stopped. The driver was near the river. The driver carefully turned the car so the lights shone directly on Joe's house and through his window.

Joe tensed and pressed his lips together. His eyes grew dark and cold. A puzzled expression covered his face. Something was very wrong. Thirty years of experience had his senses on alert.

He rarely had unexpected company, never after dark. With caution, he took his time getting up, folded the blanket and placed it neatly back on the stack with the others in the basket.

His heart raced. He looked around the tiny house to make sure nothing was out of place and his cover was intact. He debated for a split second as adrenalin rushed through his veins.

Grabbing a flashlight, he slipped from the state of a psychologically depressed old man back into his second-nature cover role. He stepped into his old worn shoes and shuffled toward the door.

"What do you want?" Joe called. He aimed the beam from his bright flashlight at the passenger side of the stopped car. His raspy voice sounded unusually loud in the cool night air. He shook his long silvery hair back from his eyes and crept out from behind the shadows.

The driver moved the car forward slowly and then stopped. The bright headlights flooded the entire yard. A car door creaked as it was being opened, and then someone appeared to step out.

Joe stepped backward, set his flashlight on a nearby lawn chair and shielded his eyes with his hands. He squinted and watched a shadow move toward him.

To the right, the familiar sound of the Truckee River slapped against the large rocks on the riverbank. The splashing added to Joe's tenseness.

The stranger's shoes made a strangely loud shuffling sound as he walked toward Joe. The car door closed. A clicking sound vibrated and magnified in the cool spring air. Without a word, the driver backed the car several feet down the long lane. He stopped directly under a dim yard light keeping the headlights on.

The moon moved out from behind a large cloud and Joe saw an unusually tall man move toward him. Joe clenched his teeth together and pushed his hands deep into his dirty overall pockets. For a split second, he took his eyes off the tall man, stepped back out of the headlight beam and glanced past the figure toward the mysterious car.

The stranger continued walking toward Joe. Closer now, his fingernails made a scratching sound when he brushed them against his long tan camel hair overcoat.

The stranger turned his head slowly, while his eyes seemed to dart back and forth along the riverbank. He clamped down on his teeth with a grinding sound. His expression hardened as he stepped directly into Joe's flashlight beam.

"I just want to talk to you and ask you a few simple questions," the stranger said, relaxing his jaw slightly. He spoke slowly and distinctly while he studied his freshly manicured nails in the moonlight, holding each nail out in front of him for close inspection.

Joe kicked at the small loose pebbles on the side of the riverbank and shook his head. He moved the flashlight beam up and down over the well-dressed man and then he glanced down at his own shoes.

"Damn," he said in disgust when he saw the gray duct tape flopping from the toe of his left shoe. Squatting down, he pressed the tape back around his loose sole. He made several noises, stood back up and stared at the stranger.

Joe knew that he had met the man before, but wasn't sure when or where. There was something familiar about the way the tall man moved his long legs, as if they were stiff or his feet hurt. Joe rubbed his chin a couple of times, looked up at the tall man and wheezed.

"I didn't tell nobody about nothing and I don't know nothing about nothing."

"Oh, but I think you do know something," the tall man answered. A broad smile covered his face revealing a perfect set of white sparkling teeth.

The stranger took a small step toward the dirty man, but stopped jerking backward. He frowned and made a face. His expression showed that he was obviously taken aback by the strong smell of sweat and decay coming from Joe and his clothing.

Joe continued to stand and stare. His eyes widened. He gulped as he remembered where he had seen the tall man. Nervously, he slid his feet slowly backward on the loose gravel.

Joe's eyes locked onto the stranger's face. He took a deep breath, trying desperately to hide any recognition in his expressions or actions. Turning slightly, Joe pressed his arm against his body releasing a mechanism inside his shirtsleeve.

A cold, sharp knife moved from under his arm and slid down into Joe's open hand. His long, heavy denim sleeve concealed the blade. With a new sense of security, Joe the Knife stalled by scratching first his crotch, and then his chest, as he juggled with the flashlight.

Finally, he said, "What is it I'm supposed to know?"

The tall, freshly shaven man flicked a small crawling bug off his coat sleeve. He jerked his head backward and pushed a long strand of bleached hair out of his face.

He said, "Rumor has it that you were Charlie McGuire's best friend and Charlie told you everything."

ASSIGNMENT: RENO, NEVADA

Joe gasped aloud. His hands began to sweat. His mouth felt dry and he tried to swallow but his throat felt as if it had a hard rock lodged in it.

"Why you asking about poor old Charlie now? He never hurt nobody and he's long gone to his final reward," Joe stammered.

The tall man walked toward Joe, leaned down, and placed his large hands on Joe's thin shoulders. With enormous force, the stranger pressed his thumbs deep into Joe's flesh. He smiled as Joe cringed with pain.

"Charlie had some things of mine and I want you to help me get them back," he said. His eyes never left Joe's face.

"Hell, man," Joe sputtered as he tried to pull away. He weaved a bit and his words were now purposely slurred. "I've been drinking ever since Charlie's funeral. I don't remember saying anything about old Charlie's death. If I did, it must have been the liquor talking."

The tall man released the pressure on Joe's shoulders. He rubbed the bony shoulders gently. "I also heard you were saying that Charlie had been murdered."

Joe jerked away from the man and started zigzagging back and forth across the yard. He dropped his head forward onto his chest, looked around, saw a big rock and stumbled toward it.

"Old Charlie never hurt nobody," Joe kept muttering. "All he ever wanted was to be left alone so he could work with his stuff."

The tall man sighed. "Do you know who I am?"

Joe caressed the cold blade in the palm of his hand with his fingers. He stood still and stared at the tall man, then moved slowly away from him. He cocked his head, closed one eye and asked, "Are you a cop?"

The tall man chuckled and rubbed his hands together. He glanced back at the car, then at his watch. "What makes you ask that?"

The dirty man looked at the tall man's shoes. A pale light reflected off the toes. Joe said, "Cops always shine their shoes." Reflecting his light off the tall man's shoes. "They learn that at the academy."

The tall man looked down at his feet. He lifted each foot and rubbed each shoe against his creased tan docker trouser leg and smiled. "Actually, I'm old Charlie's friend. We did business together. I'm hoping you can also help me. Do you have keys to his vaults or storage sheds?"

Joe jumped up and sighed with relief. He opened his toothless mouth and smiled. "Sure, I've got keys to old Charlie's units. What is it you want from there? Must be pretty important for you to come out at night like this?"

"Yes, it's very important," the tall man said. He pointed toward the road. "My car is parked there. Are you ready? We'll go now."

The tall man looked toward the old falling-down shack and shook his head with disgust. He turned and took a couple steps toward the car.

"I'll be just a minute," Joe answered quickly. He darted back toward his house and disappeared. The sound of a door opening, someone bumping into things and a door closing filled the late night air. Within seconds, Joe was back, waving a large key chain. The clinking of the heavy keys could be heard as he moved into the yard. Joe chuckled and said, "I'm ready."

The tall man waited for Joe to walk toward him. Rolling his eyes, he stepped down wind. "The car is straight ahead," he said, fanning the air in front of him as he trailed behind the foul smelling man.

"You never did say what you need from Charlie's vaults," Joe said. He walked with a quick step; all evidence of his heavy drinking seemed gone.

"When we get there, I'll tell you," the stranger answered. "Hurry up, it's getting colder than Siberia out here." The tall man took long steps and arrived at the long black car seconds before Joe.

"Nice car you got here," Joe commented. He kept both of his hands deep in his overall pockets. Without displaying any concern for his safety, Joe stepped closer to the car and began walking around examining it. He stopped for a second and memorized the California license plate.

The tall man stood back, shook his head and watched Joe. He glanced at his watch and made a hissing sound.

"Came from quite a ways?" Joe asked. He spit on the ground. "I don't remember old Charlie telling me about his doing any business with anyone outside of the state of Nevada. Least of all from California."

"Well, he did," the tall man answered. He brushed something off his coat and cringed. "I'm quite sure old Charlie didn't tell you everything he did." He motioned toward his driver. "Open the door for our guest. He's going to go with us to Charlie's vaults." He turned back toward Joe and continued. "You do have the keys to Charlie's storage units with you, don't you?"

"Sure, I've got them all right here. I have them all numbered and tagged," Joe said, patting his overall pocket. "Which unit did you want to see?"

The driver moved quietly from the front of the car to where Joe was standing. His broad shoulders and big build towered over Joe. He stood directly behind Joe and asked in a deep, loud voice, "How many places did this Charlie have anyway?"

Joe jerked backward. The unexpected words startled him. Joe hunched his shoulders forward and said, "Hey, I thought you said you knew all about old Charlie's stashes?"

The driver grunted and shuffled his feet back and forth on the gravel, his eyes never leaving Joe's face. "We do," he said. "I just wanted to know which ones we were going to visit."

Joe moved his head back and forth between the driver and the tall man. He began backing away from the car. His eyes filled with fear. His fingers caressed the knife he had slid into his pocket.

The driver took several quick steps toward Joe. With his eyes fixed on his boss, the driver slid his hand into his coat pocket. He glanced back at his boss and nodded.

Joe saw the two men exchanging glances. He knew something was horribly wrong. He needed time to think. As a ploy, he began coughing and bent over. It gave him a chance to judge the distance to safety.

After several seconds, he stood up wheezing. "Well, what say I give you the keys and you two go on to Charlie's storage units? I really don't feel too good. Think I'm coming down with the flu." He took a couple of steps sideways, trying to get out of the driver's way.

The tall man looked across the top of the car, moved his head slightly and opened the rear car door on his side. He hissed, nodded again and climbed inside the car without another word.

The driver stepped behind Joe, patted him on the shoulder and said, "I'm a stranger to Reno. You'll have to come along and help me with directions."

He reached across in front of Joe, opened the rear car door, stepped aside and grunted, "Get in!"

Joe stepped forward. He had seen the men exchange nods and knew it was too late to back out. He turned and glanced toward his shack. He silently looked up and hoped Charlie was watching him from the heavens.

Feeling his knife again, he sighed, said a silent prayer and took another step forward. He cringed when he felt the driver's hand push against his back trying to hurry him forward.

Joe's eyes widened with fear. He tried to move away but couldn't. His arm jerked and he tried to get his hand out of his pocket, but his knife caught on the key chain. It was too late.

With his free hand, Joe grabbed his neck as he felt the pain. With a sudden burst of strength he tossed his flashlight behind him into the bushes. His warm blood hissed and bubbled down his hand. "What are you really after? Who sent you?" Joe asked gasping as he slid to the ground.

CHAPTER THREE

It was early spring. The sun moved slowly behind the clouds over a small isolated village in Switzerland. The shops had just closed and the owners had all walked down the narrow cobblestone streets to their homes. Thin swirls of chimney smoke covered the landscape as the local residents settled into their normal evening activities.

On the edge of the town, hidden among tall pine trees upon a large rolling hill sat a black six-foot iron fence. An elderly guard could be seen inside a weathered wooden hut at the end of a narrow stone driveway entrance. A stack of daily newspapers from all over the world was spread out on the table in front of him.

He glanced at his watch and looked toward the low, sprawling white buildings at the end of the secluded driveway. Squinting through a pair of half-rim glasses, he could just make out the roof of the compound hidden from the street by a hedge.

An old black telephone hanging on the wall behind him rang. He glanced again at his watch and moved a white sheet of typed paper out from underneath his stack of newspapers. "Ja," he answered with a strong German accent.

For several seconds he listened without saying a word. Occasionally, he would shake his head and turn his face back toward the buildings.

After he put the phone back in the cradle, he took a wool gray loden jacket from the back of his chair. He carefully buttoned all of the buttons and reached into a drawer and pulled out a set of keys. With the typed instructions in his hand, he opened the small door and stepped out into the cool spring evening air.

For a few seconds, he stood and listened to the growing night sounds. Everything was quiet. Only the whistle of a distant train broke nature's symphony.

Again, he glanced at his watch. Turing on his heels, he walked several steps behind the hut and opened the door of a shiny new black Mercedes sedan. Quickly, he put the key in the ignition and started the vehicle.

Without thinking, he turned on the car's lights and slowly crept up the long driveway toward the buildings on the hill. As he drove, he watched through his rear view mirror, never changing his facial expression.

As the car neared the long, low main building in the middle of the complex, he glanced toward the entrance. It was lit with a single ornate hanging light. On cue, a tall man stepped out of the shadows and walked gingerly down the steps.

The man was dressed completely in dark clothing and carried a small black overnight bag. He glanced past the car, staring at the driveway. Slowly, he swiveled around, turning his head carefully as he scrutinized the hospital grounds.

The old guard stopped the car in front of the tall man. Then, exiting the car, he opened the trunk of the Mercedes, and turned toward the man. He asked, "Would you like to put your bag in here?"

The man nodded, not saying a word. He walked around the car and held his small bag out for the old man. Opening the rear door of the car that was directly behind the driver, he got in. The light from the entrance reflected off of the tall man's head. His face was covered completely in white bandages.

The older man shut the trunk and got back into the driver's seat. Without turning toward the patient in the rear seat, he said, "This is going to be a long, all night trip. Please make yourself comfortable."

The tall man extended his long legs across the rear seat. He kicked off his black leather slip-on shoes and reached for a pillow and blanket on the seat beside him. He grunted.

As the Mercedes crept along through the village and headed for the highway, the old man reached over and turned on the radio. The sound of easy listening music filled the car breaking the silence.

It was a few minutes before five in the morning when the black Mercedes pulled into the Hilton Hotel parking lot in Vienna, Austria. The streets were almost deserted.

"We have arrived," the old man announced, stopping in front of the main door. He immediately went to the trunk and delivered his passenger's bag to the doorman at the hotel. He then walked back and got into the Mercedes.

He glanced back at the rear seat through the rear view mirror, shifted his eyes forward and looked straight ahead. Several minutes later, he heard the rear door open and felt the rider exit the car.

As soon as the car door shut, the driver started the car and pulled out of the parking lot. He never looked back. Without thinking, he drove down Linke Wienzeile and followed the signs toward the Sudautobahn that lead to Salzburg.

Glancing at the car's clock, he knew it would take him an hour to drive to Melk. That was his next scheduled stop.

Again holding the instructions in his hand, he read them and nodded. For the past twenty years, he had made many similar trips. He always dropped off a passenger and picked up another one.

But, today, it was different. This time he felt as if he were doing something wrong. A shiver ran through his body. Shaking, he rubbed his hands together, then reached over and turned the heat on.

Over the years, he had never wanted to know who his guests were for fear of getting involved. To him they were always just a number.

Feeling a bit tired, on the outskirts of Vienna he stopped at a rest stop. As a part of his normal routine, he opened the trunk of the car and took out a large plastic bag. Then, he opened the rear door of the car and put the discarded bandages into the bag.

He examined the pillow and hit it a couple times against the side of the car. Checking it again, he smiled and picked off some blond hairs that were still clinging to the fabric.

After returning it to the seat, he took the blanket and shook it with all of his energy. He checked it carefully for any hairs or fibers, then folded it and put it neatly on the pillow on the back seat. As he shut the rear door, he noticed a small white notepaper had fallen to the ground.

Without thinking, he reached down, picked it up and glanced at it. It read, "HAVE A SAFE TRIP BACK TO MOSCOW" in bold, black letters.

Quickly, he tore the paper into several small pieces and held the pieces up for the wind to catch. With wide eyes, he watched as the tiny shreds of paper floated through the air, landing in the tall trees near him.

Nervously, he put the trash bag into the trunk, got back into the car and started down the highway. At Melk, he would make sure the bag was put into a container to be burned. With the latest testing techniques, he didn't want anyone tracing anything back to him, the hospital, or his passengers.

CHAPTER FOUR

Johnny Collins threw his tan lightweight jacket over the corner of the chair and walked into the family room. He had just returned from his walk that took him from his home on North Shore Drive down to the main street of Clear Lake and back. Despite the hour walk and cool brisk air, he still felt depressed.

It had been over a month since he had left the Central Intelligence Agency in Langley, Virginia. Officially, he was on administrative leave. He knew that was just polite paperwork terminology. It was really the agency's way of telling him that he was burned out.

After returning to the states from his assignments in Belgrade and Vienna, his heart just wasn't in his work anymore. With the fall of the Iron Curtain, things had changed. During the communist regime, he could tell the bad people from the good people but now it was confusing.

Former KGB agents were everywhere. Some were legitimate businessmen, some were agents for Arab or South American countries, and some were mercenaries that sold their services to the highest bidder. Many were still working with the Russian government.

Johnny wasn't stupid. He knew former Russian agents both in Belgrade and Vienna had used him to accomplish their goals. He was tired. He just didn't feel like playing the game any longer.

Walking to the front door of his house, he looked out toward the lake. He pushed the patio door open, stepped out on the deck and looked around.

His wife was standing by the big oak tree in their front yard. She was talking to a neighbor while the neighbor's two small children played near them. For a moment, he thought of joining the two women, but made a face, shook his head, turned and walked back into the house.

He loved his lakeshore house. It was a large two-story, four-bedroom home with a double car garage. He knew he had the better of two worlds because his home was on a corner directly across from the lake. He had no one in front of him blocking his view of the water. And, he owned several feet of the sand beach lakefront directly in front of his house yet he didn't have to maintain a seawall.

His main worry was having his houseguests and family members shake the sand off before they walked through his front doorway.

After closing the sliding glass door, he walked to the kitchen and glanced up at the clock on the wall. Accidentally, he caught a glimpse of his face in the microwave door. Smiling, he brushed back his hair from his eyes and noticed that his worry lines were almost gone.

ASSIGNMENT: RENO, NEVADA

Unconsciously, he opened the refrigerator door and turned to look inside. Unexpectedly, the phone rang. He jerked, stepped back and looked around the room.

Knowing no one else was in the house, he took the few steps to the countertop and reached for the phone. "Yes," he said as he palmed the phone and glanced at the open refrigerator.

He turned around looking through the floor-to-ceiling windows of the living room and saw his wife still talking outside. He held the phone close to his ear and listened. The voice on the other end stopped talking and Johnny stared into space and asked, "Are you sure?"

Johnny drew his lips into a tight line and his eyes grew misty. Nodding a couple times, he finally said, "Yes, I will leave as soon as possible. Yes, I'll be in touch."

He walked back to the countertop, put the receiver in the cradle and sat on one of the bar stools. He glanced up and saw the Hans Meyer-Kassel painting that Joe had sent him for Christmas. The memories flooded forth. With closed eyes, he put his head in his hands. Resting his elbows on the countertop, he started to cry.

Within twenty-four hours, Johnny Collins had parked his rented Ford and was standing outside an antique mall just down from the strip in Reno, Nevada. He looked up at the large neon sign. Pulling a paper out of his brown leather jacket pocket, he reread it, nodded and walked through the door. Five steps inside the store, he stopped and looked around.

His right leg ached. He bent slightly and rubbed the old wound, recalling the night the KGB agent shot him and left him for dead. As always, he wondered if the old memories would ever vanish.

The trip from Mason City, Iowa through Minneapolis to Reno had been long and tiring. Now, he wished that he had checked into his motel first. He could have showered and taken a couple of hours to rest and collect his thoughts. His stomach growled and he took a deep breath.

Today, he was acting strictly on impulse and gut feelings. It was totally different from the way he had been trained and how he had operated for over twenty years.

He couldn't remember ever having started a project or operation without some type of a plan. Before, there were lives at stake, but this time it was completely different. This time, he had to take care of family matters. This time, it was personal.

There was no one else that mattered. Just him. No crew. No support team and no reporting to anyone. Just plain old Johnny Collins, the brother of the recently deceased Joe Collins. Not agent Johnny Collins on assignment for the CIA.

Johnny took a deep breath and started forward. The world of antiques, flea markets, even Reno was completely new for him. He could find his way around Europe easier than he could find his way around his brother's small house.

He surveyed the large building and saw aisle after aisle of shelves and racks. What little he did know about antiques, he had learned from watching television shows.

Pictures, rugs, dishes, linen, lamps, cans, bottles, furniture and household items were everywhere.

Johnny smiled as he looked around. He thought many of the things in the mall should have been thrown in the trash, long ago.

Out of curiosity, he walked to an old fifties lamp and looked at the price tag. He gasped. He had no idea that someone could be expected to pay such a high price for such an item. He remembered his mom having one in the house when he was growing up.

At first appearance the rooms all looked cluttered, but as he studied them more carefully, he was surprised to find that everything was really quite organized.

There were things piled on chairs and on top of shelves, things hanging on the walls and from the ceiling. A mixture of dust, old magazines and musty clothing filled the air with the aroma of time.

He stopped, sighed and gathered his bearings. Halfway down the aisle, directly in front of him, was a long, old wooden counter with two ladies behind it.

He held the paper in his hand, glanced at it, looked up, took a deep breath and walked toward the counter. The sound of his footsteps echoed through the silence as he moved forward.

"May I help you?" a middle aged blonde lady asked. She turned her head slightly, politely looked at Johnny for just a second, and then turned her attention back to the pad she was using.

Johnny glanced at the lady and wondered if she owned the place. She looked to be in her mid-fifties, with tiny laugh lines on her face and a figure that showed she either did physical labor or spent many hours in a gym.

"Yes, the Reno police department referred me to you. I've been told you're holding some of my brother's property." He held out his hand.

The lady smiled and slapped the counter top and grabbed his hand. She shook it vigorously and chuckled softly. "Well, I'll be damned. You have to be Joe, the Knife's, little brother, Johnny Collins."

She held Johnny's hand and shook her head. When she finally released it, she stepped back several steps away from the counter, looked at Johnny and continued. "My heavens, just look at the size of you. You certainly look like Joe, but you're a big one and Joe was just a little whippersnapper."

Johnny blushed, leaning against the glass counter top, he glanced down at a display of guns and answered, "I haven't seen Joe in quite some time, but the last time I saw him we looked about the same, just like brothers." He nervously took several paces back and forth, and then asked, "What can you tell me about his property?"

"No, your sure not built like Joe," the lady answered. She turned her head, ran her fingers across her mouth and studied Johnny's face from all sides. "But then, maybe there is a family resemblance. I'm Sarah Cummings and that lady over there is Blue Jean Peggy. I suppose if anybody can help you, we can. Why don't you step back here behind the counter and we'll try to answer your questions."

She motioned for Johnny to walk around the long display counter to an opening. Her short, stubby fingers pointed toward an empty wooden chair pushed back against the wall.

ASSIGNMENT: RENO, NEVADA

Johnny put the paper back in his pocket and followed Sarah's instructions. He pulled the chair closer to the counter, sat down and looked up at the two ladies who glanced back and forth from him to their report.

"Well, we can talk as we work, if you don't mind?" Sarah said. She shifted her chair and positioned herself so she could look at Johnny and still see what she was doing. "It's almost the first of the month, and this work report has to be done so the bills can be ready for mailing by tomorrow night."

"No, go ahead," said Johnny. "I can wait until you're finished."

For several minutes the two ladies talked and Johnny sat and waited. He studied the two ladies and the aisles of old antiques around him.

Finally, Sarah glanced toward Johnny and motioned for Blue Jean Peggy to finish the report. She stood up, stretched her shoulders up and down and walked over to Johnny's chair.

She moaned and said, "Getting old. These old shoulders are starting to ache from all of this." She moved her head back and forth and rubbed her neck and shoulders.

Johnny glanced at her but had no idea what to say. He didn't want to cause any friction between the two of them and knew that he needed her help to settle Joe's estate.

She walked to Johnny, stood directly in front of him and said, "So, Johnny Collins you've been one hard son-of-a-gun to find. That creepy lawyer friend of Joe's was down here a couple times in the past day or so and must have called a dozen times. He was trying to get information about Joe's things." She frowned, bent her head down toward Johnny's face, squinted and continued. "Is it true that you worked for the Central Intelligence Agency?"

She studied Johnny's face, put her hands on her hips and stared right into his eyes. Her expression was frozen.

Johnny jerked, shifted his legs and tried to avoid both ladies' eyes. Finally, he nodded and said, "I'm what you might called semi-retired. Now, I'm living on the lake in Clear Lake, Iowa, and spend almost every waking hour fishing."

Blue Jean Peggy stood, put her pencil down, ran her fingers through her short gray hair, wiggled, adjusted her tight jeans and walked toward Johnny. Reaching him, she leaned forward and spoke softly. Her full breasts pushed against her tight blouse as she talked.

Grinning, she said, "Why would a young man like you be retired? Hell, Joe was just over sixty and he told me you were years younger than him." She shivered, moved her hourglass figure closer to Johnny and waved her heavy perfumed arms in front of his face.

Johnny chuckled and answered, "I'm what you might call semi-retired."

Blue Jean Peggy laughed and continued, "You're too damn young to even be semi-retired. What happened? Did you get your sweet little butt kicked out of the CIA?"

Johnny smiled and shook his head. He could feel his face getting warmer. He wondered what else his brother had told these two ladies about him. "Hell, I haven't seen Joe in almost ten years. I'm surprised that he even remembered how old I was."

Sarah turned on one foot and shook her finger at Johnny. "Now, you listen here. Don't you dare bad mouth our Joe! He was a good man and there was nothing wrong with his memory."

Johnny jerked backward and almost tipped over in the chair. He was happily surprised to hear such loyalty to his brother and wondered what he was stepping into. He held his hands up in front of his face and said, "Whoa! Let's start all over, at the beginning. I just stopped in to find out about Joe's belongings." He looked back and forth between the two ladies. "Then, I'd like to take the two of you to dinner and we can finish our conversation." He looked at his watch. It was almost five. "What time do you close?"

Sarah turned around and looked up at a large old beer clock hanging over the entrance door. She squinted and said, "If that clock's right, we close in about ten minutes."

She turned back toward Johnny, leaned backward and then put her arm around the other lady. She asked, "Blue Jean Peggy, shall we go to dinner with this here stranger?"

Blue Jean Peggy pulled on her flannel shirt and attempted to tuck it into her skintight blue jeans. She shook her short gray hair, twisted her lips and looked at Sarah. Finally, she answered, "Don't see why not."

She turned back to Johnny and asked, "You got any money?"

Johnny smiled and said, "Sure do. If you don't mind, I'll walk around this place while you two finish. Did Joe have anything here?" He looked around and couldn't imagine what Joe might have wanted to sell in an antique mall.

Instantly, Peggy answered, "Yes, he had booth number twenty-four. It is down that aisle straight in front of the counter, back there in the corner." She pointed toward the booth and watched Johnny's eyes follow her arm.

"He usually sold knives, but he'd occasionally put in antique paintings that he found. Since you're his heir, you'll have to tell us what you want us to do with his things."

"I'll let you know later," Johnny answered. He shook his head and walked toward Joe's booth. He gasped. The walls inside the booth were lined with Hans Meyer-Kassel paintings. Johnny was surprised to see such a large collection. It had only been since Christmas that Johnny had become familiar with the German artist's works.

Then, Johnny moved to the two large cabinets full of knives. He knew Joe had always respected his knives, but it was hard for him to believe that Joe owned so many of them, all sizes and shapes.

With all that Joe knew about knives, Johnny couldn't believe that one had been used to kill his brother.

CHAPTER FIVE

"Have you found the items?" Director Korovkin asked. He frowned, looked down at his telephone, pushed a small silver button and switched to his speakerphone. Instantly, the telephone connection became perfectly clear.

Standing, he walked to the window and looked down on Kremlin Square directly below him.

"Well, have you?" he asked again raising his voice. He shivered and shook his head, watching the snowflakes fall. By the calendar it was spring but in Moscow it was still snowing.

Director Korovkin was built like a bear. He had a full head of thick black hair. Although, for the past couple of years he could see a few white ones were creeping in just above his ears.

He stood tall with broad shoulders, a sharp square face and small dark, piercing eyes. With dark facial hair he constantly looked as if he needed a shave. He brushed a strand of hair back from his eyes and turned his attention back to the box on the corner of his massive oak desk.

He walked back to his desk, flipped a switch and watched the computer come to life. After moving the keyboard slightly, he hit a series of keys. The machine hummed and he smiled. He walked back to the window, waiting for the party on the other end of the phone line to answer his question.

"No," Chris Gannon finally answered. His voice quivered slightly as he spoke.

"But, you did talk to Charlie's friend, Joe, didn't you? That is before you killed him?" the Russian asked, raising his voice again.

Korovkin walked back to the desk, sat down and leaned back in his worn leather chair. He glanced at the fish swimming on his computer screen, closed his eyes and tried to organize his thoughts for the upcoming cabinet meeting. He knew it was going to be a difficult one.

He would have to admit in front of all the other agencies' representatives that the merchandise was still missing. He glanced first at the marble clock on his desk and then to the massive antique grandfather clock across the room in the corner. He had less than an hour to come up with an excuse that would be believable.

Chris Gannon said, "Yes, we got the keys from Joe. We knew a couple of addresses and checked them out but we couldn't find anything pertaining to the shipment. We checked all of the warehouses that we know about."

Director Korovkin sighed. "Did you check the obvious places, like his house and place of business?"

He made a face in disgust. He knew he should have sent one of his former KGB agents rather than relying on this "Solder of Fortune" recruit. However, the committee had insisted that it would be cheaper to hire within the United States than send someone from Europe. Now, he knew that the committee had made a mistake in judgment.

Korovkin rubbed his forehead and muttered softly to himself. "When am I going to learn to trust no one?"

"I looked in all the obvious places," Chris answered. His words were crisp, but his voice was still shaky.

"Yes. Yes, I'm sure that you did," the Russian Director answered quickly, not believing a word that the man was saying. He pressed several keys on the computer and then pushed a button on the edge of his desk.

A tall Army-uniformed woman instantly appeared from a door to his left. He took the top file from a stack on his desk and held it out for her. She hurried toward him, took the file, nodded and left without a word.

"I'm going to send someone in to help you search," Korovkin said directly into the telephone. He glanced at his watch. "What time is it there now?"

"It's almost midnight. I was just about to go to bed when the phone rang," Chris Gannon answered.

"His name for this assignment will be Victor Smith. He will be on an Austrian Airline plane to JFK in a couple of hours. With good scheduling, he'll be in Reno within twenty-four hours."

Chris answered quickly. "It really isn't necessary to send someone else here. I can handle this by myself. I still have Oscar working with me."

There was a long silence. Finally, the Russian said, "It has been almost two weeks since Charlie's untimely death. We must find that merchandise. It is settled. Victor will come. Make hotel reservations for him in another hotel somewhere in the city. Then, I want you to move out of that expensive hotel where you are staying and move into something more reasonable in price. I will no longer authorize such extravagant expenses."

Chris Gannon muttered, "Alright."

Korovkin said, "Oh yes, I want you to have Oscar call me."

Gannon questioned, "Tonight? I'm not sure that I'll see him yet tonight. He's probably already gone to bed."

"Yes, tonight," Korovkin answered. "Find him."

Chris Gannon sighed softly. "I'll find him. Do you want me to meet Victor at the airport?"

"It will take ten to twelve hours for him to get to New York. Keep the cell phone with you. He will call you when he makes his arrangements in New York."

"Why don't you e-mail me when he leaves Moscow?" Chris questioned.

The Russian scratched his forehead and then smiled widely. He knew with CIA and NSA's modern technology it was easy for them to trace both cell phones and computer e-mail addresses. He delighted at the prospect of tying up several agents from both agencies as they try to run down a message that he had sent to the states.

With the smile still on his face, he said, "I'll have an e-mail message sent when I know he is in the air.

Be sure and check your cell phone for the text message."

Korovkin again looked over toward his computer and watched the fish on the screen saver. He reached and clicked on the enter button and immediately a screen appeared that gave him access to several of his agents throughout Moscow.

Gannon answered, "I will."

The Russian spoke softly. "In the meantime, before Victor arrives, make a list of places where you haven't looked. The items are small and could be kept almost anywhere. If they haven't been taken out of the cases you will have a better chance of finding them. Check out Charlie's friends and recheck everything about Joe Collins. If I remember correctly he was always good at hiding things."

Gannon asked, "Did you know Joe Collins?"

Korovkin looked down at his hands and rubbed them together. They felt exceptionally cold. After a few seconds, he answered, "Yes, I knew Joe Collins. In fact I was probably the last person to have seen his family. Collins was an old diehard CIA agent."

"Oh," Gannon answered.

There was silence for several seconds and then Korovkin asked, "What do Americans do when they have to store something? Do they have places like we do here in Russia, where they can put things and go back and get them whenever they wish?"

Chris Gannon answered, "Yes, they do. I'll make a list of such places here in the Reno area. Before Victor gets here, I should have some good solid leads."

"Please do," the Russian answered, detecting hostility in Gannon's tone. Korovkin hung up the phone, leaned back and stared at the newspaper that was spread out on his desk. He pulled a file out from under the stack and began staring at it. Off to his side, he could see his computer screen once again return to fish swimming.

After several seconds of studying the file, Korovkin reached for the phone again and pushed a red blinking button. He said, "Victor, were you trying to call me?"

"I just returned to my room and saw the flashing light. What's up?" the agent asked.

"Are you ready for an assignment?" the Russian director asked.

"I've finished packing. Everything is a go on this end. How about on your side, still a go?"

Korovkin shook his head. "Pack a few western style things. There is a slight change in plans."

"Am I still going to the states?" the agent asked.

"Yes, the original mission is still on, but will be delayed a week or so. I'll notify Washington now. I need you to head for the airport. I'll have a messenger take a packet and meet you there. He'll go directly to the phone booth by the check in counter. Watch for him. He'll be carrying a big canvas, dark-blue Nike bag."

Victor Schmitz, the dedicated old KGB agent sighed. He asked, "What name am I going under?"

The Russian laughed. His cheeks shook. "This is easy. You are going as Victor Smith. I doubt whether the Americans will ever get the connection. They are so accustomed to seeing your name spelled the European way."

ASSIGNMENT: RENO, NEVADA

Victor laughed. "That will certainly make it easier for me. Western, you say?"

The old director answered, "Yes. The messenger will have your passport, all necessary information and your funds. You are to be on the next flight to JFK via Frankfurt. I want you arriving in the USA on Austrian Airlines. Switch to Austrian in Frankfurt."

"Where am I headed?" the agent asked.

"Your assignment is Reno, Nevada," the Russian answered. "You are to be on per-diem and if you need clothes for the climate, you can buy them there. Blue jeans should work rather nicely, I would think."

"I've never been to Reno. Sounds like fun. I've heard it's a great party town with lots of women and gambling."

"Just remember you're on a job, not there to eyeball the women or play in the casinos. Any questions?"

Victor laughed. "I understand. Do I go to Washington D.C. when I finish with Reno?"

"Yes, of course," the Russian scolded. "You're just taking a slight detour, but your original assignment is still active. Let your beard grow until you get to Washington. I don't want anything to change that assignment. Shouldn't be any problem. Have you had your shots?"

"I'm fine," Victor answered. "I even had my flu shot when I was in London earlier this winter." There was a short silence and then he asked, "What's the Reno assignment?"

"It has to do with a "shipment" that was supposed to have gone to a buyer in California but ended up with an antique dealer in Nevada," the Russian said.

"That doesn't sound too serious."

"Normally, it wouldn't be. However, this shipment contained items that we need to get back." The Russian grimaced and swayed back and forth in his chair. "I don't even want to think what might happen if we don't recover the items."

"I'm on it. Am I working alone?"

"No, I'm sorry to say. We have a "Soldier of Fortune" recruit on site by the name of Chris Gannon. This is only the second time we have worked with this man so he is rather inexperienced. However, he will brief you. You will be in charge. Make sure he knows that. There is also a "sleeper" who has been reactivated for this. His name is Oscar and he can be used as a driver, bodyguard, back-up and overall gopher."

Victor chuckled. "Sounds like an army is there already. Do they know I'm coming?"

"Yes," the Russian answered. He held the phone away from his ear and looked very worried. Victor was almost like a son to him. The last thing that he wanted was for something to happen to Victor.

Finally, the Russian said, "Victor, be careful. Don't take any chances. It's imperative that we retrieve the merchandise, but it's also extremely important the Americans not discover that you are in the states. You must not attract attention. Your upcoming mission to Washington is even more important."

"I won't. I'll keep a low profile. On the plane, I'll practice my Texas drawl. Do you want me to keep in touch?"

The Russian looked up as a tall, slim man walked into his office. The man was wearing blue jeans and a heavy black leather jacket. He was carrying a brown leather briefcase and looked like an American tourist. "Yes the courier's here now. He'll have a palm computer for you. Are you wearing your ring?"

"Yes, I'm ready. Everything is in place," the agent answered.

Director Korovkin held the phone against his ear. "Great. We'll man our site immediately and monitor your trip." A big smile crossed his face when he thought of activating the Moscow safe house across the street from the American Embassy Housing Compound.

"Is using the computer safe?" Victor asked.

"Very," the Director answered. "During all of the new American Embassy construction we were able to tap into one of their regular home telephone lines with one of the latest wireless devices. If the number is traced it leads to the American Housing area."

He smiled because he loved to play cat and mouse with the Americans. Normally, he had them chasing their own tails.

"I'll be in touch," Victor said.

The phone line went dead. The older Russian motioned for the newcomer to place the brown leather briefcase on his desk. He said, "Come back in five minutes. Ask my secretary to come here immediately."

After his secretary had been briefed and left, Director Korovkin opened the briefcase and pulled out a large envelope filled with documents. The packet included a passport, valid Texas driver's license, birth certificate, social security number, a high school diploma and a college graduation certificate. He placed them in a pile on the side of his desk.

He unzipped a side compartment and took out a packet of new American one hundred dollar bills and Visa and American Express credit cards. They joined the pile. All of the documents had the name Victor Smith on them.

He turned the briefcase over, pushed a button on the bottom and took out a piece of paper. For several minutes, he read and reread the words. Finally, the paper was placed on top of the pile.

The Director pushed the briefcase and the pile of documents across his desk and then glanced at the other file that his secretary had brought in. He rubbed his fingers over the bold red letters.

"TOP SECRET," he said smiling. He flipped open the file and unhooked two of the top pages that were stamped 'DIRECTOR'S EYES ONLY."

For several seconds, he reread the papers and turned his chair toward his computer. After scanning the pages into his computer, he put them back in the file and pressed an intercom button. He leaned on the desk and rested his head in his arms. Everything was falling into place.

He had only learned about the shipping mistake a couple of days earlier. The one thing he was thankful for was that Reno was not a heavily populated city.

He stood and walked back to the window. The traffic outside of the Kremlin walls was stopped. Huge trucks were moving what appeared to be new background settings into the Bolshoi Theatre. He wondered what was coming. It had been months since he had taken his wife to the ballet.

ASSIGNMENT: RENO, NEVADA

Startled, he jumped when he heard the loud knock. "Come in," he said, letting out a big sigh of relief as the courier came back into his office.

CHAPTER SIX

While standing outside in the antique mall parking lot, Johnny Collins opened his car door, turned toward the two women and said, "I'll follow you. Since you're familiar with the city, you pick someplace where we can get a decent meal and still have room for privacy."

Sarah Cummings called across the roof of her black shiny Mercedes, "I know just the place. It's called "Desert Oasis" and is on South Virginia not too far from the mall. Both of you just follow me." With her elbow, she pointed to her right.

Johnny nodded and folded his long body into his car. Being semi-retired, he had thought he'd save money by renting an economy car, but now wished he'd sprung for a larger roomier, model. With an unexpected pang he realized he missed the perks of being a full-time employee and on an expense account.

He drove his white Ford Taurus out of the parking place and kept his eyes on Sarah's Mercedes. He wondered if the antique business was so profitable that she could afford such a luxury car from just selling antiques.

He thought of Joe and wondered what kind of a car he had driven. He smiled when Blue Jean Peggy drove along side of him in her dusty covered jeep.

Johnny followed Sarah, and Peggy followed him. They drove across the rear of the Antique Mall and pulled out onto the street near a stoplight. When the light turned green, Sarah indicated with her hand toward the right and pulled out. Johnny nodded and followed.

They drove at a moderate pace down the street passing several small motels. All had "no-vacancy" signs lit. Johnny looked at the license plates on the cars in the parking lots and saw that most were from states several hours away.

He mentally shivered remembering the cold weather he had just left in Iowa. Smiling, he glanced down at the leather coat he was wearing and thought about the heavy parka that he had left locked in his pick-up. The pick-up was parked in long term parking at the Minneapolis International airport. He was sure that it would still be snowing when he returned to Minnesota.

Sarah slowed, turned on her directional signal this time and turned onto a side street. Johnny glanced up and saw the Desert Oasis sign directly in front of them. At first sight, Johnny wondered about the place. The outside of the building looked weather- beaten and heat drenched from the hot sun, but the parking lot was full.

He grinned as he thought that was usually a sign that the food was good. At least, that was what it meant in the restaurants he frequented in the Washington, D.C. and Midwest areas.

"So, what do you recommend?" Johnny asked once they were settled at a table in the back of the restaurant. He held the small menu up to his eyes and glanced at both of the ladies sitting across from him. "Anything special this chef is known for?"

Sarah leaned forward and whispered almost directly into Johnny's ear. "Just don't order anything that has the red dot beside it unless you like really hot spicy food. It'll curl the hairs on every part of your body!" She chuckled softly, nudged him with her elbow and pointed to one of the red dots on his menu.

Blue Jean Peggy shifted in her chair and said, "I'd recommend everything. They broil the best steaks and serve the best country fries for miles around." She looked around the room and waved at a couple of men sitting near the window and then added, "Their mixed drinks are great, too. Personally, I'm having a Margarita and a rare t-bone." She didn't even look at her menu and with great familiarity, threw it over her head. It landed with a soft whoosh on a small serving table directly behind her.

Johnny nodded and handed his menu to Blue Jean Peggy. "Sounds good to me. But, I'll take a beer. Margaritas always give me a splitting headache."

"Sissy," Blue Jean Peggy said with a wink taking his menu and pitching it in the same way she had discarded hers.

Johnny laughed and unzipped his jacket. He leaned on the table with his elbows and said softly, "Let's talk about my brother."

Sarah looked at Blue Jean Peggy then back at Johnny. She brushed her blonde hair away from her face. Her eyes grew misty. She shook her head and said, "I still can't believe he's gone. The newspaper said that his funeral was pending. Have you decided when it will be?"

"Remember? I just flew in today," Johnny answered. He glanced back and forth at the two women. Moving his shoulders up and down, he sighed and continued. "Before I left Iowa, I did phone a funeral home located here in Reno. I'm going over there tomorrow to make arrangements. The police were to have released Joe's body after the autopsy, but there seems to be some kind of a hang-up. I'm hoping they'll be able to tell me more in the morning as I'm planning on going straight from the police station to the funeral home."

Johnny stopped and again looked directly at his two companions. He could see tears running down both of their faces. He turned away and looked at the other customers in the restaurant before he spoke. "I'm supposed to see a Lieutenant Bob Larson. He's in charge of Joe's case."

He waited for the women to wipe their tears and then asked, "Do you know this Larson?"

Sarah rolled her eyes and avoided looking directly at Johnny or Blue Jean Peggy. Finally, she said, "Yea, I know "holier than thou" Larson."

Johnny smiled. "Is that good or bad?"

Sarah sighed and shrugged. "He can be a son-of-a-bitch when he wants to be." She looked at Blue Jean Peggy and winked. "I guess he really doesn't have to work too hard at it either. He is one most of the time."

Blue Jean Peggy lightly hissed under her breath and turned directly toward Sarah and whispered, "There's a couple of cops sitting over by the door." She pointed with her head. "Keep your voice down." Turning back to Johnny she asked, "Will Joe be buried here in Reno?"

Johnny glanced toward the table where the two men were eating. They didn't appear to have heard the conversation about the Lieutenant. "No, I'm planning on taking him back to Iowa and burying him in the family plot. However, I do intend on having a service at the funeral home here in Reno before he is shipped home."

Johnny watched both the two women as he talked. Although Joe was his brother, he felt as if he were talking about someone he barely knew.

Sarah sighed and a single tear flowed down her cheek. "I'm glad you're having a service here in Reno. He had so many friends here that it will be nice for all of us to have an opportunity to pay our last respects."

With a great deal of emotion, she reached down and pulled up her large brown leather purse from the floor. She dug through it and brought out a small box of tissue. After placing the box on the table in front of her, she pulled out a tissue, sniffed and dabbed at her nose. The entire act took several minutes.

Johnny just sat silently and stared. It had been years since he had seen anyone make such a production out of a simple thing. Remembering his intelligence training, he knew he'd have to go slow if he was going to find out exactly what Joe had been involved in.

He asked, "Can either of you tell me why Joe might have been killed or who may have done it?" He watched their faces and studied their reactions as he questioned. There was a long silence.

Finally, Sarah said, "We've talked about this subject for hours. From his behavior, I suspected Joe to have been hiding something for all the time that I knew him. He always avoided anyone or anyplace where there would be any type of confrontation. He didn't like arguments or any form of violence. He told me once that you were the only member of his family that believed in guns."

Johnny leaned back and shook his head. As he remembered Joe, a soft smile filled his face. "Ever since Joe was a kid, he didn't want anything to do with guns. When we were young, Dad took us hunting, but Joe would always stand back when we shot the animals. However, he'd clean them in just a few minutes flat because he was great with knives. He just couldn't bring himself to actually kill the animals."

Blue Jean Peggy said, "Yes, it was a strange fate that he dealt mainly with knives and was then killed by one."

Johnny said, "The only way that I can think that it happened was that someone came up from behind him unexpectedly. He just couldn't have seen it coming."

Blue Jean Peggy sniffed again. "You're probably right. I had a booth beside him at the flea market on the Sunday before he died. He surely didn't appear to be worried about anything other than old Charlie's death. I think that really hit him hard."

Johnny's heart began to race. "Who is this old Charlie you just mentioned?"

Sarah pointed to Blue Jean Peggy with a smile on her face. "She knew Charlie better than I did. Didn't you, Peggy?"

Blue Jean Peggy squired in her seat. She grinned and looked at Johnny out of the corner of her eye, her face turning a bright pink.

Johnny had never seen an older woman blush before, and wondered if his wife still blushed. He winked at Sarah and turned toward Blue Jean Peggy and asked, "Can you help me?"

Peggy took several deep breaths to help her regain her usual rough manner. "Charlie McGuire and I were special friends, just like Joe and I were. He died a couple of weeks ago, under what Joe and I thought were strange and suspicious circumstances."

Johnny frowned, wiped at an invisible spot on the table and asked, "Are you saying both Joe and Charlie were murdered?"

Peggy shrugged and grimaced. "I think so, but the police don't. They say that Charlie died of natural causes." She looked around the room and turned to stare at the two policemen who were still eating at their table on the other side of the room.

Johnny leaned closer toward Peggy. He whispered, "Why don't you begin at the beginning and tell me why you think Charlie's death wasn't natural?"

He leaned back and studied her eyes and face. For no reason that he could think of, he felt chilled and a shiver ran though him. He rubbed his arms to calm himself.

"Well, it all began about two months ago when Charlie bought this big shipment of antiques from some passing picker from California."

Johnny raised his hand. "Whoa, you'll have to speak English or translate as you go along. What's a picker?"

Blue Jean Peggy looked at Sarah and shook her head. She turned to Johnny and smiled. "That's a person that goes around to auctions and various places, buys things and then goes around to antique or junk dealers and sells what he has. Understand?"

Johnny nodded his head and answered, "Ok, thanks. Now, continue."

Blue Jean Peggy took a deep breath. "Well, a couple of days after Charlie put the furniture and items in the mall, he told me that he felt as if someone was following him. I told him he was getting old and was only imagining things, but Charlie said he was sure he had seen a car following him. He just felt it in his bones."

"What happened?" Sarah asked. She turned to Johnny and said, "I've never heard this story from start to finish myself."

Peggy nodded. "Actually nothing happened right away. A couple days later Charlie started coming down with the flu. He said he ached all over and really felt awful. I tried to talk him into going to the doctor, but he was too stubborn. I even told him I'd take him to the clinic, if he wanted to go. Well, I finally convinced him to at least take some Vitamin C and he said he was feeling better. That didn't change his feelings. He still kept insisting that he was being followed."

"What made him think that?" Johnny asked.

"Charlie said that every time he'd go in or out of his warehouse storage sheds, the same dark gray car was parked close by. He said a man was always sitting in the car and turned away when he looked toward him. I told that old rooster he was just getting paranoid."

Johnny asked, "Did he say if anyone else saw this gray car or did he mention that anything in his storage units had been searched or if anything was missing?"

Peggy made a face. "Charlie was always thinking that someone was stealing from him. He did say he felt that someone had been in his units, but I was there once and I honestly don't have a clue how Charlie could have noticed if anyone had ever been there. His sheds were a mess and there was stuff piled around everywhere."

Johnny frowned. "Actually, with some people having things in a mess is best for them and they can accurately tell if something isn't where it should be. I had a boss one time that had a desk that was a disaster. However, if you asked for a specific paper, he could get it immediately. Usually, these type of people notice or recall the smallest details."

"That was Charlie," Sarah answered. "His things were always messy, but he could tell you what he had and how many of each."

Peggy nodded in agreement. "I recall that one night when Joe was at my house and Charlie stopped by, the two of them were discussing the fact that someone was following Charlie. Joe said he remembered seeing the car."

Sarah gasped. "Why in the world didn't you say something about this sooner?"

Peggy patted Sarah's arm. "Really didn't think it was important. Anyway, Charlie still had some of the shipment to unpack. He and Joe moved it to his storage unit down by the airport."

Johnny asked, "How many of these units did Charlie have?"

Blue Jean Peggy shrugged and twisted in her chair. "I really don't know. I know he always mentioned a couple here in Reno but I suspect he had several more. I know he had one over in Sparks near the Truckee River too. One night when he was on his way to the Sparks unit, he said a gray car followed him. That stash had a lot of what Charlie called his precious items, and he didn't want to lead whomever was in the car to it. He told me he zigzagged all over town that night and finally lost the car. Charlie was joking and laughing about it."

Johnny leaned on the table and glanced back and forth at the two women. He asked, "Did Charlie say if he ever saw the car again? Can you remember when the last time he mentioned seeing it?"

Peggy studied the ceiling and finally answered, "He said he saw the car at his house one night. He lived in a small duplex off of Monroe Street. Not sure of the number but it was white with red trim. It is a neat clean place with a couple of small lilac bushes in the front yard. There was an unattached garage around the back that you entered from the alley." Peggy pointed to her right. "You go out to the stop light and turn right. His place wasn't close to the police station." She looked at Johnny and added, "Normally, security wasn't an issue with Charlie."

Sarah shook her finger at Peggy. "Good heavens, lady, tell us what you know. Why do you think Charlie was killed?"

Blue Jean Peggy leaned on the table. She motioned for Sarah and Johnny to lean toward her. "Charlie thought that whomever was in the gray car was after something that was in the shipment he got from that picker. He didn't even see the car until after he got the shipment." She paused and looked at each of them and whispered. "That very next day, Charlie was found dead in his pickup in front of his house. The police said he died of a heart attack. I don't believe it, I'm telling you I think that he was killed."

Johnny frowned and slid back in his chair. He rubbed his chin and asked, "How old was Charlie?"

Sarah answered quickly. "He was about sixty. Right, Peggy?"

Peggy shook her head. "Yep, he'd be sixty, day after Christmas. And, before you ask, he hadn't been sick other than that flu he had. He didn't smoke and only drank once or twice a week. Not ever day like some of those "fleas" do."

Johnny felt completely out of place. He raised his eyebrows and asked, "Now, what is a "flea"?"

Sarah laughed. "We keep forgetting you don't know the business. A "flea" is someone that sells merchandise at the flea markets or swap meets. A "dealer" is someone that sells at a mall. Both Joe and Charlie would have been called "fleas" because they were seen at all the flea markets. Very few people knew that they had booths at the mall that I own."

"Why was that?" Johnny asked.

"Well, at my mall, both Joe's and Charlie's booths were listed under their real names. That would be Joe Collins and Charlie McGuire. Most of the people that either one of the men associated with knew them as

"Old Charlie" and "Joe, the Knife". I doubt if there were five people other than Blue Jean Peggy and me who even knew what their real names were."

Johnny raised his hands and laughed. "This is a new world for me. Now, what kind of items did Charlie buy from this California man? Where did the shipment come from?"

Peggy wiped a tear from her eye. She sniffed and said, "I only saw some of the things, but I'd say that most of it came from Europe. It was old village. Rough farmer style. It wasn't the elaborate style that you get out of England. It was mainly pine, walnut and oak furniture that came from Germany, Austria or maybe Eastern Europe."

Johnny thought for a moment and asked, "Could it have come out of Russia?" He remembered reading a memo before he left the CIA about the large amounts of Russian antiques that were being smuggled out of the old Soviet motherland and being sold around the world for hard currency.

Peggy shrugged. "Might have been, but it wasn't any of the black lacquered stuff that I've seen from Russia. It was more the peasant look, which is very popular here in the states now, especially here in the West and particularly in California."

"What kind of a car was it that you said Charlie had seen?" Johnny asked.

Peggy looked at her fingers and answered, "Charlie never said. He just said that it was a dark gray, long one. I think Charlie would have said if it had been a pickup or a van. I think it was probably a sedan." Once again, she looked toward the policemen and then continued. "Charlie didn't like to admit it, but he was a bit color blind. It could have been blue, black, dark maroon or something that looked dark gray."

Johnny groaned. "How did Charlie die? Did the police do any investigating?"

Peggy shook her head and answered, "Hell, no. I never was able to get anything from the police. I heard about his death on the noon news. The report said he was found in his pickup and that he was a fixture in the antique world. He was born here in Reno. His dad was a doctor and one of the first men to sell ranch land to developers."

Johnny smiled and shook his head. "Was Old Charlie rich?"

Blue Jean Peggy shrugged.

Sarah said, "Who could tell with Old Charlie? He acted as if he didn't have a penny, but I suspect he had a good cushion stuck away somewhere."

Johnny took a notebook out of his pocket and began making notes. He looked back at the women and asked, "How long ago did he die?"

Sarah answered, "A couple weeks, definitely less than a month."

Johnny made more notes in his book. "Did you both go to his funeral?"

Sarah nodded.

Peggy said, "They only had a service. They wouldn't let me see Charlie's body. They had his casket closed. From what Joe said, Charlie just died, but no one has ever been able to prove it one way or the other."

Sarah looked around the room and then commented, "Peggy and I both called the police after we heard of Charlie's death. Both of us were told that it wasn't a police matter."

Johnny looked confused. He made more notes in his book. "Who took care of the funeral arrangements and claimed his effects?"

Peggy's eyes blazed. "That is what's so odd. Some guy out of California came and said he was Charlie's brother. He took the body as soon as the service at the funeral home was over. I have no idea what happened to poor Charlie's body."

Johnny turned to Blue Jean Peggy and asked, "How come you didn't get to claim the body if you were such good friends?"

"Hell," she said. "I would have but by the time I heard about his death, this self-identified brother who appeared already had all the arrangements made. What could I do?"

Johnny rubbed his chin and then said, "I don't know what the state laws are here. Did Charlie ever talk about having a brother in California?"

"Nope, not to either of us," Sarah answered.

"Strange," Johnny said. "So, why did Joe think Charlie had been killed?"

Blue Jean Peggy started to speak but saw the waitress and leaned back in her seat. The group silently watched as the waitress placed steaks in front of each person and finished serving the side dishes.

After she left, Peggy spoke in a very soft voice. "Joe told me one night when he was drinking, that Charlie got something in the shipment that Joe thought was really strange. He said that after Charlie died he tried to find it, but he couldn't. He thought the killers took it."

Johnny's hand began to shake. He could feel the sweat running down his back. Joe had been in the Korean War and Johnny knew that Joe would be able to recognize various weapons. He took a drink of water and asked, "Can either of you take me to Charlie's and Joe's storage units tomorrow?"

Sarah said, "I can't but Peggy probably could. How about it, Peggy?"

Blue Jean Peggy ran her hand through her short gray hair. She pulled at her flannel shirt and picked up her fork and knife. She looked around the room, nodded her head and began eating.

Johnny picked up his silverware and glanced around the room. He felt as if he was being watched. He opened his mouth to ask something else, but thought better of it and said, "Let's eat before everything gets cold. This looks and smells great. I'm anxious to compare this steak to good old Iowa beef."

ASSIGNMENT: RENO, NEVADA

CHAPTER SEVEN

Victor Smith stepped off the Air West flight and walked down the terminal. He stopped halfway toward the baggage area. A wide smile covered his face. Every thing he had heard about Reno flashed through his mind.

The new blue jeans and boots felt tight and stiff. They made a crunching sound as he moved. He stopped near an empty seat in one of the waiting areas, put his new Texas wide brim hat on the seat, adjusted his tan coat, dug into his jeans for loose change and checked the faces of the people who were waiting for their flight.

He brushed his curly blond hair and ran his fingers gently across his face. Just as a flight attendant passed, he rolled his baby blue eyes at her and took a deep breath. He loved the United States and practiced "ya'll" on all of his connecting flights. Now, it was almost second nature. With his hat back on, he stood up straight and walked to the nearest slot machine.

He had never played a machine before, but had seen it done in several western movies. With his long leg extended, he pulled a stool towards him. Once settled, he unbuttoned his barn coat, rolled his shoulders back and forth and began feeding quarters into the machine.

Victor watched a seven fall into place and lock. He glanced around the departure area. No one was paying any attention to him. He sighed with relief.

Suddenly, the machine began ringing and clanging. Victor's heart pounded. His eyes grew wide. He gasped. Quarters began flowing from the machine and a couple bounced against his leg and onto the floor.

A short, gray haired, elderly lady hurried toward him and the ringing machine. "Well, I'll be. You hit the jackpot," she yelled into his ear.

Victor jerked backward, put his hand over his ear and nearly fell off the stool. He turned and looked directly into the old woman's eyes. He shrugged, looked confused and whispered to her. "What do I do now? I've never hit a jackpot before."

The lady bent down and whispered. "Be happy, sonny. You're fifty thousand dollars richer. Just sit there. The machine will only pay so many quarters and someone will be around with the rest of your money. See the words on the screen. PLEASE WAIT FOR ATTENDANT."

Victor looked at his watch and asked, "Will it be long? I have an appointment."

The old lady said, "You might want to pick up the ones that fell on the floor while you're waiting. We don't want to start a stampede here."

Victor felt unusually warm and uncomfortable. He didn't like all the attention but felt if he walked away it would create more attention. He smiled at the woman and with a single scoop with his long arm grabbed the fallen quarters and put them back into the hopper.

The old woman put her hand on Victor's shoulder. "Just take a deep breath and sit still. Smile. You look like you're scared to death."

Victor answered in his strongest Texas accent, "Thank you, ma'am. Ya'll here in Nevada are really most hospitable to us Texans."

The old woman slapped Victor on the back. "Hell, sonny, these damn people took all my money, it's about time that they're paying some back."

Within a few minutes, a short young man with a large curved mustache, carrying a large book and notepad, came rushing out of a nearby door. A tall teen-age looking boy followed on his heels. They both ran toward Victor and the ringing machine. The boy carried a camera.

Someone behind Victor yelled, "Here they come now."

Victor turned just as the boy snapped his picture. Before Victor would say a word, the boy ran back through the door and out of sight.

The man stood beside Victor, opened the big black book and placed the notepad on the machine. He said, "Looks like this is your lucky day. May I see some identification?"

Victor took a deep breath, looked around at the gathering crowd and took out his wallet. His hand shook. He smiled a broad wide smile and said, "Ya'll sure know how to make a guy feel welcome."

"From Texas, I see," said the man as he read Victor's driver's license. "Well, just sign here by the X's and I'll give you a form for your taxes and the money." He studied Victor's eyes and then added. "I have to file tax papers on my end and then you will have to declare the winnings when you file your taxes in April."

Victor nodded. He glanced into the faces that had gathered around him. A strange winding noise caught his attention and he let his eyes sweep over the area.

He saw a beautiful tall woman standing on the side with a video camera. Quickly, he turned his head away from her and held his head down close to the book and signed. Without looking up, he said, "Did I sign my life away?"

The man laughed. "No, that's just for Uncle Sam. Now, if you'll move back I need to make a couple of adjustments to the machine. I have to see how much money it has already paid out."

Victor moved the stool back slightly and kept his face in the shadow of the man's body. He could hear people talking behind him, but he didn't turn around or look up.

"Well, with the money in the base of the machine here, I still owe you a lot of money. Do you want it in cash or a check?"

Victor spoke softly. "I'd like it all in cash if I could. I really don't want to have to mess with a check."

"Not a problem. Have you taken out any of the quarters?"

The old woman tapped on the young man's arm and said, "No, I've been here ever since he hit the jackpot. Some of the quarters fell on the floor but he picked them up and put them in the hopper. It's all there."

ASSIGNMENT: RENO, NEVADA

The attendant turned and looked at the old lady. "Well, Mrs. Larson. I thought I recognized your voice. How are you? I didn't see you standing there. Have you been in town visiting your son again?"

Mrs. Larson looked at Victor and said, "I really don't know if it is good or bad being recognized." She slapped Victor hard on his back and whistled.

The man looked up from the machine. "Mr. Smith, if Mrs. Larson says that all the money is here, that is good enough for me." He gathered all the quarters from the hopper and then pulled a bag out from around his neck and counted out crisp, new one hundred dollar bills.

He turned back to Victor and said, "Please, stay here a moment, I have requested an armed escort you when you exit the airport."

Victor laughed and answered, "I think I will be just fine." He took the pile of hundred dollar bills and handed five bills to Mrs. Larson. He smiled. "Here. Go buy yourself something nice."

Mrs. Larson gave out a loud yell, started crying and gave Victor a big hug and a kiss. Immediately, the crowd clapped.

Victor stood up. Out of the corner of his eye he saw the lady still videoing the scene. He leaned down and hugged the elderly lady. Carefully, he turned his back to the video camera, and kept the old woman between himself and the crowd.

The male attendant whispered, "Come with me. The Security men are on their way. We don't want anyone mugging you in the airport." He nudged Victor's arm, picked up the bag of quarters and started down the hallway.

Victor felt trapped. He didn't want an escort but knew he had to follow the man. "I sure hope not," he sighed. He turned slightly and waved to the large crowd gathered around him. He continued to keep his face turned away from the lady and her video camera.

Within minutes, he was escorted down the hallway between two tall, muscular uniformed airport security men. In a group, they walked to the baggage claim area, picked up Victor's suitcase and marched together to a cabstand.

"Who are you?" the cab driver asked as he watched the two bodyguards help Victor into the cab. "You must be someone famous to have an escort here in Reno."

"No one special," Victor answered. "Just a Texan." He closed the cab door and waved to the two guards as the cab pulled away.

CHAPTER EIGHT

Two hours later, Victor was sitting at a table in a small Chinese restaurant on Virginia Street. There were very few people at the other tables.

"You'll never guess what happened to me today!" Victor stated after Chris Gannon walked up to his table.

Chris shook his head, rolled his eyes and glared at the newcomer with cold green eyes. "I have no idea."

He placed his camel hair coat carefully over two chairs taking care to spread the coat so it wouldn't wrinkle.

Victor adjusted his barn coat on the empty chair beside him and returned Gannon's cold stare. He moved his eyes slowly around and caught his reflection in the mirror across the room.

Holding his chin higher, he moved his head back and forth, admiring his new face. A recent girlfriend told him that he had a classic Greek profile and since then, he thought of her when he saw his reflection. He smiled and sighed. The memory was good, and he enjoyed thinking about her admiration of him.

For several minutes, neither man spoke as they tried to judge the other. Finally, the waitress appeared and took their orders. Victor's eyes followed the petite and attractive female form as she moved back toward the kitchen.

"Well, what happened?" Chris finally asked. "That is, if you can take your eyes off that waitress' derriere."

With a wide smile, Victor showed his sparkling white teeth. "The meal is on me. I hit a jackpot at the airport today."

"You what?" Chris hissed loudly. His eyes grew wide and he winced as he looked around the room. He leaned back in his chair and rocked back and forth on the chair's two back legs and added, "That was pretty stupid."

"Yea, stupid. I hit three sevens on one of the slop machines," answered Victor.

"You idiot!" Chris sputtered almost tipping over in the chair. He rubbed his cheek and shook his head. "First of all, it is a slot machine, not a slop machine. Second, you are supposed to keep a low profile, not attract attention."

Victor laughed. "I didn't put the quarter in to win on purpose. I had a quarter and I simply put it in the slot and pulled the handle. How was I to know it was going to win?"

Chris thought for a moment and then answered, "Well, I suppose that isn't too bad. How much did you win? Was it around two hundred dollars or so? That would at least make it worthwhile."

Victor frowned, shrugged and waved his hand at Gannon. "You act like an old woman. There couldn't

ASSIGNMENT: RENO, NEVADA

have been but a couple people there. I got my money and left."

"Well, how much?" Chris asked.

Victor looked toward the kitchen and whispered, "Fifty thousand dollars. Do you want to see it?" He started to reach into his coat pocket.

Chris gasped. "Fifty thousand. Holy cow." He thought for a moment and then asked, "You said there weren't many people around you?"

Victor shrugged and answered, "Only a couple."

Within seconds, the waitress arrived and placed a large helping of General Tso's chicken and a plate of mixed fried rice in front of Chris.

He smiled, touched her hand and leaned over and smelled the food. Looking up into her eyes, he caressed her hand and said, "This looks and smells great. Honey, can you bring me some more tea?"

The waitress blushed and hurried away giggling.

"Was that necessary?" Victor asked, as he stared at Chris. After a long silence he continued. "What have you found out about the missing items?" Instantly, his carefree expression changed to a hard business frown. He tapped on the table with his fingers and waited while Chris stuffed rice into his mouth.

"Not now," Chris said between bites. "I want to eat this while it's hot. We can talk later."

The waitress reappeared carrying a large tray. She avoided Chris' smile and placed a large serving of rice and chicken with cashews in front of Victor. A young oriental boy followed behind her with two steaming pots of tea.

After they hurried away, Victor asked, "Can you at least tell me if you found where the cases are?"

Chris shook his head. "Later. Eat and then we'll go see."

Victor smiled and picked up his fork. "Well, that's the first thing you've said since we've met that I agree with."

In a little over an hour, the two men were in Chris' car and heading down West Fourth street toward the main part of the city. Chris was driving. He rolled down his window and rested his arm on the windowsill.

He said, "My informer told me just before I met you at the restaurant, that Charlie McGuire had another storage shed near the airport."

"Well, let's go check it out," Victor said. "Is it far?"

"No, but I thought I'd drive you through the downtown strip area first," Gannon answered. "Then, we'll go out to the airport and check out the shed."

Victor kept his eyes fixed on the streets and the people. "That's fine with me. This is my first time in Reno and before I go back, I'd like to see as much of the city as I can."

Gannon looked over at Victor and smiled. They drove for several blocks without talking.

"Is that ringing from the slot machines?" Victor asked as they passed the front of a large older casino.

"Sure is," Gannon answered, turning the corner next to one of the newest hotel casinos. He smiled and pointed directly in front of him. "Look over there at that arched sign that reads "The Biggest Little City in The World". It's a Reno trademark. They use it in a lot of the western movies." He slowed the car so

ASSIGNMENT: RENO, NEVADA

Victor could read the large sign hanging in the middle of the street.

"I want to come back and go into some of these places before I leave," Victor said, patting his wallet in his coat pocket.

Chris rolled his eyes and nodded to his left. "That's one of the latest hotel casinos and over there on your right is the National Bowling Stadium. Now, that place is something else. It makes the bowling alleys you have in Europe look like toys."

As they waited for the light to turn green, two attractive young ladies walked out of the stadium. They looked directly at the two men. Chris slowed the car.

"Shall we ask them if they want a ride?" He looked at Victor and winked.

"No, not now. After we find the merchandise we'll have plenty of time for that." He watched the ladies for a moment and then added, "But those are some great looking legs."

Chris turned onto Interstate 80 near the University and followed it past Interstate 395. The traffic was light. "That's the airport turnoff," he said. "I was told the storage sheds are on South Rock Boulevard. Help me look for the exit."

"What kind of buildings arc they?" Victor asked as he squinted to see the signs in the dark. He could only imagine the type he had seen recently in Vienna, Moscow and throughout Europe. There, they were large, old rundown buildings in a dark, dingy part of the city.

Chris turned toward Victor and answered, "I have the impression that they are new. Probably individual ones like the ones that are popping up all over this part of the country." Suddenly, he tramped hard on the brakes and whipped the steering wheel around as he gasped, "Here's our turnoff."

Victor grunted as he slid forward in the seat. He hit his leg against the dashboard and muttered to himself.

"You should wear your seat belt," Chris Gannon said. "That's the law here in the states."

Victor turned, eyed Gannon and answered, "It is the law almost all over the world." He rubbed his knee and made a face. "I thought you knew this city?"

"Hell, I live in California." Gannon pointed to a grouping of small one-story sheds directly to their right. "There's the storage units over there."

The sheds were completely surrounded by a high wire fence. Inside the fenced area were row after row of small, connected one-story buildings. Each one had a large black number on it."

Chris stopped the car along the side of the fence and turned off the lights and motor. He put his hand on the door.

"What's next? Did you get any keys?" Victor asked. "These buildings all look alike."

Chris turned quickly toward Victor. His shoulder bumped against the steering wheel and sounded the horn. He jerked away from the noise.

"I have the damn keys but have no idea which is which. They're not marked in any way," he whispered holding up a large key ring with several keys on it.

Apparently aroused by the horn blast, two large Doberman dogs ran out from behind the sheds and raced toward the parked car. They stopped at the fence and growled. Their eyes flashed red in the moonlight.

"Unless you brought some meat," Victor said, "I think you'd better get back in touch with your informer." He ran his hand over his forehead. "Better yet, let me talk to him. There are a lot of things we apparently don't know."

Chris ran his hand through his hair, looked at his watch and made a discouraging sound. "I won't be able to get in touch with him until tomorrow. We'd better get out of here. I don't want those dogs getting our scents memorized. Also, I have no idea of where any cameras may be located."

He started the car, backed around and headed toward the interstate. As he swerved in and out of traffic he asked, "Do you want to go back to the strip?"

A smile filled Victor's face. Although, he had a girlfriend in Moscow, he answered, "Sure, I can sleep when I'm dead."

CHAPTER NINE

It was a cool crisp morning when Johnny parked his rental car around the corner from the Reno Police station. He glanced at his watch and walked into the large brick building.

The clock on the tower of the building down the block began to chime eight. He patted his chest to make sure that he had the list of questions he had compiled before leaving his hotel room.

"I need to talk to a Lt. Bob Larsen," he stated as he stood in front of a uniformed policeman sitting behind a large gray metal desk.

This morning Johnny was dressed in blue jeans, a light blue denim shirt, brown leather jacket and white sneakers. He watched as several plainclothes policemen dressed in suits and ties passed him. He smiled, nodded and felt completely relaxed. The idea of not having to wear a suit and tie pleased him.

The Desk Sergeant held a black ballpoint pen, squinted, turned his head slightly and looked at Johnny. He asked, "What do you need? Maybe, I can help you."

Johnny pulled a paper out of his pocket and glanced at it. "I'm supposed to see Larson about my brother, Joe."

"What's your brother's full name?" asked the desk officer. He held the pen over a yellow legal pad and glanced down at the file he had spread out on the desk in front of him.

Before Johnny could answer, a door opened to Johnny's right and several uniformed policemen walked out of the room. Their voices and heavy footsteps filled the quiet space.

"Joe Collins," answered Johnny. He waved the paper in front of the policeman.

The desk officer frowned and Johnny repeated the name louder against the noise and confusion.

The policeman made a note on the pad. Suddenly, he stopped and looked directly at Johnny and asked, "Are you Joe the Knife's brother?" The office spoke louder than necessary and pronounced his words slowly and clearly.

Suddenly, a hush filled the entire room. Without looking around, Johnny sensed everyone looking at him. He turned around, smiled widely exposing his teeth.

"Yes," he answered. He nodded to the entire room as every policeman stared back at him.

Johnny turned back toward the desk officer and grimly asked, "Now, may I see Larson?" His smile had disappeared and a cold hard stare had replaced it.

The desk officer's face turned red. He squirmed and stammered, "Yes, please take a seat over there. It may be a couple minutes." His short stubby fingers pointed toward a worn wooden bench against a wall in the narrow hallway.

Johnny took a seat and stared at the wall in front of him. The room continued to be quiet. A door creaked and opened at the end of the long hallway. Johnny turned toward the sound. He noticed the other policemen look in the same direction.

A large linebacker sized man stood in the open doorway. His shoulders almost touched the doorframe on both sides. He glanced around the room.

The large man waved his hand and the other policemen resumed their business. The big man took a couple long steps toward Johnny and motioned toward him.

"Are you Lt. Bob Larson?" Johnny asked as he walked toward the big man.

The tall man squinted and raised his hands. His flaming red hair caught Johnny's attention. Johnny blinked several times when the light reflected off of Larson's head. It looked as if Larson's head was on fire.

The policeman smiled and extended his hand. He looked down at Johnny and studied him for several seconds. Finally, Larson said, "So you're Joe's brother?"

"Yes," Johnny nodded.

"Well, I'll be," Larson answered.

Johnny took the man's hand and asked, "Why is that so strange? Everyone I've met so far in Reno seems to think there is something funny about me."

The big man laughed and clapped his hands together.

Johnny recoiled backward as the sound reverberated off the walls.

Larson chuckled. "I think it's just hard for any of us to believe Joe had relatives. That's all. He hadn't mentioned anything about any family whatsoever that I knew." The man walked back into his office and pointed to a chair near his desk. He kept his eyes on Johnny as he walked around the room toward his desk chair.

"So, what can you tell me about Joe's death?" asked Johnny once he was situated in the office. He felt uneasy. It had been years since he had felt intimidated by another person's stature.

"Call me, Bob. I think we're going to be seeing a lot of each other and this Mister or Lieutenant bit isn't needed for me." Larson leaned back in his chair, gazed at the ceiling for a moment and then slowly shook his head. Finally, he opened a desk drawer and pulled out some files. "Here it is. Joe Collins." He held the thick manila folder up.

"Well, what can you tell me?" Johnny repeated staring at the file.

The officer lowered his head, put the file upon his desk, flipped it over and ruffled through it, then looked back at Johnny. He began reading from the file, moving his lips and muttering as he went. "Let's see." He stopped and glanced toward the calendar on the wall. "It says that he died almost four days ago. Says here that they had trouble finding any next of kin." He read through a couple more papers and then looked up at Johnny and asked, "When did they get in touch with you?"

"I got a phone call about a day and a half ago. Then, a telegram. I caught a flight out of Minneapolis and here I am. I arrived yesterday." Johnny shifted in his chair and studied the room around him.

"Who contacted you?" Larson asked. "There is no notice here in the file that you were contacted."

Johnny squinted. The reflected light glared in his eyes. He tried to watch the policeman's eyes, but it was impossible for him to read anything in the expression on the man's face.

Johnny thought for a second or two and then answered, "Joe's lawyer." He reached inside of his pocket and pulled out a paper. He read the name aloud. "A Mr. Terrance Ruddick."

"Huh!" the policeman said. "Were you ever contacted by the police?" Larson rested his large hands on top of his desk and twirled his thumbs.

"Not directly," answered Johnny.

"Well, I guess this notation is correct." Larson took a pencil and made notes in the file. He put the pencil back, closed the drawer and looked back at the file. "I suppose now you want to know all the details about your brother's death?"

Johnny sighed. "You supposed right." He unzipped his leather jacket and rested his arms on the arms of his chair. When the officer didn't continue, Johnny studied Larson's office more closely.

A gray metal desk and a chair filled one side of the office. Numerous gray file cabinets covered the walls that weren't covered by the door and two small half-windows. Under the windows were two gray straight-back metal chairs.

ASSIGNMENT: RENO, NEVADA

It was an extremely small office compared to the offices Johnny had used in the CIA headquarters in Langley, Virginia. It was even smaller than any of the storage rooms in the Agency basement.

Johnny's head swayed. Almost every bit of space in the room was filled with the large man, furniture or the cabinets. He was beginning to feel claustrophobic. He knew he had to calm himself and concentrate on the Lieutenant.

The officer finally looked up from the file and answered, "I see here they found your name but no address among Joe's personal things. Have you claimed his belongings from the morgue?"

Johnny was trying hard not to stare at the large man in the small room. He kept moving his eyes away from the man's face. "No, I told you that I got in yesterday and came here this morning. I was told to check with you first. Later today, I plan to stop by the funeral home that I contacted by phone before leaving Iowa. No one said anything about going to the morgue." Johnny glanced at his watch and started to stand.

"Whoa, that can wait." Larson indicated with his hands for Johnny to sit back down. "We need to have a little talk first. Besides, I don't think the examiners are finished with the body yet." Larson put the thick file down, leaned across the desk and asked, "Why do you think Joe was killed?"

Johnny settled down and sighed. "I have no idea. It has been years since I've seen him. I'm not sure what he might have been doing."

The officer looked at Johnny and then toward the open door. He got up, walked around Johnny and closed the door. He walked back to his desk but stopped and studied Johnny's face before he sat down. He asked, "Could he have been involved in drugs?"

Johnny laughed. "Hardly. Joe might have smoked or drank, but he would never have used drugs."

Larson thought for a bit, drew a deep breath, and slowly asked, "How can you be sure? You admitted that you hadn't seen him in years."

"I might not have seen him but I usually talked to him at least a couple times a month. When Joe got back from Viet Nam, he told me that one of his best buddies died from an overdose. Joe was so shook up that he swore he'd half kill any of his family if he heard they were using drugs." Johnny looked at his fingers and blinked several times as he remembered. He could still hear Joe's screaming words.

The officer nodded. "Maybe," he said. His expression showed that he neither believed nor disbelieved what Johnny had said. "Did you know how Joe made a living?"

Johnny pulled the envelope out of his pocket. He tossed it on the desk in front of the policeman. A deep wide frown covered his forehead. "I went out to the antique mall last night after I got settled in. Sure, I know Joe dealt in antiques and knives. I said I hadn't seen Joe in a few years, but that doesn't mean that I didn't know anything about him. As I said, we did talk often."

After the officer read the attorney's letter, he handed it back to Johnny. Smiling, he nodded and asked, "Did you know Charlie McGuire?"

Johnny squinted and looked directly into the officer's eyes. "I've heard the name, but I have never met him."

The officer took a pad from his desk and made a couple notes. Looking back at Johnny he commented, "He was one of Joe's best friends."

"Oh, that's right," answered Johnny as he put the attorney's envelope back into his pocket. "Last night the girls talked about Charlie."

"What girls?" the officer asked. His eyes scrutinized Johnny's face as he waited for an answer.

"Let's see?" Johnny answered. He looked at a corner of the wall and paused like he had to work at trying to remember their names. Finally, he said, "There was Peggy and Sarah, I can't remember Peggy's last name but I think it was Sarah Cummings. We went out to dinner together at some restaurant over by the big mall."

Larson pursed his lips together several times and opened the file again. He glanced up at Johnny and then at the file. He read for several minutes without making a comment. Finally, he said, "Yes, it says that Cummings owns the mall where Joe rented a booth. There isn't any mention of this Peggy person. Who is she?"

Johnny laughed. "She is some colorful lady that works at the antique mall with Cummings. She was working there last night when I stopped by. I'd judge her to be in her late forties or so. I recall now, she is called Blue Jean Peggy. From her name I would imagine that she always wears blue jeans. She has short gray hair and a full figure. I found her to be very friendly and just a nice lady. She's the one that told me about Charlie McGuire."

Larson closed the file and leaned his large hands on his desk. "What did she say?" he asked.

Before Johnny could answer, Larson pulled open a drawer and took out a clean yellow legal size pad. He dug through another drawer for a ballpoint pen and glanced up waiting for Johnny to continue.

Johnny shrugged. "Not much, actually. Just that he died."

Larson put down his pen and leaned back in his chair. He ran his fingers through his hair and contemplated Collins. "Did they tell you McGuire had also been murdered?"

Johnny jerked. His mouth dropped open. "Murdered? No, they said that he died and they didn't express any opinion about how he had died. Was he killed in the same way that Joe was? With a knife?"

Larson spoke softly. "I'm not positive how McGuire was killed and I don't have the file here on my desk. I just remember that we suspected that he was killed." He looked at Johnny with a serious expression and asked, "I can find out if you wish. Do you want to know?"

Johnny shrugged and stood up. "I not concerned with how he died, unless, of course, his death is connected to Joe's. Then, I do want to know all the details."

Larson made a note on his yellow pad and put his pen down. "I suggest that you drop by the Coroner's Office after leaving here and pick up your brother's things. I'll call down and let them know that you are coming. They are just a couple blocks from here."

ASSIGNMENT: RENO, NEVADA

He made another note on the file and then closed the file and looked back at Collins and asked, "Are you still with the CIA?"

Johnny turned back toward Larson and answered with a wave of his hand, "Semi-retired." He looked at Larson for a few seconds, then turned and walked out the door.

Larson jumped up and quickly followed Collins. "Keep in touch." He took a couple steps behind Collins and asked, "Are you going to the funeral home now?"

Johnny kept walking down the hall. "Yes," he answered without looking back.

"When's the funeral?" Larson called.

"I'll let you know," Collins said and turned the corner out of Larson's view. He kept walking and was starting down the steps when he heard Larson call to the Desk Officer.

CHAPTER TEN

The snow was sticking to the windshield and making the roads dangerously slick when Bill Weaver pulled his car into the CIA Headquarters parking lot in Langley, Virginia. It was almost ten in the morning. He glanced down at his watch and shook his head.

It was still two hours until he could eat his banana. His stomach growled. He hated being on a diet. It always made him irritable. He opened the car door into the cold, freezing wind.

Weaver, a tall heavy-set man, stepped out, and his foot went into a puddle under the thin layer of snow. His black loafer sank to the concrete and instantly filled with water. He silently cursed the weather, his diet and the doctor that ordered it. He shook his shoe trying to get as much water off and out of it as possible.

He grabbed at his overcoat, pulled it around his bulky frame and hobbled for the nearest entrance. The snow and his cold foot made him shiver. Now, he was not only hungry but also wet, cold, and exasperated as well.

ASSIGNMENT: RENO, NEVADA

Mentally, he counted off the months until his retirement. Just knowing it was near made him feel better. In six months, he'd be away from both the National Security Agency and the Central Intelligence Agency, the agency doctor and these lousy Virginia winters.

"Get the group together. I want a meeting in my office in five minutes," he barked when he passed his administrative assistant in the hallway just outside his office.

"Yes, sir," she sighed. She knew by his tone of voice that his meeting at NSA Headquarters at Fort Meade, Maryland had not gone as he had hoped.

By the time everyone gathered in Weaver's office, he had changed his shoes and socks and felt warmer. His wet socks were on the radiator and his shoes were propped on their sides behind his desk. This was one of the rare days that he really didn't care how things looked in his office. He had more important things on his mind.

"Well, we have a problem," he said, once everyone had taken a seat. He stood up, held a cup of steaming coffee between his hands and began walking around the room. "Our friends to the East have done it again."

Everyone looked at him with blank expressions. They looked at one another and shrugged.

Weaver ignored his staff's reactions. He said, "Our dear friends over at NSA intercepted a message yesterday from Moscow. It seems that one of our dear old friends, Viktor Schmidt is back on the scene and is expected to be on his way to the states." Weaver looked at his watch. "He's probably here by now, if he made good connections." He paused for a moment, looked at each of the members and continued. "I'm betting he did and is."

"Do we have any idea why?" Bruce Wilson asked. "He's been off the scene for almost a year. Are there any thoughts on where he's been and why he's suddenly reappearing?" Wilson was second in command and although somewhat new to the group was always a key figure in the intelligence loop.

"No, I was hoping that one of you had heard something and could tell me where he's been and why he's suddenly back in the picture." Weaver looked around the room, carefully studying each member's reaction to his words. "Did any of you hear anything about Schmidt's visit?"

Weaver could only see blank expressions and negative shrugs. He turned his face away and studied the picture hanging behind his desk. It was a large, tinted watercolor of the CIA Headquarters building by Martin Barry, one of his favorite local artists.

"Surely, we have the same listening devices that NSA has, why didn't we pick up the message?" He turned back toward the group and his voice went louder. His face showed no expression except for a glint in his eyes.

Margie Clark, the tall, blonde linguist, asked, "Where was the origin of the message? Any idea what time?"

"Our friends say that it came from an area around the American Embassy in Moscow and was transmitted a couple times during the day. They weren't able to trace who was receiving the message and they could only narrow it down to west of the

Mississippi river. This snow storm was coming and they couldn't get a better reception fix."

Sam Reed, the newest member of the team and a former military terrorist expert, looked puzzled. He questioned, "Is this the same Viktor Schmidt that we believe was responsible for the those bombings at the Cairo and Athens Embassies?"

Weaver placed his cup on his desk and clapped. Sarcastically, he said, "The one and only."

"Shit," Sam muttered. "Have we alerted anyone on the West coast? That evidently is where he's heading."

Weaver chuckled and shook his head. He made a whistling sound with his mouth and finally answered, "No, we haven't. He could be heading for Washington, D.C. or anyplace. The message could have been relayed just to throw us off. Why do you think the West coast?"

Sam shrugged. "Don't know. Just a gut feeling."

All heads turned toward Sam. Although, Sam was the new man in the group, everyone knew he had more years of actual experience working with terrorists than all of the people in the group combined, other than Weaver.

"Well, gang, what do we do?" Weaver asked.

Wilson answered, "Guess, we'll try and find out what's going on around the states that would be large enough to get Moscow's attention to bring in someone of Schmidt's caliber. I don't think that Schmidt is selling his talents on the open market just yet."

Weaver shook his head and grunted. "I doubt if Moscow is that understanding. I want the latest pictures of Schmidt sent to our field offices around the world. Someone might know something." He waited for a few seconds and then added, "Where's Collins? He'll want to know about this."

Margie Clark answered, "Remember, he's in his home state of Iowa."

Weaver put his lips together and said, "Damn, that's right."

Wilson stood and walked toward the door. He turned back toward Weaver. His voice was low. He stared at Weaver for a few seconds and then asked, "What does Collins have to do with this?"

Weaver looked at Wilson and said, "I know you're new to this unit so you wouldn't know some of our past history." He held his cup to his lips and took several sips. Finally, he turned back to Wilson and said, "As far as we know, Collins was one of the last people that ever saw Schmidt. It was Schmidt that left Collins to die along the Iron Curtain border in the late eighties."

Wilson shrugged. He frowned and then said, "You mean no one saw Schmidt in regards to the embassy bombings just a couple of years ago?"

Weaver commented, "That's right. We all deduced from the evidence that Schmidt was behind it. But, no one saw him."

Wilson thought for a moment and then said, "Maybe, we shouldn't tell Collins about Schmidt now."

Weaver sat down in his desk chair, leaned his elbow on the desktop and ran his finger along the side of his coffee cup. Finally, he muttered, "I don't know." He shook his head several times. After a moment, he smiled. "Johnny would want to know. If I were in

Johnny's shoes, I'd sure as hell want to know that Schmidt was in the states. Hell, maybe he's on his way to Iowa to finish off Collins."

Marge said, "I thought Collins was retiring."

Weaver put his hand up and nodded slightly. He said, "Semi-retired. He's on call if we need him. I want all of you to put out feelers. Try and find out why Schmidt is in the states. While you are doing that, I'll check with someone higher up the command chain before I contact Collins about Schmidt."

The rest of the group stood to leave. As they started out the door, Weaver added. "I want to know the instant any of you find out anything. We want to know what's going on before NSA does. I sure as hell don't like finding out this kind of stuff from them. Now, get busy."

CHAPTER ELEVEN

Johnny Collins walked out of the police station and paused. He stood still for a moment, looked around at the buildings, glanced toward the street sign on the corner and wondered why he hadn't thought to pick up a street map at the airport. He took a couple steps forward then stopped. With a deep sigh, he turned and walked toward a tall gray haired man that had just crossed the street.

With a bewildered look on his face, he asked, "Can you point me in the direction of the Coroner's Office?"

The man stopped and looked directly at Johnny. He turned his head and looked back down the street toward the police station. "Sure. What did you need? Maybe I can help you."

Johnny smiled and answered, "I really hate to bother you. Just point me in the right direction. I just need to go talk to them for a few minutes."

The man pulled at his navy blue suit coat and said, "Say, don't I know you? You look and sound awfully familiar."

ASSIGNMENT: RENO, NEVADA

Johnny laughed and started to walk away. He answered, "No, I rather doubt that. I'm new to Reno."

The man turned back and then turned again began to follow Johnny. He called, "Hey wait!" and walked in front of Johnny, turned and looked directly into Johnny's eyes. "I do know you. You're Johnny Collins. You're Joe's brother."

Johnny stepped backwards and hesitated. He frowned studying the older man. Finally, he said, "Yes, I am, but I'm positive I've not met you before."

The man chuckled and slapped Johnny on the back. "Hell, I'd have know you anywhere. My name is Tom Clausen." He extended his hand and smiled. "Joe and I were poker buddies. I feel as though I met you years ago and grew up with you."

"You and my brother were friends?"

Tom laughed, "I guess you might say that. Many a night I felt as if I were supporting him. He was lucky at poker, but you probably already know that."

Johnny answered, "Actually, I don't remember Joe every saying anything about playing poker. But, I'm glad to hear that he won occasionally."

"Huh, I wish it had been only occasionally," Clausen laughed and once again slapped Johnny on his back.

Johnny smiled. "Would you like to walk with me over to the Coroner's Office? I have to go claim Joe's personal things."

The stranger shook his head and brushed some invisible dust off his suit sleeve. "Darn, I'd like to help but I have to go to work. I think the boss would frown on me taking time off just now." Clausen turned around and pointed back down the street. "The office you need is down there. Go to Mill Street and turn right on Kirman Avenue. You're only a couple blocks from there. You'll see a brass plaque beside the door."

"Thanks. When do you get off work?" Johnny asked after he turned around and faced the direction to the Coroner's Office.

"I'm supposed to be off at five, but who knows?" Clausen took a step forward and stopped. "Want to get together later? I'd love to talk to you about Joe."

Johnny nodded. "I'd like that."

Clausen reached into his pocket and took out a small spiral notebook and pencil. He looked up at Johnny and asked, "Where are you staying? I'm sure you're not staying out at Joe's place."

Johnny reached into his pocket and searched for a business card from his hotel. "I'm staying at a hotel near the bowling center. It would help me if you would go with me to Joe's place. Would that be possible?"

Clausen shook his head. "You need to go out there in the daylight. I don't think I can get away in time today. Have you talked to Sarah or Peggy yet? One of them should be able to get away easier than me."

"Well, old poker buddy of my brother, give me a call and maybe we can get together and go out to eat or have a drink." Johnny dug around some more in his pocket. "Thought I had a business card with the hotel address on it but I can't seem to find it."

Clausen laughed. "If it's near the bowling center, there are only two in that area. I'll find you and if you aren't in when I call, I'll leave a message." He turned and took a couple steps back toward the police station. Turning again toward Johnny, he asked, "Do you have a car?" Before Johnny answered, Clausen glanced at his watch.

"Yes, a rental. It's parked over there." Johnny pointed to the other side of the street. He turned and took a couple steps forward. "Please, be sure and call me. I'd like to reminisce about my brother with you. I'm only going to be in town for a couple of days."

"Sure will. If you run into any problems, give me a call here at the station." Clausen started walking away, but turned back and added. "My name is Tom Clausen. Remember that."

"I will," Johnny answered. He stood and watched the older man walk through the door into the police station before he turned and started down the street. He smiled as he walked. Something about meeting a friend of Joe's made him feel better.

CHAPTER TWELVE

Victor Smith stood outside his motel waiting for Chris Gannon to arrive. He had a frown on his face and his small suitcase was on the sidewalk in front of him. He tapped his foot on the sidewalk and studied the cars as they passed. When he saw Chris arrive, he pushed his suitcase closer to the side of the street.

"Say, what's with the suitcase?" Chris asked as he jumped out of the driver's seat of a jeep and opened the back hatch. "Are you leaving already?"

Victor left the bag sitting on the sidewalk and got into the jeep. "Just put the bag in the back. I'll explain as we drive."

Chris shrugged and did as he was told. "So, what gives?" he asked once he was back behind the wheel.

Smith raised his head and stared at Chris. "What did you tell the hotel people when you made the reservation?" Didn't you tell them that I would be staying indefinitely?" His blue eyes locked on Chris Gannon's face as he waited for an answer.

Gannon frowned. "I don't remember what I said. What's wrong?"

"I have been evicted. They told me about twenty minutes ago that I had to leave. They are expecting some type of a convention and all the rooms are reserved."

"Ha, is that all?" Chris answered. He started the vehicle and slowly moved out into the morning traffic. "Well, if worse comes to worse you can move in with me. I've got two queen beds in my room."

Smith winced. "Before we go out to the storage shed, I need to find a place to stay. What's around here that's respectable? I don't want to stay in any flea bag place, but I also don't want the hotel management breathing down my neck."

Gannon shrugged. "They're all pretty good. Say there is one not far from the strip that's supposed to be quite reasonable. It's new and has several floors. Since it's new, I've heard they are willing to do almost anything to get their rooms filled. Would that be alright?"

Smith smiled. "That sounds fine. I think being up a couple stories would be best. I could look down on the city. Let's go there and see if they have any vacancies."

Gannon wove in and out of traffic, slowed and pulled into a parking spot in front of the new hotel. He said, "It has a couple different entrances. This is probably the least busy side. Do you want me to register you or do you want to register yourself?"

"You register me in your name and get the key. We can keep my suitcase in the car until we're finished with the storage shed." Victor leaned back against the seat and sighed. "How come you're driving a jeep this morning? What happened to the sedan?"

"Oscar had some errands to do and wanted to use it. We have a couple different vehicles that we keep in a garage just off the strip. I thought this might be better if we found our items. Since there aren't any seats in the back, we'll have more room to carry the cartons."

Smith looked at Gannon and asked, "That's if we find it, isn't it?"

Gannon glanced at Smith and looked away. It was obvious to Smith that Gannon didn't like him but he really didn't care. To Smith, there were few men that he cared whether they lived or died and Gannon was certainly not one of them.

Smith shyly watched Gannon out of the corner of his eye. He saw Gannon grit his teeth. When Smith first heard that he was going to the states he was excited. But now he didn't appreciate the change in his original plans and this side trip to Reno. A little thing like having to change hotels was a nuisance and something he really didn't like having to do. Remembering how assignments had gone sour, he knew that small details were often just the beginning of bigger problems.

Gannon slid out of the driver's seat and said, "I'll be a minute. I'll leave the keys here just in case you have to move."

Smith nodded and watched Gannon go into the door. He scratched the side of his nose slightly and pulled down the passenger's sun visor mirror and studied his face. Taking both hands, he touched his face with his fingertips, taking care to stroke the edge of his face near his ears. Turning his face, he smiled.

He liked what he saw. He thought even his mother would not be able to recognize him now.

Within minutes, Gannon returned and scooted behind the wheel. He said, "You can go in whenever you want. I already signed in and paid cash for seven days in advance. I explained that I was going to be working here in Reno and would be working long hours and split shifts. I gave the address of a company that is located in Sparks as my working address. It would be very unusual for the hotel management to check it. They said that if I were to use the telephone I would have to give them a credit card. I gave them an extra fifty dollars as a deposit to pay for any phone calls "I" might have to make."

He started the jeep and pulled out into the traffic and stopped at a red light on Virginia. He turned to face Smith and said, "I'd suggest you go outside the hotel to a public telephone if you need to make any personal phone calls. Ever since the World Trade Center attacks and establishment of the new Homeland Security Agency, the phone companies and the government have instigated all sorts of abilities to trace calls."

Smith grimaced and glanced out his window. It was times like this that he missed the old communist ways. Then, there was only one way of doing things.

The men continued in silence. They passed several warehouses and small industrial offices. When Gannon got close to the storage sheds, Smith asked, "There shouldn't be any problem getting into the shed, should there?" He looked at the gated area and added, "You have identified the right key, haven't you?"

Gannon turned and irritated looked at Smith and answered, "Yes, of course I have the key." As Gannon slowed down to make the turn into the gateway, he licked his lips and glanced back at Smith. "You might want to check for a guard?"

Smith twisted in his seat and leaned forward to study the area. He could see several rows of attached sheds and small pathways between them. As he turned back he noticed a shed that protruded out further than the rest. "Is it customary for such places to have guards? I would think that dogs would be enough?"

Gannon drove the jeep through the open gate. He slowed down and studied the numbers on the side of the buildings. "Some do and some don't," he said as he squinted in the bright sun. "Most of these places people come and go as they wish."

Smith sighed and leaned back. "That's good. I certainly don't want to have any problems."

Gannon tipped his head in agreement and drove slowly in front of the buildings in order to read the numbers as he passed.

Smith glanced at Gannon and noticed Gannon had a confused expression. "You know what we are looking for, don't you?"

Gannon quickly glanced back at Smith. "Yes, of course. I'm checking the numbers looking for the one that we want." As he talked, he rotated the steering wheel clockwise. He looked back at the road and slammed on his brakes. The jeep stopped on top of a steep embankment.

Smith pushed himself up and looked out the driver's side at the sharp drop. He leaned back in his seat and took a deep breath. "You had better keep your eyes on the road. You'll get us killed."

Gannon silently put the jeep in reverse and crept backwards. When he knew he was safely away from the edge of the road, he moved back closer to the sheds. "There it is over there," he said as he got his voice back. He slowed down and inspected the deserted area in front of them.

Smith started to open the door, then closed it and asked, "Do you suppose they have those dogs wandering around during the daytime?"

Gannon laughed. "Doesn't look like it. I haven't seen any since we drove onto the property. They probably only release them at night when the gates are closed and locked."

Smith took the ring of locker keys off the dashboard and held them up to his face. "Which one is it?" he asked.

Gannon answered without looking at Smith. "It's the one that reads "Airport units."

Smith studied the keys carefully and found the correct long silver key. He could barely read the imprint of the number. He licked his finger and rubbed it a couple times across the indent. "It's a good thing those dogs are not out. At least we have that on our side. It looks like we need locker 827. I'm going to try and find it." He opened the door.

"Wait," Gannon said. "Close the door. I'll drive to it. That will create less attention." He put on his left directional signal.

Just as he started to turn a red station wagon pulled out from the driveway, passed directly in front of them, narrowly missing the jeep.

Gannon slammed on the brakes as the men stared at the car. Gannon asked, "Was the driver a woman or a man?"

Smith turned and saw the driver spin the car's tires and heard the sound of several small pieces of stone fly up and hit against the jeep's windshield. He answered, "I'm not sure but I think it might have been a female."

Both men stared as the station wagon disappeared around a corner.

Smith gasped, "Damn, she sure is in a hurry. Women drivers."

Gannon stretched his head around and watched the red vehicle pull back out onto the main road. "I wish I'd gotten a good look at the driver."

After taking a couple deep breaths to settle himself, Gannon drove the jeep along the driveway and stopped in front of number 827. "That's it," he pointed. "The one on the right."

Smith jumped out and quickly opened the storage-shed door.

Gannon rolled down the driver's window and glanced back through his rear view mirror. "Blasted. We must have tripped some type of an alarm. There's a man with a clipboard coming around the buildings and walking directly toward us."

Smith walked over to the jeep and hoarsely whispered to Gannon. "Don't say a word. I'll handle this. You turn this thing and park it near the door and open the rear while I talk.

Smith walked down the pathway, turned and, without pausing in his stride, glanced back at Gannon who had done as he was told. Smith continued toward the man. "Good morning," he called as he walked.

ASSIGNMENT: RENO, NEVADA

The apparent storage manager was dressed in faded blue jeans and a light blue denim shirt with a sleeveless, light blue vest. He was a short but wild looking man with wind burned skin and short gray hair that stood straight up. He had a Minnesota Twins baseball cap sticking out of his vest pocket.

"How can I help you?" Smith asked with his best Texas drawl.

"I'm the manager, and I need you to sign in," he said. He walked toward Smith and held the clipboard up and waited for Smith to take it. "We've been having some problems recently and the boss wants everyone to sign in and out." He pulled a ballpoint pen out of his vest pocket and handed it to Smith.

"No problem," Smith answered. He took the board and scribbled his name on the line and handed it back to the man. "Boy, that lady that just left here sure seemed to be in a hurry."

The manager made a face and commented, "Yeah, she buzzed right by me but I got her license plate number."

Smith laughed. "Women drivers." He turned and began walking back to Gannon and the jeep.

The manager glanced at the clipboard and called, "Hey, wait just a minute. I need to see the key with the number of the shed you want to open."

Smith turned and held up the key. He called, "That would be shed 829."

The manager pulled the clipboard up and began writing and then shouted, "What was that number again? My pen seems to be skipping."

Smith called out loud automatically as he walked. "829".

97

Smith turned and moved back to the shed. As he walked he shook his head and kicked pebbles. He hoped that the manager didn't ask to see the key because he had purposely given the wrong shed number.

The manager called back, "Just honk when you leave and I'll make a note of the time. That way you won't have to stop back at the office." He turned and began walking back around the corner.

Smith turned, stood for a moment and watched the manager. He was pleased that the manager never looked back to see exactly which shed they were opening.

"Damn, I don't have a good feeling about this," Smith said when he walked up beside Gannon. "When we leave I want to stop back at the office."

Gannon frowned. "Why? The manager said just to honk."

"Just because," Smith answered and helped Gannon push the large overhead door up.

Gannon walked inside and swore under his breath. "There doesn't seem to be anything here but furniture. You know what we're looking for, don't you?"

Smith smiled. "Yes, I know what we are trying to find but I am not sure what it will be in. You go back to the jeep and angle it so that it faces the road and stay in the driver's seat with the motor running just in case we have to leave in a hurry. I want to check this place over carefully."

Gannon stomped out to the jeep. He told himself as he walked that this wasn't working out to his liking. He had a bad feeling.

Smith pulled a pair of leather gloves out of his pocket and slipped them on. He moved around the dark warehouse, pulled at the furniture and opened every drawer. He walked back to the doorway and slammed his hand against the doorframe. He opened a couple of boxes that he found in a far corner.

"Damn," he said. Then, he walked out onto the driveway and looked around. He went back to the shed, pulled down the door and walked back to the jeep.

Gannon left the engine running and got out of the jeep. "Find anything?" he asked.

"Go lock everything up," Smith said handing Gannon the key ring. He walked around and got into the passenger side and waited for Gannon to return.

Finally, Gannon returned, got in and put the jeep in gear and asked, "What next?"

"How in the hell do I know?" Smith answered. He hit the dashboard with his fist and sent the maps flying in the air. "You're the one that was supposed to find out where Charlie stashed the shipment."

"Well, it looks as if I don't know," Gannon answered with a shrug. He avoided looking directly at Smith. "Do you want to go back to the hotel now?"

"Do you have manure for brains?" Smith asked. He was totally frustrated and his face was warm. "Now, for sure, I have to stop at the manager's office. I don't want him telling anyone that we were here."

Gannon didn't say a word. He headed straight for the storage unit entrance and parked directly in front of the manager's office. "Do you want me to go in with you?" He pointed across a dusty driveway, "That must be his old pickup over there."

Smith glanced around and pointed up at the top of the doorway. "I want you to throw a rock at that surveillance camera. Break it and check to make sure that there aren't anymore around. Also check to see if there is some type of a timer by the gate. If so, take it out too."

Gannon didn't say anything but pulled the jeep back into the shadows. "What are you going to do?"

Smith laughed. "I'll be back in a couple minutes. You make sure that no one comes in."

Gannon felt uneasy but did as he was told.

Smith took his time walking to the office. His eyes darted around from object to object looking for any sign of anyone else in the area. Carefully, he opened the office door. When he entered, he heard the manager in a back room talking on a phone.

Smith froze in place and then stepped into the shadows and listened.

"Yes, someone is here now," the manager said. His words carried clearly. "There are two of them. They went to Old Charlie's shed. They're going to honk on the way out so I can mark the time they leave on the paper. I'm not sure I can hold them long enough for you to get here."

Smith rubbed his gloved hands together. The leather made his hands feel warm. Carefully, he tiptoed into the office and crept up behind the manager just as he lowered the telephone back on the cradle.

Carefully, Smith raised his hands and put them around the manager's throat. He pressed his fingers together, locking them.

ASSIGNMENT: RENO, NEVADA

The manager struggled, turned his body and stared directly into Smith's face. He fought Smith's hands and tried to speak, but couldn't.

For several seconds, he struggled to get free but Smith pressed harder and harder. Finally, the manager's eyes rolled back into his head, and he slumped forward on the desk with a soft plunk. A small stream of blood trickled out of his mouth and nose. It made a slight red stain on the white paper on the desktop.

Smith rearranged the man's body to look as if he were sleeping. He found the clipboard, released the papers and took all of them.

He glanced around the room, threw books on the floor and opened several desk drawers. He walked back to a file cabinet, opened the drawers and fingered through the papers. He found a gray metal box, opened it and took out a stack of bills and several rolls of coins. He put them in his pocket along with the papers. Then, he walked back out the door.

He stopped to think and remembered the surveillance camera. He turned and walked back into the office and found a small video recorder attached to the wall directly over the door. He reached up, ejected the tape, pulled the wires off the unit and put the cassette into his pocket. Satisfied that there wasn't anything else, he turned and walked on out the door.

Gannon waited until Smith was in the jeep and they were a couple miles away from the storage units before he asked, "Why did you take all the papers? Why not just the one that you wrote on?"

Smith was looking through the papers and glanced toward Gannon. "The police have ways of reading the slightest indent on paper. Normally, if you just shine a flashlight on the paper you can read any imprints. I didn't want to leave the smallest clue."

Gannon looked impressed, rolled his eyes, and asked, "Where to?"

Smith took off his leather gloves and placed them on the dashboard. He rubbed his hands together and finally said, "Stop at one of the big chain restaurants. Let's have something to eat. That'll give me a chance to figure out what we'll do next."

CHAPTER THIRTEEN

Johnny Collins walked down Mill Street and stopped in front of a large store window. He stepped close to it and pretended to be looking at the store display. The hairs on the back of his neck itched. That was normally a sure sign that something wasn't right.

For several seconds, he stood and studied the display of computer parts. He kept his head forward and turned his eyes to see the reflections in the glass. His glance moved slowly over the people passing.

A tall man dressed in a wrinkled blue business suit stopped and stood by a parking meter several feet behind Collins. The man appeared to be fumbling in his pants pocket for change, but kept his head turned slightly toward Johnny.

Johnny watched the man's head and avoided meeting his glances just in time. Moving forward a few steps, Johnny glanced back toward the man. When his eyes flicked over the waiting man, Johnny started forward. The man turned and began following Johnny.

Keeping the man's full attention, Johnny turned and continued walking down Mill Street. He stepped lightly to listen for any sound of footsteps behind him. At the corner of Mill and Kilman, Johnny turned right, keeping on the right side of the street. He looked up and checked street numbers. The Washoe County Coroner's office was directly across the street from where he stood.

He stepped to the edge of the sidewalk and stopped. An ambulance went roaring pass, barely missing him. Johnny jumped backwards bumping into someone.

He spun to try to regain his footing, and looked directly into the face of the man that was watching him.

"Sorry," Johnny said automatically. He moved smoothly out of the man's path and adjusted his leather jacket. His heart was pounding.

"Do you have a minute?" the stranger asked taking a step closer to Johnny. "I'd like to talk to you."

Johnny stopped and looked directly into the stranger's face. He studied the stranger's eyes and asked, "What about?" A deep frown covered his forehead because the stranger was twice as wide as Johnny was and he was blocking Johnny's movement.

"I knew Joe and I want to find out what happened to him," the stranger whispered with a husky voice.

Johnny's eyes went wide. When he regained his composure, he asked, "How did you know Joe?"

The stranger took a step closer to Johnny. "Joe and I often had tables beside each other at the Flea Market on Saturday mornings." The stranger took a deep breath, bent over and coughed several times.

ASSIGNMENT: RENO, NEVADA

For a second or more, Johnny thought he should pat the stranger on the back, but, instead, stood quietly and waited for the coughing spell to subside. When the man stood straight again, Johnny meaningfully glanced at his watch and remarked, "I have to go to the Coroner's office now."

The stranger took several deep breaths and looked up and down the street. "I can wait for you. There's a park over there a couple blocks. It's called Pickett Park. I'll go there and wait for you." He pulled a dirty blue handkerchief out of his back pocket and wiped his lips. "I'll wait as long as it takes. You don't need to hurry on my account."

Johnny looked into the older man's eyes. They were bloodshot and the whites had a yellow cast. Johnny couldn't decide whether the man had been drinking. He watched the man as he turned to start down the street. He said, "I shouldn't be too long. Is the park large? Will I be able to find you?"

As the man started walking away he answered with a wheeze, "You won't have any problem. I'll be on one of the benches near the pond."

Johnny took a couple steps forward and then turned and looked back toward the man. His sixth sense training kicked in, and he felt uneasy. There was no one on the street except the man, who now was almost a block away. He couldn't see any reason for his worry.

Taking a deep breath, Johnny stepped closer to the edge of the curb, then reared backward as a speeding jeep flashed passed him. It had been so close that Johnny could feel the exhaust fumes against his skin.

His stomach turned over as he muttered and regained his step. Now, he looked both ways, hurried across the street and headed directly toward the Washoe County Coroner's Office. Before he entered the Coroner's Office he turned and looked down the street at the tall man who was just rounding the corner.

He again looked at the sign on the door, then reached up and turned the handle.

"I'm here to claim my brother's personal property." He leaned forward and spoke through a small opening to an elderly lady sitting behind a desk, filing her fingernails.

The gray-haired lady looked up. Her dark blue eyes flashed as she smiled and asked, "Who would that be?" Her voice was husky and scratchy from years of heavy smoking.

"Joe Collins," Johnny answered as he leaned against the opening.

The lady sadly smiled and pointed toward a door at the end of the hallway. Johnny turned and looked just as the door opened. Lt. Bob Larson stood in the open doorway. Larson looked at Collins and motioned with his hand.

"You have to fill out this form first," the receptionist said, when she saw Collins take a couple steps away from her window. "You can't do anything without filling out the paperwork." She pushed a clipboard and pen through the opening.

"Do I have to do it now?" Johnny asked.

"Now," the lady stated firmly. "You can go over there and sit down and fill it out." She pointed with her long fingernails toward two wooden chairs placed against the side of the wall. "The paperwork has to be done before you can do anything else. The staff inside will just send you back here to do the paperwork so you might as well do it now." She stood up and put her hands on her hips and sympathetically looked at Johnny. Her gray hair flipped from side to side as she shook her head in disgust.

Johnny glanced at the woman and then at Larson who had stopped to talk to someone in the room he was just leaving. For an instant, Johnny considered filling out the form where he was, but took the clipboard and walked to an empty chair as he was instructed.

"Collins, is there anything that I can help you with?" Larson asked, as he neared the chair where Johnny was sitting.

Johnny looked up; smiling he looked at his watch. "You sure got here fast." He brushed back at the paperwork and continued, "No, I think I'm fine. I'll finish this and then get Joe's things and move on."

Larson shrugged and took a couple steps away. Then, he turned and looked Johnny straight in the eyes and asked, "Where are you going next?" He moved to stand in front of Johnny and shifted his weight from one foot to the other as he waited for an answer.

Johnny held the pen and twirled it a couple times in his fingers. He pursed his lips together appearing to be in deep thought. Finally, he answered, "Probably to the funeral home and church. I want to make arrangements for some type of a local service. I think that his friends would appreciate that."

Larson nodded. "That's good. Be sure and let us know when the service is. I'll post it on the bulletin board. I'm sure there are some of the men that will want to attend."

Johnny laid the clipboard on the empty chair beside him. He looked up at Larson and asked, "When are you going to tell me everything that you know about Joe's murder?"

Larson took a step backward and frowned. He put his hands up to his chest and said, "Whoa. I have told you all I know, which is almost nothing. I just don't know anything more." He was studying Johnny's face as he talked.

"Maybe, I should be doing some investigating on my own," Johnny answered sharply.

Larson laughed. "I hardly think so. I really doubt if you can find out anything that we haven't already discovered." He turned and took several steps toward the door.

Turning back toward Johnny, he asked, "What do you plan on doing, calling some of your buddies at the CIA to help you?" The tone of his voice was filled with sarcasm.

Johnny stared at Larson and then quietly picked up the clipboard. "If I have to," he answered. His words were barely above a whisper.

Larson turned and walked directly back to Johnny. His face had turned a shade of beet red. Putting his hands on his hips, he stared at Johnny and said in a cold tone, "Now, don't you come in to my jurisdiction and tell me what you can and can't do. Stay out of this. We'll find out why your brother was killed and who was responsible. I don't want any blow hard big shots from Washington, Langley or California, nosing around my city meddling in our affairs. Do you understand me?"

Larson pointed his finger in emphasis at Johnny and shook it several times as he spoke. "I can promise you that if you start digging into this, I will slap your sorry ass in custody faster than you can spell CIA. Do you hear me?"

Johnny chuckled and smiled. He frowned at Larson and then turned his attention back to his clipboard. He didn't say another word.

Furiously, Larson turned and thundered down the hall. A loud bang shattered the silence as Larson slammed the door behind him.

CHAPTER FOURTEEN

Johnny turned the corner of Ryland and Kilman and walked into Pickett Park. He brushed his hand against his pocket and felt Joe's wallet and watch that he had been given at the Coroner's office. For a moment, he hesitated and wondered if he should check the wallet, but decided that a couple more hours wouldn't make any difference one way or the other.

"I'm sorry it took me so long," Johnny apologized, stopping in front of the man that he had met earlier in the day. "Thank you for waiting."

The older man pulled his wrinkled blue suit tight around him and slid over to the edge of the bench. He patted the wood.

"Sit down, if you like. The wood's only cold for a moment." He smiled and his bright blue eyes followed Johnny's movements carefully.

Johnny sat halfway on the bench. He glanced at the shabby man and then let his eyes move slowly over the park around him. Turning back to the man, he asked, "Well, what did you want to talk about?"

The man opened his mouth and said, "First, I want to introduce myself to you." All of a sudden, he closed his mouth, took a deep breath and began coughing. His face flushed a bright color.

Johnny glanced at the man. "You should see a doctor about that cough. You sound as if you have walking pneumonia or something." Johnny reached over and popped the man hard on the middle of his back.

The man looked up at Johnny and took a deep breath. "Sorry, about that. My name is Terry Granger." He took several more deep breaths. "Maybe, I should go see a doctor? I think the clinic is open until four today. First, I need to talk to you about Joe."

Johnny relaxed and let his back touch the wood of the bench. "Well, talk slowly. I've got plenty of time. Would you feel better if we went to that restaurant across the street and had something warm to drink?" He pointed to the Embers restaurant across the street and down the block.

"No, I'm fine." Granger stiffened and looked around the park. He gulped involuntarily when he saw a red car turn the corner in front of them. His eyes darted from the street to the sidewalk and back to the park. "I want to get out of here. It's probably best that we're not seen talking like this."

The remark startled Johnny and he asked, "Why in heaven's name would anyone care if I talked to you?"

Granger leaned forward and whispered. "Somebody cares. Believe me. They killed Joe and Old Charlie, and they'll kill me if they see us together." He pulled his coat around him, trying to pull his long neck down into the collar.

Johnny laughed. "Hardly. I think you're seeing make believe boogie-men." For the first time, Johnny caught the smell of whiskey on the old man's breath.

"This is real, man," the old man grunted. He nervously flexed moved his shoulders as he talked and rubbed his arms briskly. "These guys want the stuff that Old Charlie got from those Russians. They'll kill anyone and everyone until they get it."

Johnny's eyes went wide. "What stuff from the Russians?"

Granger cringed and his lips quivered. He looked as if he had seen a ghost. "I really don't know but I overheard Joe and Charlie talking about some old stuff that Charlie bought from this guy from California. Charlie told Joe that he knew the guy was Russian. Charlie also told Joe that he was sure that someone had broken into his storage places."

"Did you hear what Charlie had bought and why Joe was concerned or involved?" Johnny asked, leaning closer to the man. Johnny looked around to see if someone could be near enough to hear them talking.

The old man surveyed the area and finally answered. "No, they caught me listening, then they turned and moved away from me."

Granger looked at Johnny and then rubbed his hands together. His nose was red and moist and his cheeks were scaly.

Johnny glanced at the old man's dirty hands and then, toward his face. "Have you told anyone else about this?"

The old man looked at Johnny as he spoke, "No, I stay away from the police. I was going to say something to Clausen at Charlie's memorial service, but didn't when I saw Joe talking to Clausen. I figured that Joe was telling him. When they both looked my way, I turned and slipped into a group of people leaving the funeral home."

"What have you heard about Joe's death?" Johnny asked as he stood up, stamping his feet a couple times to get the blood circulating again.

The old man shrugged. "Only that he was killed. I don't even know how he was killed. The streets are pretty quiet about it." He bent his head toward his shoulder and looked up at Collins. "How was he killed? Was he shot or what?"

Johnny leaned over toward the old man and whispered, "His throat was cut."

Granger recoiled, shivered, and started coughing again. When the fit passed, he started to cry. "I know it. I know it. I'm going to be next. I just know it." Hugging himself tightly, he shook his head back and forth; tears streaming down his face.

Johnny reached down and put his hand on Granger's shoulder. "I doubt if anyone knows anything about you." He patted the man several times and looked around the deserted park. "Where do you live? Do you want me to take you there?"

Granger's teeth began to chatter. He pulled away. "No, I'm fine," he finally sputtered out. "It's best that we're not seen together. I'm sure they know all about you and I don't want to end up like Joe and Charlie."

Johnny stepped back, paused, and looked down at the obviously frightened old man. He reached into his pocket and took out his wallet. He handed Granger a twenty-dollar bill. "I want you to go get something warm to eat and then go to the clinic and see someone about that cough."

After the old man took the money, Johnny helped the man stand up. "Are you sure you don't want me to go with you?"

Granger pulled his wrinkled suit coat around his chest and his hands back into his sleeves. He looked up at Johnny. "I'll be fine. You don't have to worry about me. Just look out for yourself. Always, look over your shoulder."

Johnny leaned over and whispered. "Where is the storage place that Charlie used? Did he and Joe share the same shed?"

Granger laughed a deep, hacking laugh. "Hardly. Neither of them trusted one another, or anyone else. I'm not sure where Joe's was, but one time I followed Charlie to his."

"Will you take me there?" Joe asked.

Granger pushed one of his hands out of a sleeve. "Sure, I'll take you there." He looked up toward the sky and thought. "It's about noon. Do you want to go now?"

Johnny shook his head. "Unfortunately, I can't go now. I've got to get over to the funeral home. Can we go later in the day? We could stop by Joe's house. Can we do that?"

Granger rocked back and forth several times. He rubbed his hand against his pocket where he had put the money that Johnny gave him. He asked, "When?"

Johnny eyed his watch. "I should be free in a couple of hours. Say three this afternoon? Where can I meet you?"

Granger shifted his body under the loose coat. He nodded his head in thought and said, "I'll meet you at the Golden Nugget. Do you know where that is?"

Johnny shrugged. "I don't have the faintest idea. Is it a casino?"

"Yes," Granger answered quickly. "There should be lots of people around. It'll be safe. You would be better off parking in the ramp-parking garage. I'll meet you on the first floor, by the steps. There's a row of nickel machines there. I'll be either playing one of them or standing near them. About three?"

"That's fine," Johnny answered, checking his watch again. He started to walk toward the old man. "Where are you going now?"

Granger bent over slightly and started walking away. "It doesn't matter. I'll be at the Golden Nugget at three." Without a look back, he turned and started toward the street.

Johnny waited a couple of minutes and started walking. Passing the Embers Restaurant, he moved back toward the police station where he had parked his car. He sauntered casually to let Granger get a good head start.

He observed Granger turn on Mill Street. Johnny swept a swift look at the old man and was barely conscious of the passing cars. He saw Granger stop at the red light at the intersection.

Johnny turned the corner and headed directly for his car. He had just opened the car door when he heard a distant cry cut shout, a loud thud, then a crash and squealing tires.

    Surprised, he turned, looking up and down the street. He couldn't see anything unusual. As he put his key in the ignition, he heard a police siren in the distance. Remembering the traffic on the East Coast, he knew that only the city's name changed; traffic was the same no matter where he went.

CHAPTER FIFTEEN

Chris Gannon drove the jeep into the parking lot of Embers restaurant after driving down Virginia Street. He swerved in and out of the cars and nearly hit a man crossing the street.

Victor Smith rode in silence. He stared directly in front of him and kept his hands folded in his lap. Once the car stopped, he unhooked his seat belt taking his time opening the door. As he stepped out of the car, he turned and for the first time in twenty minutes spoke. "I'm driving from now on."

Gannon laughed and slammed the car door. "I don't think so. You don't know the town like I do." He thought for a moment and then asked, "Do you even have a stateside license?"

"Damn right, I have one," Smith answered sharply. He walked around the front of the vehicle and turned and glowered at Gannon. "Then, you had best drive slower if you value your life." He patted his chest and walked into the restaurant without looking back.

After the waitress showed the men to a corner booth, Victor smiled at her and said, "I'll take an omelet with everything you have on it. Also black coffee."

The waitress appeared to be a young college student. She had soft brown eyes and shoulder length brown hair. She smiled, flipped her hair slightly when she heard the Texas accent and answered slowly, "I'll get you just that." She turned toward Gannon. "And, sirs, what can I get you this morning?"

Gannon flipped open the menu and looked back at the young lady. "How about you?" he asked with a smile.

The student politely smiled, but only answered, "I hardly think so. I only started the shift. I'll bring coffee and you can have a few more minutes to read the menu." She turned to walk away.

Gannon reached for her skirt and tugged at it. She stopped, brushing his hand away. He immediately grabbed her again and said, "I'll take a ham and cheese omelet and black coffee."

The waitress pushed Gannon's hand onto the top of the table. She held her pad and pencil and wrote down his order. "Is that all?" she asked looking at each of the men.

Both men nodded and watched her walk away with a naturally swaying motion.

Smith looked at Gannon and said, "Stop acting like a sex-starved college boy. We have serious business to attend to."

The waitress reappeared just as Gannon was about to speak. Instead, he turned his attention back to the waitress and grinned broadly. After she put the coffee on the table, he said, "Thank you, my dear."

ASSIGNMENT: RENO, NEVADA

She turned, winked and headed back toward the kitchen.

Once she was out of range, Smith turned back toward Gannon. Leaning across the table he looked directly into his eyes. "What are we going to do next? We have to find that merchandise."

Gannon shrugged. "We will have to find out where else McGuire stored his stuff. Maybe we should go out to Collins' shack and look around?"

For the next several minutes, the two men discussed all the possibilities that they had. Smith finally leaned back and directed his attention out the window. It was still morning and the tourists and gamblers were starting to fill the sidewalks.

His eyes aimlessly roamed up and down the sidewalks and watched for several minutes, casually noticing the differences between American tourists and the European ones he normally saw in Moscow. Totally absorbed in the scene around him, he felt a sudden vibration against his chest. He yanked his legs back and spilled some of the coffee.

"What's wrong?" Gannon asked grabbing a couple of extra napkins. He quickly placed them over the coffee puddle.

Victor looked startled and then sheepishly felt his pocket. He reached inside his coat, bringing out a small black box. He flipped the cover to reveal a small portable cell telephone with a tiny screen.

"Wow!" Gannon exclaimed. "What's that? I've never seen one of those."

Victor stared at Gannon and turned his head to read the screen in front of him. "I need to get to a secure phone right away," he said, raising his eyes slightly but

119

sucking his cheeks against his teeth so that Gannon couldn't see any expression on his face.

"Hell, man, you can use any of those over by the door. Here in America, we don't have to worry about that crap of being secure." Gannon laughed and signaled for the waitress to pour more coffee.

Victor looked at Chris and pulled himself to the edge of the seat. "Stay here. I'll be right back."

Smith walked to the phones, looked at all three of them for a couple of seconds and then walked to the one whose side was open on the street. He took the receiver off the hook, read the small print on the base of the phone and dug a quarter out of his pocket.

After he dialed the number, he put the coin in the slot and held the receiver away from his ear. Hearing the phone ring, he massaged a thin piece of metal that he had extracted from his small black box. Holding the metal against the phone, pressed the ring on his finger against the top of his black box computer phone, punched enter and waited for the connection to click through.

He felt uneasy, but the feeling wasn't unusual. It was times like this that he always had a feeling someone was watching. He passed it off. Being Russian had an effect on the way he thought and acted no matter where he was.

"What's up?" he asked as soon as he heard a click on the line. He placed the small black box on a shelf by the phone.

He held the receiver close to his lips and spoke once the ring was answered. For several minutes, he stood and talked. Nodding his head now and then, and trying to keep his voice low so no one would pay any special attention to him.

As he talked he kept his body turned slightly so he could see what was going on around him. He wanted to watch Gannon and see the people that walked by the window. In a flash of ghostly recognition, he turned pale as he pressed the phone closer to his lips and blurted out, "I thought you told me Johnny Collins was dead?"

His eyes grew wide. He licked his lips while he listened. He could feel his temper rising. "Well, I don't give a damn what your files say. I was sure that I had seen him earlier this morning and just now he walked by the window of the restaurant where I am eating!"

He listened for a few more seconds and without saying another word, Victor put the phone carefully back on its cradle and disconnected his equipment. His eyes darted around the restaurant as he took a step back to his table.

Victor walked carefully as if he were unsure of his steps. His thoughts swirled in his brain. The last time he had seen Johnny Collins was several years earlier near the border of East and West Germany.

Their misadventure was still fresh in his mind although it was over ten years old. Victor could vividly remember the chase Collins had led him from Budapest to Prague and into Hof, Germany. Sharp pangs of tension ran up and down his spine as he remembered catching up with Collins near Hof Air Force Base just across the five-mile safety zone in West Germany.

They fought, and he was able to retrieve the book with the names of all the European KGB agents. Victor thought he had left Collins for dead. The thought that he had failed to kill Collins shocked him.

Victor had only briefly seen a man walk past the window, but in those few seconds, an inner alarm shrilled. He was sure the man he had seen was Johnny Collins. There was something distinctive about the way that Collins moved, an animal swaying of the arms, and the way he walked. It was like seeing an old movie film.

Rapidly making the connection, he now surmised that Johnny Collins was related to Joe Collins. His heart raced as he considered the possibility as he hurried back to the booth and Gannon.

"What's up?" Gannon asked. "You look as if you have just seen a ghost?"

"Come on. We're going," Victor answered after taking a couple forks full of the omelet. "Pay the bill. We have things to do."

Gannon's mouth dropped open. He stared at Smith and the food in front of him. Hurriedly, he shoveled the last few bites.

"Get moving," Victor hissed. "Now!" Grabbing his coat off the seat, he headed for the doorway without looking back.

Gannon took a sip of coffee, rose hurriedly to obey and accidentally shook the table. A glass of water went flying and crashed to the floor. The water flew every which way landing on an elderly man eating at the next table.

Gannon grabbed the check and his coat and briefly called, "I'm sorry."

ASSIGNMENT: RENO, NEVADA

Without looking back, he scurried toward the other side of the room with the check flapping back and forth in his hand. As he moved, he managed to put his coat on.

CHAPTER SIXTEEN

Johnny Collins took a deep breath, perused the area surrounding the machines and looked at the big clock on the wall. It was just three. Once again, he scanned the first floor of the Golden Nugget and carefully searching for Terry Granger.

He waited for a moment and then began walking. A parking validation sign caught his attention. While still studying the area, he handed his parking ticket stub to the young lady. He didn't say a word. She efficiently stamped it and handed it back.

"Enjoy your visit to the Golden Nugget. Good luck," she said with a big smile.

Johnny smiled back. "Thanks. I could sure use some good luck."

He stuck the stub into his leather jacket pocket and spotted the place by the stairs where he had agreed to meet Granger. Since Granger was nowhere in sight, he walked around the short row of nickel slots, moved to the end and leaned against a pillar. From where he stood, he was able to watch the entire area.

ASSIGNMENT: RENO, NEVADA

A skimpily dressed waitress passed and he stopped her long enough to order a soft drink. Glancing back at the large clock, he slowly rotated his view, checking the crowd once again. It was then that he noticed that everyone was staring at the television screen behind the bar area directly on his right.

A somber looking announcer was talking. Johnny leaned forward and began to read the headline running across the bottom of the screen. Unable to see it clearly, he took a several steps closer to the bar.

The television announcer said, "A fatal traffic accident on our city streets has claimed another victim earlier today. The dead man has been identified as Terry Granger, a lifetime resident of Sparks. The details are still incomplete. As reported earlier from the scene of the accident, Granger was crossing the street when hit by an on-duty plainclothes policeman. The officer said that he was on his way to investigate a previous murder between Sparks and Reno when Mr. Granger darted out in front of his vehicle. He swerved to avoid hitting the man but was unable to do so. The officer's name has not been disclosed due to further investigation. More news on today's fatal accident at five this evening."

Johnny's eyes grew wide. His emotions turned his stomach and he placed his hand over his mouth as he stared at the television screen. Finally, he set his drink down on the counter and wondered aloud. "Hells bells. What is going on here?"

CHAPTER SEVENTEEN

Johnny hurried out of the casino and ran up the stairs of the parking garage. He sat in the empty car for a few minutes collecting his thoughts.

For some unexplained but highly suspicious reason, people were dropping dead all around him. He knew somehow the deaths must all be related. For several minutes, he scanned the radio searching for an updated news bulletin regarding Granger's death. He wanted to know which police officer was involved. As he surfed, he heard reports relating to the accident but nothing new.

Nothing made sense. He took out a map from the glove compartment and studied the city. With a pen, he began marking various places. Somewhere there had to be a connection.

He checked the time. It was now almost four. A plan began to form in his mind. He started the car and once again checked his watch.

It was only a few minutes after four when he parked in front of the Antique Mall on Vasser. He was surprised to see several cars parked in the parking lot behind the mall and he could see the parking garage across the street was also busy. Sarah Cummings black Lexus was parked directly in front of him. He glanced at the vanity license plate with her name on it and smiled.

"Hey, big man. I thought you had forgotten about going out to Joe's place," Peggy called as he walked through the antique mall door. She was arranging a display of old fashioned clothing in the mall window.

Johnny nodded. "I've been quite busy today. May I ask which one of you can go with me?"

Peggy raised her hand. "I'm going to ride with you and Sarah's going to come by as soon as she can after she closes." She stood up, adjusting her tight sweater and looked up at the clock. "It won't be long until closing."

Johnny turned and followed her eyes. It had been almost twenty-four hours since he had entered the Antique Mall for the first time. He spun his keys around. "That sounds fine with me. Are you ready?"

"Let me freshen up a bit first." She hurried down a long aisle that was filled with row upon row of colored pottery.

Johnny sighed and walked toward the customer service counter and saw Lt. Clausen talking to Sarah. He took his time walking because the couple looked as if they were in the midst of an argument.

Johnny wished they would talk a little louder so he could hear what was making Sarah so upset. As if on clue, she began flailing her arms around as she talked.

Not wanting to interrupt, Johnny moved toward an ornate glass cabinet and leaned forward to study the display inside. Using the reflection, he could watch the couple. After a bit, Clausen walked away from Sarah and started to the back of the building. Johnny turned and walked up to the customer service counter.

"So, how are you today?" Sarah called when she saw him move toward her.

"Just fine. How about you?" Johnny answered quickly. He moved directly in front of the counter but still was several feet from where Sarah was standing at the far end of the counter.

When Sarah frowned, Johnny realized that she hadn't recognized him. He repeated his greeting.

"Well, Johnny Collins," she answered after a few seconds. She moved to close the gap between them.

Johnny heard footsteps and turned and saw Clausen returning back to the counter.

Sarah smiled at Johnny. "We almost gave up on you. I thought you were going to come in earlier so you could pick up Peggy and go by Joe's place. What kept you?"

"I've been a bit busier than I thought I'd be." He turned toward Clausen who had walked up to the couple. "Nice to see you again, officer. What brings you out here? I thought you were going to be busy today?"

Sarah stepped between the two men. She looked at each of them and then to Johnny. She grimaced, "Clausen's been warning me to watch out for stolen antiques. He stops by every once in a while to make sure that we stay honest."

Johnny laughed. "Guess that's as good a way as any to keep people informed." He looked around the room and scanned past several large pieces of furniture that he hadn't seen during his visit the previous evening. "Seems as if you have more things today. Does your stock turnover that quickly?"

Sarah laughed a loud long laugh. "Don't I wish? Yes, we did have a new dealer move in this morning. He's going to display some of his merchandise out here in the open area and in a booth. We highlight special articles every month. This month, we're stressing primitive works; of furniture, paintings, pottery and the like."

Johnny walked over to one of the new pieces and ran his hand over the top of a dresser. "This piece looks quite rustic." He turned around, held his arms out and asked, "Are these American?" Without waiting for an answer, he walked to a plain log plank table and carefully ran his hand over the top.

When Sarah didn't answer right away, Johnny turned around looking directly at her. Finally, she said, "I think they are from a combination of places. Quite nice, aren't they?" She walked to where Johnny was standing and took a cloth out of her back pocket and ran it over the top of the table.

"Yes, they are," answered Johnny. He flipped over a price tag and whistled. "Wow, I didn't know this style of furniture could command such a high price."

Sarah laughed again and led Johnny back toward the customer service counter. Clausen stood; watching watched the couple and then walked toward the door exiting without a word.

"You men." Sarah chuckled, shaking her finger at Johnny. "You always spoil things by bringing up what things cost."

Johnny grinned at Sarah and then turned around and paced toward the front store window. He observed

Clausen get into Sarah's black Lexus. He opened his mouth to say something, but Peggy grabbed his arm.

"Come on," she said. "Let's get going before the sun does down. It'll be hard enough to look around Joe's house with the sun up."

Johnny followed Blue Jean Peggy without saying a word. He stopped and edged back toward the counter just as Sarah picked up the phone. He called, "Do either of you know a guy by the name of Terry Granger?"

"Sure," Peggy answered instantly. "He's a friend of Joe's. What's that crazy old kook done now?"

Sarah didn't say a word. She held the phone up and silently stood staring at Johnny. Her face now was a ghostly white.

Johnny frowned, studying Sarah's face. "I thought I heard on the news earlier today that he had been killed in an accident? Did either of you hear anything about that?"

Peggy dropped her arm gasping aloud. She looked at Johnny and then at Sarah. "Are you sure? I didn't hear any such thing. Did you, Sarah?"

Sarah dropped in her chair. She was shaking uncontrollably, and her breathing was raspy. Her head dropped to her lap as if she were having some type of an attack.

Johnny and Peggy ran toward her. "Sarah, are you alright?" Johnny asked concerned.

Peggy slapped Sarah on the back several times. "Sarah, take deep breaths." She pulled her head up and striking her between the shoulder blades. "Sarah, take a deep breath." She pleadingly repeated her advice over and over.

ASSIGNMENT: RENO, NEVADA

Johnny looked around for something to drink. He spotted a soft drink can on the counter, grabbed it and shook it gently to see if any thing remained; then, he offered it to Sarah. He held it up to her lips. After she took a of couple sips, he asked, "Sarah, what is wrong?"

Sarah threw her hands up in the air and motioned for the couple to back away. "I'll be fine," she whispered, her eyes streaming. She looked frankly at Johnny, her eyes wide, and asked, "Are you sure Granger is dead?"

"Yes, I heard it," Johnny answered. He leaned his back against the counter. "I was supposed to meet him earlier today and he never show up. I just happened to catch a TV news bulletin about his death."

"How?" Sarah whispered. Her face was slowly regaining its color.

"It was a car accident near the police station. The reporter said a plainclothes policeman hit him hurrying to answer a call. Evidently, Granger darted out in front of his car."

Peggy gasped. She looked at Sarah with tears in her eyes. She opened her mouth to say something but stopped short when she saw Sarah signal with her eyes.

Johnny saw Sarah exchange looks with Peggy. He wondered what the two women knew that they didn't want to share with him.

"Maybe, we should put off going out to Joe's place until tomorrow," Johnny said.

"No," Peggy said quickly. "The sooner we get this over, the better." She turned to Sarah. "Are you still going to come out after you close?"

Sarah nodded, regaining her strength. "I should be there about five thirty or so. Then, what say, I treat you both to dinner?" She bounced off the chair and grabbed Johnny and Peggy's arms.

Johnny shrugged in agreement and looked at the two ladies. "Sounds fine with me. We'll see you out there in a few minutes." He glanced up at the clock. It was almost four forty-five.

CHAPTER EIGHTEEN

Victor Smith and Chris Gannon pulled into the antique mall parking lot as Johnny Collins and Blue Jean Peggy were pulling out. Victor stared at Collins, blinked several times and shook his head in disbelief. He was amazed that he had seen Collins three times in the same day after so many years.

"Now, let me handle this," Victor said as the two men walked through the mall entrance. "Why don't you look around and see how many other people are in the building? Try and keep them away from the front counter if you can."

"Sure. No problem, I'll stay out of your way," Gannon sarcastically replied.

Victor flashed a look at Gannon, and headed for the service desk. He called in a low voice, "I'll meet you back in the car."

Victor stopped and waited for Gannon to disappear down an aisle, then, he continued toward the salesperson that was standing near the counter. "Good afternoon, Ma'am. I wondered if you could..." He stopped in mid sentence when he saw the rustic peasant furniture.

Sarah followed his glance. "It is quite unique, isn't it?"

"Yes, ma'am, it surely is. May I ask where it's from? It looks too old to be American?"

Sarah walked out from behind the counter and walked directly to Victor. She leaned close to him and confidentially whispered, "I'm really not sure either, but I believe it's from Europe."

Victory looked down at the lady and smiled. He put his hand on her arm and held her as he walked toward the furniture. He removed his hand from her arm and walked around the table and chairs. After he ran his hands over the table, he walked back to Sarah. "Yes, I'm inclined to believe it is."

He got down on his knees and looked under the table and inspected all of the pieces more closely. Standing up again, he brushed off his knees and smiled at Sarah.

"I'm authorized to make you a handsome deal, if your interested in several of the pieces," Sarah smiled, obviously pleased with his interest.

Victor extended his hand. "I'm Victor Smith from down Dallas way. I've been looking everywhere for pieces similar to these. Do you have anymore around?"

Sarah leaned back and put her hands out in a plea. "Good heavens, man. There must be fifteen pieces here. What exactly are you looking for? A specific item?"

Victor laughed and gently touched Sarah's arm. He turned his head so his hair moved slowly with the motion. "I'm not quite sure," he laughed. "But, I will know it when I see it."

"You dealers!! That's what they all say," Sarah answered as she moved away from the furniture.

"Oh, ma'am, you have me confused with someone else. I'm a serious collector, not a dealer. Sometimes, I think we are even more dedicated." He prompted Sarah slightly. "Well, do you have any more pieces?"

Sarah sighed and turned looking up at the big clock. "Yes, I know where there are several more pieces, but they are in another storage location. Not here in this mall. It's too late to go there today, what say, we meet and go there tomorrow? I'll have to get the key to the shed first anyway."

Victor's palms began to itch. "Are you sure we can't get to it tonight? Now, you have my juices flowing. I really want to see those other pieces."

Sarah sadly shook her head. "It's getting late and I'm supposed to be meeting a friend in a few minutes. I'm not even sure that the warehouse has lights." She thought for several seconds and then added, "No, tomorrow would be best."

Victor sighed and shrugged. "Well, if that's the best you can do. You realize that I won't be able to sleep a wink tonight wondering about the pieces I'm going to see tomorrow."

Sarah looked troubled. "Are you in town for long, Mr. Smith?"

"I'm in for a bit of gambling, resting and seeing the sights. Not sure, but definitely until I see the pieces you have."

"Well, I'm Sarah Cummings. I own this mall and let me officially welcome you to Reno. Where are you staying?"

Victor looked toward the entrance. "At one of the new hotels in the heart of the city."

Sarah looked at her clock again. It was almost five. "I really have to be going, but if you're alone in the city, why don't you meet me and a couple friends for dinner? We're going to the Liberty Belle for steaks about seven. Would you like to come?"

Before Victor could accept, he heard footsteps and looked up. Chris Gannon was walking toward them. As he neared, Victor said, "Sarah, this is my colleague, Chris Gannon. He's visiting Reno with me."

Gannon didn't say anything but extended his hand, smiling. Sarah shook it and said, "Why don't the both of you join us? The steaks are great and we won't be out too late, so you can still have time to see the night life if you wish."

Gannon looked at Victor with a confused look. Victor said, "Yes, that would be great. What did you say the name of the restaurant was?"

Sarah looked pleased and walked to the service counter. On the back of her business card, she wrote the name Liberty Belle and the address. "Here, we'll see you about seven. The reservation is in my name, Cummings."

The two men started to walk away. Victor stopped and asked, "Sarah, you forgot to tell me where to meet you tomorrow?"

"I'll give you the details tonight at dinner," she answered. She had already turned off the background music and was holding a microphone in her hand.

As the men walked out of the building, Sarah announced the mall would be closing in five minutes.

"I want you to drive around so she can't see us when she leaves the building," Victor said.

He thought for a moment. "That Ford looks as if it's been parked there for a while, so I doubt if it's hers. I'd take odds on the jeep. She doesn't strike me as a pickup truck person."

Gannon laughed. "I don't think she looks like a jeep person either, but there aren't many choices left."

Smith put on a pair of sunglasses. "Maybe not, but that's the one I'm betting on." He looked around, studying the layout of the buildings. "Go over there behind that gas station. It's a perfect spot. We can observe this area clearly from there."

Gannon did as he was told. After they sat silently for several minutes, he asked, "Did you find out anything?"

Smith kept his eyes fixed on the mall parking lot. "Yes, didn't you recognize the furniture they had so prominently on display?"

Gannon shrugged. "Not really. Should I have?"

"If I'm not mistaken, some of those pieces were in the shipment that was sold to Charlie. My gut feeling tells me we are getting warm."

Gannon's stomach growled. "I'm getting hungry. We didn't get to eat much when you hurried me out of that restaurant. Can we stop somewhere and get something to hold me over until this evening?"

Smith smacked Gannon hard on the leg. "There she is getting into the jeep. Follow here, but keep behind her. I don't want her to notice us."

ELIZABETH JUNG

Gannon rubbing his leg didn't say a word. His stomach growled again as he pulled out onto the street.

CHAPTER NINETEEN

"While I drive, why don't you see if you can catch some local news on the radio?" Johnny suggested.

Peggy slid forward in the seat, pulling at her seat belt. "These doggone things always make me feel as if they are going to cut me in two." She pushed several buttons but could only find music and static. "We must be between signals or something. It's a bit unusual. Normally I can pick up a local news station anywhere in Reno or Sparks at this time of day."

Johnny glanced at Peggy and then into the rear view mirror. He had the strangest feeling that someone was following them ever since they had left Joe's place, but he didn't see any suspicious cars behind them. "We can try again. I put Joe's mail in that plastic bag on the back seat. Will you look through it as we drive? If there are any bills that need to be paid, I want to make sure that I pay them before I leave back to Iowa."

Peggy unhooked her seatbelt and pulled herself up on the seat, she extracted a large grocery store plastic bag from the rear seat to the front seat. Once she had the seat belt hooked again, she began thumbing through the items one by one. A large single tear rolled down her cheek.

Finally, she said, "There isn't much here. There's another letter from the city; like the ones we saw in Joe's house. Did you bring those with you?"

Johnny pointed with his head. "There, in that pillowcase full of things on the floor behind me. I'll go through it later tonight at the hotel. Are you sure there wasn't anything at Joe's that you wanted other than that old quilt you took?"

Peggy looked at Johnny and wiped a tear from her eye. "No, I just wanted something to remind me of him. That's all I really need."

Johnny shrugged and stopped at the stoplight below the Nugget. He glanced at the flashing billboard. "Hey, want to go see Charlie Pride tomorrow night? I see he's playing here at the Casino. Might be fun?"

She smiled. "I really don't think so. I'm not much of a country music fan. I like the golden oldies myself." She reached over patting Johnny on the thigh. "But, thanks for asking."

Johnny nodded. "What do you think ever happened to Sarah? I thought she said that she was going to stop by Joe's place?"

"Something must have come up at the shop," Peggy answered, looking out at the nightlights flashing to life. "I should have taken my cell phone out of the jeep. She might have called us."

Johnny flipped on his directional signals and moved into the left hand traffic and pulled onto Interstate 80. "Where do you want me to drop you?"

"Can you just take me home? I live off Virginia up by the college. It really isn't far from here and I'd like to wash my face and freshen up."

Johnny looked at the time. It was already almost seven. "No, problem. But, didn't you leave your car at the antique mall?"

Peggy laughed. "No, Sarah's using my jeep today. She loaned her car to someone for a couple days." She slid back on the seat and leaned her head against the headrest, closing her eyes.

"Are we still going out to eat?" Johnny asked.

Peggy gave a relaxed sigh.

"Say, don't you fall asleep on me. You still have to tell me where to turn."

Peggy rolled her head toward Johnny. "Turn on Virginia by the gas station. Turn right and we go up the hill. I'm just exhausted. Seeing Joe's place like that has taken every bit of energy out of me. Didn't you think that his house had a funny smell?"

"It smelled like chemicals," Johnny answered. "Did you see any chemicals around there? I only saw a few household cleaning items. They certainly shouldn't have made an odor that strong."

Peggy agreed. "No, and I didn't see anything unusual either but it was kind of dark and dingy in there. We should go back out and check it again when you can open the door and take along some stronger light bulbs. I think he only had 20 watt bulbs in all the lamps."

Johnny laughed. "Yes, Joe was always a bit of a tight wad."

Peggy sat up and looked around. "What are you going to do with his things? Have you given any thought to that?'

The vision of Joe's house flashed through Johnny's mind. He thought he might just have someone come in, bulldoze the area and sell the land. "Actually, not much. Any suggestions?"

Peggy ran her finger along the side of her nose, thought, and looked at Johnny out of the side of her eyes. "I'd be interested in buying that desk, chair and those two oil paintings if you want to sell them."

Johnny shrugged and frowned. "I wouldn't have any idea what they would be worth."

"I'll give you ten thousand for all the pieces," Peggy said quickly.

Johnny gasped, jerked his head around and stared at the lady. "What did you say?"

Peggy waved her hands in the air. "Oh, alright. I'll give you fifteen thousand, but that's as high as I can go." She laughed. "I have to make a living myself you know."

Johnny blinked several times. He couldn't believe his ears. He stared at the road, then saw the sign for Virginia Street and turned on his directional signals.

"I turn here, right?" he asked.

"Yes. Then go on up the street." Peggy thought for a moment and then asked, "What do you think about my offer?"

As he left the interstate, Johnny checked his rear view mirror again. This time he watched to see if any one else turned behind him. As he pulled onto Virginia and headed North toward the University, he answered, "Let me think about it overnight. I don't

ASSIGNMENT: RENO, NEVADA

want to make any decisions until I have an idea what it's going to cost to ship Joe's body home to Iowa. Is that agreeable with you?"

"That's fine. But, do keep me informed on what you're doing with those pieces." She sat quietly for a moment and then added, "Turn right at the stop light coming up. My house is the first one on the corner of the next block. You can just pull into the driveway."

After Johnny stopped the car, he looked at Peggy's house. It was a rambling single story ranch style with a three door, attached garage. "Does any one live here with you?"

"Good heavens, no!" she laughed. "Do you want to come in? I want to try to reach Sarah or see if she left a message on the answering machine. I'm not sure where she wanted to eat. She mentioned the Liberty Belle." She got out of the car and looked back at Johnny. "Come on in and at least have a drink."

Johnny glanced at the dashboard clock. "Ok, but for just a few minutes. I want to call home before it gets too late. There was a ball game right after school and I want to see how it went."

As Peggy walked to her door, Johnny opened the trunk and got her quilt out. He walked into the house and put the quilt on a chair in the living room. He glanced around the room and whistled. "Wow, this is some pad."

Everywhere he looked the walls were covered with oil paintings. Each room was filled with antique carpets and furniture. It reminded him of a museum.

Peggy chuckled. "As you can see I love antiques, especially good ones. See that corner over there. I'd move that oriental chair and vase. That is the perfect

143

spot for Joe's desk and chair. Don't you think so? When the blinds are open, the sun would warm my back."

Johnny nodded. "I have to admit you have the space for it. Have you collected all these things yourself?" He talked as he walked around and lightly touched the priceless pieces.

"I and my late husband. He loved fine things as much as I do." She walked into the kitchen and called, "What would you like to drink?"

"Just a soft drink is fine with me. I have to drive and don't want anything stronger."

"I have several kinds, come out in the kitchen and pick out one you want." She turned and walked back to the doorway. "Oh, look the answering machine is blinking."

As Johnny walked to the kitchen and opened a drink, she pushed the machine button.

When Peggy returned, she relayed, "Sarah left a message before she closed the mall. She said she invited two Texans to join us tonight at the Liberty Belle around eight thirty. She said she had some unexpected errands so wasn't going to make it to Joe's place to meet us."

"Does she often change her plans suddenly like that?" Johnny asked, flipping the tab on the can and taking a long drink.

Peggy gave a coy laugh. "Listen, in our business, we follow the almighty dollar. If she thought she could make money by doing something else, she'd do it. She mentions two Texans, so she probably had a deal brewing. It's not so unusual. She knows I'm a big girl and I'd get back some way or the other."

ASSIGNMENT: RENO, NEVADA

Johnny set the almost empty can on the sink. "I'd better be going. Where's the Liberty Belle?"

"I'll pick you up," Peggy answered. She walked over to a large grandfather's clock in the entrance hall. "How about an hour from now. We should be about on time. That'll give you a chance to call your family first. Which hotel are you in?"

"Darn, I still don't know the name of it but it's by the Amtrak Station. Why don't I call you when I get back to my room and tell you?"

"Sure, here, have one of my business cards. My home number is the last one." She reached into a silver mug and pulled out a white engraved card with her name and several phone numbers, but no address.

Johnny took the card, glanced at it and stuck it in his jacket pocket. He walked to the door and then stopped. "How are you going to pick me up if Sarah has your car?"

Peggy laughed and slapped her hands together. "Do you think I'm a pauper and only have one car? Man, in that garage I have three more. Which would you like to ride in tonight? I have a red Mustang convertible, a yellow Volkswagen Bug and a light blue Cadillac for you to choose from. I'll probably drive the Caddie. I really don't like driving the other two in at night." She thought for a moment and added, "Sarah also has four cars. She buys a new car like some people buy shoes."

Johnny laughed. "That would fine. I like traveling in style. I'll call from the hotel."

He walked out the door just as Peggy's phone rang. He was backing out of the driveway when he saw a black Lexus turn the corner behind him. It looked like Sarah's car but he couldn't see the license plate.

For an instant, he considered staying to see whom it was, but decide he needed to get back to the hotel. He still wanted to talk to his family before dinner. He missed them.

CHAPTER TWENTY

"What time did you want me to pick you up for dinner?" Gannon asked. He looked hungry and patted his growling stomach.

"Find out for sure where the Liberty Belle is. I'll call you later. I want to take a shower and make some phone calls first." Victor Smith opened the car door in front of his hotel, walked around the back and got out his bag. He leaned into the back of the car and asked, "How much money do you have?"

"Do you mean personally or at my disposal?" Gannon looked into the rear view mirror as he talked.

"I want to know how much money you can draw on for emergencies?"

"Oh, if I need any money I just ask Oscar. He gets it. I don't have any idea what his arrangements are, I've never asked. All I know is that he has always been able to get all the money that I've ever needed." He ran his fingers through his hair and turned slightly toward the back. "Do you want me to ask if there is a limit?"

"No, just tell Oscar to call me. I want to arrange a meeting with him." He slammed the trunk down and walked around to the driver's side. "Can you do that?"

"Well, yes!" Gannon nodded. He shifted into gear. "I'll tell him. He should be back at the hotel by the time I get back. He has been busy today on some kind of special assignment, but I don't know what."

Victor asked, "What room did you say I had? I don't want to have to dig through my change to get the key card."

"It's 615. I asked for a room in the back where it would be quieter."

Victor nodded. "On second thought, you call me about the dinner arrangements. Call in about thirty minutes or so." As Gannon drove off, Victor picked up his bag and walked through the back door just as another hotel guest was leaving. He looked for an elevator and when he didn't see one, took the steps up one flight. When he stepped into the hallway, he saw an elevator sign and within minutes was in his room.

After a quick inspection of the room and checking the bathroom, he threw his suitcase onto the empty bed and took out a small codebook that he had packed in a corner. Flipping through its pages, he located the hotel Bible that was in the drawer of the desk. He saw that it was the King James Version and smiled. He turned to a specific passage.

With the bible spread out on the desk beside him, he now took out his palm computer. He pressed a piece of thin metal to the phone, punched several numbers on his computer and waited for an answer on his computer screen.

ASSIGNMENT: RENO, NEVADA

For several seconds the screen stayed blank, then, a message flashed up saying that the line was secure. He pressed the clear plastic once again with his thumb and waited for the screen to recognize him. The words "pick up the telephone," flashed across the screen.

"I'm in my hotel room but I still don't have anything positive to report," Smith uttered into the mouthpiece. He held the phone away from his ear and studied his new room. It was more spacious and elegantly decorated than the room he had used the previous night.

"Have you found anything?" Director Korovkin asked. His voice was perfectly clear.

"Nothing. This Gannon character didn't have any usable leads. We are starting over at the beginning. However, today I did find some of the furniture that I believe was in the shipment. It was out at the antique mall. I studied the inventory list while I was on the plane and several of the pieces I saw match the list."

"When will you know for sure?" Korovkin asked in his strong Russian accent.

"We are meeting the mall owner for dinner this evening at some steak house. She said she has a warehouse with more of the pieces and she'll take us to it tomorrow. Hopefully, by tomorrow night we will have an answer." Victor fiddled with the pen and paper and scribbled on the telephone pad. He sketched a picture of several pieces of furniture that looked like the pieces he had seen.

"How is Reno? I have always wanted to see the old West but never had the opportunity. Did you see any cowboys?" the deputy asked.

149

Victor smiled. Although he knew the elderly Russian passionately hated Americans, he knew the Russian still liked to hear about the United States. "You see lots of people dressed like cowboys, but I think you have to go outside the city to see them on horses and chasing after cattle."

There was a short pause and then the old man asked, "Maybe you can get me some pictures? I have always heard that Reno is a great city to visit."

Victor shifted his legs. "I suppose I can. I'm sure that the hotel has those throw away cameras downstairs in the gift shop. I'll get one tomorrow and see about taking some pictures for you." He glanced down at his drawings. "I've just drawn a picture of the pieces of furniture that I saw. When we are done talking I will transmit them to you with this new built-in scanner I had installed in my laptop. Be sure and watch for it. If they are not the pieces, get back to me right away. But, I'm almost positive these were in the shipment. I could photograph the pieces tomorrow and transmit them to you via email if you needed."

"I found out some more about your friend," the Russian deputy said.

Victor Smith's heart began to race. "He is alive, isn't he?"

"Yes, he is. He is the brother of "your" Joe Collins. Your suspicions are correct. I have not been able to confirm it, but it would not be unusual for him to be in Reno looking after his brother's estate."

Smith slammed his hand against the wood doorframe. "I knew it," he said as he caught his breath. "I saw him again this afternoon. I could sense his presence. It is all too much of a coincidence."

ASSIGNMENT: RENO, NEVADA

"Well, don't blow your cover. He has no reason to suspect you are alive and in the area. We have too many things riding on you to have your identity discovered now. Remember, your main purpose is your upcoming role in Washington, D.C. This mission to Reno is something to keep you busy until we can get you situated in Washington." There was total silence, then the director added, "You do understand, don't you, Victor?"

Victor Smith twitched his shoulders in automatic obedience and nodded his head several times. A strange peace fell over him. "Yes, I understand. I will not reveal my true presence to anyone. I am sure he has no idea that I am in the area. Were you able to find out what Collins has been doing for the past couple years?"

"Yes, he is semi-retired from the CIA and is living with his family in Iowa. We have his home address and I have activated a sleeper in Minneapolis to keep a watch on the family. It is just a one-in-a-million quirk of fate that his brother got involved in this antique shipment."

Victor lightly compressed his face and turned to admire his classic profile in the mirror behind him. He smiled and studied his perfect white teeth. "Don't worry, I will not reveal my presence but I might play cat and mouse with him."

The older Russian laughed. "Just don't get him caught in your trap. Call me tomorrow. I always enjoy talking to you."

"I will. I'll send the pictures now. Until tomorrow."

Victor took the paper, pressed a button on his computer and slowly ran the paper across the screen. He pressed more buttons and closed the computer. Counting to ten, he watched the computer until he heard a buzzing sound.

He put the phone back on the stand and removed the piece of metal. He took the device into the bathroom, washed it with soap and water to remove his fingerprints and carefully wrapped it in tissue and returned it to his case.

To an unsuspecting, inexperienced person, the device looked like any other piece of metal or maybe even a gun wrapper. However, this piece was very special; it was a mini-computer with a full electronic field. Although it was still being Beta tested in the field and wasn't available to all the agents, Victor found that it worked perfectly for his needs.

With a smile on his face, he sat on the opposite bed and kicked off his shoes. He pulled a pillow beneath his head, leaned back and absently studied the ceiling. A broad smile covered his face as he closed his eyes.

Just as he started to doze, the phone rang. Turning slightly, he reached for it and answered, "Yes".".

Gannon said, "Oscar has not returned to the room but the Liberty Belle is about a fifteen minute drive from your hotel. I'll be downstairs at the back door in thirty minutes. That will give us plenty of time. Is that alright with you?"

"Yes, I'll be there. Can you leave a message for Oscar to call me when he gets in? Do you have my cell number?"

Gannon coughed and then answered, "Yes, I have it in my wallet. I'll leave a note in the room. I don't want to leave one downstairs with reception."

Victor glanced at his watch. "No. That is fine." He hung up the phone and rolled over on the bed. He still had that smirk on his face.

ELIZABETH JUNG

CHAPTER TWENTY-ONE

Johnny Collins just stepped out of the shower when he heard a knock. "Just a minute," he called hurrying into the bedroom and reaching for his jeans on the edge of the bed.

He ran to the door and looked through the peephole. He saw a short white haired man. Nervously, his vision swept around the room and paused at the nightstand. The gun he had found hidden in Joe's house was in plain view if anyone came in.

With his shoulder against the doorframe, he kept the chain lock attached and opened the door.

Before he could say anything, the old man held up a newspaper and spoke with downcast eyes. "You asked for a copy of the latest local paper, sir?" The man turned his body slightly and handed the paper through the narrow opening.

"Oh, yes. I'd forgotten. Just a sec, I'll get some change." Johnny looked back at the dresser where his wallet and change were.

The old man stepped away and turned to walk back down the hall. "It's complimentary," he called as he shuffled toward the elevator.

Johnny watched until the man got back on the elevator; he took the chain of and stepped into the hallway. No one was in sight.

Closing the door, he smiled. He couldn't remember the last time he hadn't had to tip someone for doing something that was part of the job.

He took the wet towel off the bed and tossed it on to the bathroom floor. He walked to the TV, flipped it on and clicked through the channels. It was a bit past seven. He still had some time before Peggy was to arrive.

As he waited, he picked up at the newspaper, reading the headlines. He skimmed over the local articles about city corruption and looked several minutes at a picture of a Texan who had hit a jackpot at the airport. He muttered to himself, "Why couldn't that have been me?"

He spread the paper out on the desk and scanned the pages. His eyes went up and down the columns. He stopped on an article about a manager who was strangled. The hair on the back of his neck stood up and his skin tingled. He straightened himself and said aloud, "There is murder everywhere."

Finding nothing of specific interest, he turned to the sports pages. A local news up date flashed on television. Johnny nervously recoiled, reached for the remote to turn up the sound.

Completely engrossed in the unfolding news, the phone rang several times before Johnny answered it.

He kept his eyes on the TV as he reached for the phone.

"Yes," he said, straining to hear the news broadcaster as well as the caller.

"Johnny," Peggy said. "Sarah hasn't called so I think maybe we should cancel our dinner this evening. I have called several places trying to find her, but haven't been able to locate her.

Johnny leaned toward the TV, absentmindedly, he said, "Something must have come up. Does she do this often?" He pushed the mute button on the remote control.

Peggy answered, "I don't think she has ever done this to me. I'm getting worried. I think I should stay home in case she tries to call."

"Let me know if I can do anything," he answered. "I'll probably eat at one of the places around here and get to bed early. Call me if you need me."

Peggy's voice revealed her concern. "I will. Thanks, Johnny."

Johnny turned his attention to the TV and pushed the mute button again. He walked closer to the set. For the next several minutes, he listened to the story of Terry Granger's death. He was surprised to discover that the police had already ruled Granger's death an accident and the unnamed policeman was not under investigation.

CHAPTER TWENTY-TWO

It was exactly eight in the morning when Johnny walked out of his hotel room and took the elevator to the lobby. He had taken the pillowcase with Joe's things and put it on the bed, as if it were an additional pillow. He had eaten a doughnut for breakfast and was feeling much better about everything.

He stepped out into the large room and looked around. He checked his watch against the clock hanging above the reception area.

He wondered for just a moment if he had the information correct when Tom Clausen stepped out from behind a tall pillar. Clausen walked directly toward him.

"Hope I haven't kept you waiting?" Johnny said extending his hand. "I'm glad you were available on such short notice."

Clausen took his hand and answered, "Not a problem, I just cleared up a few things and only arrived about two minutes ago."

Johnny took a quick look through the door's glass pane and slipped his leather jacket on. "Do you want to drive or shall I?"

"You drive," Clausen answered. "My car is in the shop for repairs. I'll be the navigator."

After the men were in the car, Johnny asked, "Where to?"

"You said yesterday you wanted to go out to Joe's place. Let's start there. Do you know how to get there?"

Johnny looked at the morning traffic. "I went out there last night with Peggy and she told me where to turn. I doubt I could find the way this morning without a lot of trouble. She took me out through the hills and we returned on Interstate 80. Why don't you just take me whichever way you prefer?"

Clausen smiled. "Fine. Just go straight. We will go through the University." He buckled up his seatbelt and slid back on the seat.

"If we are going through the University, maybe we should stop at Peggy's and see if she has talked to Sarah."

Clausen turned to Collins and asked, "Why?"

"Sarah planned to go to dinner with us last night, but she didn't call Peggy."

Smiling, Clausen questioned, "What is so unusual about that?"

Johnny shrugged and turned to look at the passenger. "I don't really know, but Peggy talked as if it was quite unusual." He drove a few blocks. "Be sure and tell me where to turn."

Clausen made a noise and cleared his throat, then said, "Oh, we have a long way to go on this road, just keep going straight. We don't turn until we get to McCarran Boulevard." He checked the time on his watch. "It's after eight, Peggy would be at the mall by now. They open at eight."

Slowing to a stop sign, Johnny said, "You are probably right. We can check at the mall later today."

"I hardly think that is necessary, but if it will make you feel better," Clausen answered. He was silent for several minutes. "Go straight until McCarran Boulevard. Then turn right and take it for about two miles. You won't turn again until Baring Boulevard. At that point, then turn right on Sparks Boulevard and drive until you come to the Truckee River. Joe's place is just a block off of Sparks Boulevard near the river. You'll probably recognize the area when we get closer."

"Whoa, that's a bit much all at once. Just help me with the signs and tell me where to turn a few hundred feet in advance." Johnny swung around a slow car and out into the heavy lane of traffic. "Since I left the Washington, D.C. area, I've only been doing small town driving. I've forgotten how heavy traffic can be in larger cities." He looked in his side mirror and watched the cars dash around him. It was his old training sense; he couldn't identify anyone following him, still he had a pressing feeling that they were being followed.

"Have you decided when you're going to have the memorial service here in Reno?" Clausen asked, turning slightly in his seat to face Collins.

Without looking at his passenger, Collins said, "I talked to a funeral home staff person yesterday, but the police haven't released Joe's body yet. Do you have any information on that?"

Clausen reached inside his leather jacket pocket and slipped on his sunglasses. After a short silence, he answered, "I overheard Larson tell the duty officer that he thought it would be sometime today."

"What took them so long?" Johnny turned toward Clausen as he spoke.

"I'm not sure. I know they did a complete blood analysis and they were still waiting for some lab reports."

Johnny frowned. "Why blood tests? Did they suspect he died some other way than by having his throat cut?"

Clausen grunted. "I really don't know. I've not seen the police report on the death."

"Oh," Johnny said. "Exactly, what department do you work for?"

Clausen hesitated every-so-slightly before replying, "I'm with the drug division."

"Drugs! Do you suspect that Joe was involved with drugs?" Johnny asked, forgetting to signal in his surprise as he cut into the right lane and nearly clipped the car behind him.

A horn blasted and Johnny checked his rear view mirror. He raised his hand in a wave of apology to the car behind him.

Clausen snorted. "In my section, we suspect everyone is dealing in drugs. It's like when you worked with the CIA, didn't you suspect everyone was a spy?"

ASSIGNMENT: RENO, NEVADA

"Hardly," Johnny answered quickly. "Usually the ones that we suspected were. Can you say the same for drugs?"

Clausen didn't answer, turning around to check the cars behind them. "Turn here. Joe's house is up that long lane."

Johnny slowed the car to a stop several feet from the Truckee River. He got out of the car and walked to the riverbank. He made sure that he walked around the yellow plastic barrier ribbon that had been strung between two trees. Looking down, he watched the water splash against the rocks.

After several seconds, he said, "It is quite lovely here. I can understand why Joe liked it. By chance, do you happen to know how much of this land Joe owned?"

Clausen stood several feet away from Johnny. He watched a turtle struggling to get back into the water. "I don't know. I never talked to Joe about it. I know he's been here for years, so whatever he had would have been "grand fathered" in just in case there were any future development or city code changes. I have heard Sarah talk about this land, you might ask her."

Johnny made a mental note to check for any legal land documents with Joe's lawyer as he walked around to the door of Joe's house. "You coming?" he called as he neared the front door.

Clausen edged to where Johnny was standing and politely waited behind him. "It's been sometime since I've been here. Maybe I can find something that would help with the investigation."

Johnny shook his head sideways. "I doubt it. When Peggy and I came last night we had to crawl under that yellow tape. It was obvious from the appearance of the house that the police had been here and did at least a preliminary search."

He took Joe's house key out of his jacket pocket. He had taken it the previous night from under a large rock beside the house and kept it with him. No one had mentioned a key, Joe had told him years ago about the hiding place.

As Johnny reached to insert the key, the door squeaked open. He recoiled, "That's strange. I'm certain I locked this last night after Peggy and I left," Johnny said, looking over his shoulder at Clausen.

"Maybe the police came back?" Clausen said.

Johnny dubiously sighed, "Maybe, but I can't believe they came back between dark last night and this morning."

He carefully stepped into the small dark room, ran his hand up the side of the wall and flipped on the light. Papers, blankets, dishes, pots and pans and pillows were thrown around the area. The stuffing from an oversize chair was hanging loose where it had been cut out of the seat.

"Holy cow!! Someone sure tore this apart," Johnny yelled.

Clausen pushed past Johnny. "Looks as if it has been quickly searched. Whoever did this was looking for something specific and they didn't care if anyone knew they had been here."

"Boy, I'll say." Johnny took a deep breath and walked around the room. After he had surveyed the damage, he turned to Clausen. "From my experience with this type of thing, I'd judge they didn't fine whatever they were looking for." He pointed to the

ASSIGNMENT: RENO, NEVADA

bathroom on the other side of the room. "You check that and I'll start in the kitchen. Let's go over every thing inch-by-inch and see what we can find."

Clausen asked, "Didn't you and Peggy check it last night?"

Johnny sighed. "Yeah, but I wish we could have checked it better. It was so dark that we could only see some things. I hadn't taken a strong enough flash light and the light bulbs were so small they cast shadows everywhere. I knew I would be coming back so I didn't see a need to check thoroughly."

Clausen indicated he heard and moved over and into the small bathroom. Johnny started going through the kitchen cabinets. He had done this type of search so many times it was routine. He had no idea what he was looking for but knew that he would know when he found it.

"Nothing in there," Clausen said after several minutes. He moved through the kitchen and into the small bedroom on the other side of the room. "I'll go in here now." As he walked he took care not to step on anything.

Johnny finished the cupboards and moved to the refrigerator. Carefully, he went shelf by shelf. He found nothing. He opened the freezer door and from deep in the recesses of his mind, he remembered that when he and Joe were growing up, his parents always hid their valuables in the freezer. His dad always joked about having cold cash and insisted that in event of a house fire, the casing on the freezer would keep the valuables safe.

Holding his breath, he began pulling out the frozen food. One by one, he unwrapped each piece and put the unwrapped items in a bag he had found under the sink.

He reached toward the back of the shelf and brought out a bag of flour. A knowing smile filled his face. The flour had been opened. Turning around, he checked to see where Clausen was. Quickly, he put the bag of flour in the bag without checking it. He didn't have to. He knew it contained something important.

To be on the safe side, he went through the other shelf and checked everything on it. He found nothing unusual. As he turned to close the freezer door something caught his eye. It was a piece of paper that had been stuck under the rubber molding around the door.

He heard Clausen's feet walking back into the room. With his back toward the door, Johnny reached his hand up and pulled the paper loose and stuck it in his back jean pocket.

"Nothing here," Johnny said as he shut the freezer door. He put the bag of food by the door. "I'll take this with us and throw it out at the hotel. I don't want the smell of rotting food in here since I'm going to try and sell this place."

Clausen spun around and questioned Johnny, "You're going to sell this house and land?"

"Of, course. What would I do with it? I live in Iowa." He looked around and considered the house. "It isn't big enough for my family to use as a vacation place." He shook his head. "No, I'll list it sometime or try and sell it on my own." He turned and looked directly at Clausen. "Why, do you know someone that might want to buy it?"

Clausen sighed and shrugged. "I don't know, but I can ask around. I guess I'm just surprised to hear you might sell it. Actually, I never gave thought to what might become of it." He walked back to the door and looked out at the river. "It certainly has appeal. I would imagine that someone would want it for the location itself." He was quiet for a couple seconds and then added, "The house certainly isn't worth much."

"No, I doubt if it's worth ten thousand dollars. In Iowa, it would probably be worth five thousand. But, who knows, being here on the river, it could be worth a great deal. I'll have to check with Joe's lawyer, Terrance Ruddick, and see." He moved into the living room area and stood in front of the desk and chair.

"Ah, I didn't know Joe had retained Ruddick as his lawyer. He's honest and very reputable. I didn't know that Joe knew Ruddick." Clausen remarked.

"I have no idea where they met or such. Ruddick was the one that contacted me about Joe's death. I'll find out more after I have a chance to talk with him," Johnny answered.

"Oh, you haven't met him yet?"

"No, just talked to him on the phone. I have an appointment set up for later this week."

"Well, that's great. You never know around here about the value of property. Property prices go up and down depending on the economy and the location," Clausen answered turning back toward the living room.

"Do you have any idea what this desk set and these oil paintings would be worth? Are they antique?" Johnny asked. He turned and looked at Clausen, running his hand over the wooden desktop.

"I don't have the faintest idea. That would be Sarah and Peggy's line," Clausen answered. He walked to the desk and studied it more carefully. "It looks antique. It has lots of drawers and a nice smooth finish. Probably a couple thousand dollars or so just for this piece, I would think."

Johnny licked his lips before responding. "Yeah, that's what I thought." He opened his mouth to tell Clausen about Peggy's offer of fifteen thousand for the pieces, but decided for the time being he would keep that information to himself.

It was almost noon by the time the two men returned to Johnny's car and headed back to Reno. The bag of thawing food was in the trunk of the car. This time when leaving, Johnny had taken extra care to lock the door of the house. The two men had rolled two large rocks up against the door, hoping that the barricade might keep any four and two legged critters out of Joe's house.

ASSIGNMENT: RENO, NEVADA

CHAPTER TWENTY-THREE

The black phone on Director Korovkin's desk rang as the aging Russian Director of the Federal Security Service stood at the window looking down on Dzerzhinsky Square in the heart of Moscow. Flinching his head slightly, he heard but ignored the phone. He never moved his body because he knew his secretary would answer it.

For the past hour, he had watched the people below rushing back and forth in the light spring rain. His thoughts went on the old days when the KGB had full authority, before the fall of the Iron Curtain.

In those days, he wouldn't have had to answer to a group of non-professional, committee members. In today's world, they knew almost nothing about how to ensure the security regulations necessary to keep Russia a world power.

The new "friendly" image was not his idea. He hated having to account for every ruble spent. The paperwork alone was going to bury him.

His secretary had told him that some of the committee members were asking when he was going to retire. Retiring had never even crossed his mind. Despite all the hassle regarding the lost shipment and expenses, he was determined to stay and fight for what he thought was the protection of Mother Russia.

A red light flashed on his desk, he smiled and nodded. His secretary had been instructed not to alert him unless Victor Smith was calling.

Checking his watch, he shuffled stiff-legged toward his desk. On damp days, his legs really bothered him. He wished his government could afford to keep the heat on during the cold, damp spring days, but they continued to follow the old ways. In all government buildings, heat was still only allowed from November fifteenth to March fifteenth.

He rubbed his wrists, turned the big brown leather chair around and lowered his overweight body into it. Then, slowly, he shifted his legs and put them under the desk.

Arching his shoulders up and down, he ran his hands over the cold wood. After contemplating the flashing light for several seconds, he reached for the black phone and whispered. "Yes, my dear."

"Sir, Victor Smith is on your secure line."

His secretary's brisk young voice made him smile. He pushed on the black speakerphone button. "Well, Tex, what do you have to report this time?"

"Nothing new on this end. Oscar did a search of Joe Collins' house late last night and found nothing. He said he feels like he's looking for a needle in a haystack. The dinner last night fell through. Our contact at the mall didn't show up. I am going to check back at the shop as soon as it opens."

ASSIGNMENT: RENO, NEVADA

The old man leaned on the desk and pressed his free hand to his forehead. He rubbed his hand back and forth over the deep frown that kept reappearing on his forehead.

"Sir, are you there?" Victor asked. His voice was a little louder than usual.

"Yes," the troubled man answered. "It's too late now but I knew we should have shipped the items through diplomatic pouch to our embassy in Washington. I shouldn't have listened to the others and included it in that furniture shipment. It was too precious. It is no wonder it is lost."

"Why didn't you?" Victor asked.

The old man slapped the top of the desk. A loud bang reverberated through the phone line. "Because I didn't have anyone I thought I could trust in Washington to receive it on that end. We thought we could trust our California connection. It all would have worked out beautifully, if our connection, George, hadn't decided to go to Vegas the day the shipment cleared customs. He was instructed not to tell anyone about the shipment. So, when the shipment arrived at his office, his second in command thought it was to be included in the furniture shipment for Reno and he packed it in a truck and headed out for Reno. By the time our man got back to Sacramento, the furniture had been consigned to Charlie McGuire. When George found out the shipment had been included with the furniture, he immediately headed for Reno. The rest you know."

"How trustworthy is George?" Victor asked.

The old man sighed. "Very. He is one of my most trusted agents. When he wanted to retire to the U.S.,

169

we set him up in business. The problem is not with him. It was just one of those unforeseeable freak happenings."

"Sir, I know what the container is and what it should look like, but what is so important inside it?"

"Victor, you only need to know that it is very valuable. Any more knowledge could be dangerous to you."

Static filled the line. After a brief silence, Victor said, "I will keep looking. Are you sure that it is here in Reno?"

Korovkin emphasized, "Yes, it was definitely with the pieces of furniture that was sent to California and eventually ended up in Reno, Nevada there is no doubt. You must find the crate."

"Does the entire crate have to be found intact?" Victor asked.

"There are twelve units in it, but Erzebet never lived long enough to tell us exactly how many."

"I'll find the carton," Victor answered. "If it is still here in Reno. We will search every place until we have it or know that it is no longer here."

The old man ran his wrinkled hands back and forth on his legs. "I know you will. Keep me informed. If you think you need more help, I can ask George to drive or fly from California and assist you." There was a long pause. "I really don't want to if I'd hate to risk it with a chance of blowing it. He has a wonderful cover now and I don't want to blow it."

"Let's see what Gannon, Oscar and I can do. I'll keep you updated."

ASSIGNMENT: RENO, NEVADA

The old man heard the dial tone and pushed the disconnect button. He hoped Smith could find the needle in the haystack.

CHAPTER TWENTY-FOUR

Johnny Collins walked into his hotel room and locked the door. He placed the bag of food near the door and then took everything out of his pockets and spread them out on the dresser.

Emotionally, he was exhausted. He didn't see a message light flashing on the phone. After digging around in Joe's house, he felt dirty. He lifted his arm, smelled his clothes and wheezed in disgust.

Just as he stepped out of the shower, his phone rang. Grabbing a towel, he rubbed his wet hair. Looking down at his damp feet, he shrugged and moved toward the bed. With his right hand he reached for the phone. "Yes."

"Hi, this is Peggy. I'm down in the lobby. May I come up?"

Johnny hesitated and looked around the room at the bag of melting food by the doorway and his dirty clothes that were spread helter-skelter. "Sure, give me a minute. I just stepped out of the shower."

"It will take me that long to get up there. They won't tell me your room number."

ASSIGNMENT: RENO, NEVADA

"It's 638. I'm at the end of the hall."

"I'll be right up. There is something that I want to discuss with you."

Johnny hurriedly finished drying, dressed and straightened up the room. When he heard the knock, he threw the wet towels into the shower and slid the shower door shut.

"Hi, what's up with you today? Why aren't you at the antique mall?" he asked as he opened the door and Peggy stepped into his room.

She was dressed in dark navy tight fitting jeans and a bright red western style shirt that pulled tight across her chest. Her short gray hair had been styled so it stuck straight out from her head. She had a large brown leather purse slung over her left shoulder.

Johnny smiled. He thought she looked as if someone had scared her.

Peggy looked around the room and then walked to a straight-backed chair near the window. She ran the pointed toe of her cowboy boot against the carpet. "Nice room," she commented.

"Come on, you didn't come up here in the middle of the day to admire my room and carpet. What gives?" He picked up his pocket items from the bed and placed them into his trousers.

"Sarah is holding down the fort at the mall. I told her that I wanted to run some errands. I do it every once in a while so she didn't mind." She picked up the purse that she had placed by her feet.

"Well, glad to hear that Sarah made it to work today. Where was she last night?" Johnny asked. He looked at her as he sat down on the edge of the bed and indicated to Peggy to take the only chair.

"Oh, she called about an hour after I called you. She had run into an old friend and they started talking about antiques and Sarah said she completely forgot the time."

"So, you worried for nothing?"

Peggy hesitated and slowly answered, "Yes, I guess so. I guess I was a bit on edge and thought something had happened to her." She looked into Johnny's eyes and asked, "You can understand how I feel especially after Joe and Charlie's deaths?"

"Well, everything is fine. Now, what did you want to see me about?"

"Johnny, I just can't get Joe's death off my mind. I need to find out what happened." As she spoke tears began to fill her eyes and smudged her mascara.

Johnny stood up, walked to the door, locked it and then walked over to the window, pulling the curtains apart, he looked out. He turned back to Peggy. She sat in the chair a few feet from where he stood.

Thinking, he flexed his knuckles unconsciously, in a nervous gesture. Finally, he answered, "So, do I."

Peggy sniffed and dug through her large purse extracting a tissue. She dabbed at her tears and blew her nose, then leaned forward and put the tissue in a wastebasket at the side of the desk.

"Johnny, my gut instinct tells me that Joe's death and Old Charlie McGuire's are connected." She puckered up her lips, blinked her eyes rapidly and continued. "I think both deaths had something to do with the delivery we got from that California picker."

"Picker? I've forgotten who that is?" Johnny shook his head trying to remember and leaned toward Peggy.

ASSIGNMENT: RENO, NEVADA

Peggy laughed. "Remember, a picker is someone that gets items and then takes them around to antique dealers and sells them. They are quite helpful. They attend auctions and garage sales, buy items that are sold for less than true value or that they think they can resale and make a profit. Then, they sell to us. They really help us so we don't have to attend everything and we can keep our shops open for business." She watched Johnny's eyes and added, "We also sell items to them that didn't sell in our city and they take them to another city and sell them."

"That's right, sounds like a good deal to me," Johnny answered. "Helps everyone. How do you figure Charlie's and my brother's deaths are connected to this picker?"

"Something is going on. I heard Sarah on the phone today. She was whispering and when I walked toward her, she hung up. I don't think she was finished with the conversation but she didn't want me to hear what she was saying or to whom she was talking."

Johnny smiled and shrugged. "People can be weird. We both know that. Did you ask her about the call?"

Peggy nodded. "Yes, she said it was a wrong number."

"Didn't you believe her?"

"I have known Sarah for more years than I care to admit. No, she was lying. I know it."

Johnny reached into his shirt pocket and pulled out the paper that he had gotten from the refrigerator at Joe's home. "There is something I want to show you. You tell me if this makes any sense."

He handed Peggy the folded paper. She carefully unfolded it and studied it. She shook her head.

"No idea what so ever. Sounds like a story to me."

Johnny took it back and walked closer to the window and held it up to the light. Suddenly, he cried. "Of course. Now I see it."

Peggy jumped up from her chair and rushed toward him. "What do you see?" she questioned putting her head near his hands.

"I should have known. Let me sit at the desk for a minute." He turned his head slightly and added, "You can look over my shoulder, if you want."

"What is it?" Peggy walked behind him and bent her head closer so she could get a good clear look at the paper. "What should I be looking for?"

Johnny searched through a desk drawer and found a pen and clean sheet of paper. "Joe wrote this for me. When we were growing up we often sent messages to each other in what we called "our code". Actually, what we used was a cipher."

"What's the difference between a code and a cipher?" Peggy asked.

Johnny held the pen in the air and turned slightly toward her. "A code is normally one word or group of words. For instance, you send me a message and in the message you use the words "green trees". When I receive the words "green trees", I know it means that I am to meet you at the street at nine in the morning. We even made up a codebook for certain words."

"That makes sense. But, what's a cipher?"

"That's a bit more complex. After we got bored with codes we developed our own cipher system. For instance, you send me a message that reads, "It is cold today." I know that for "c's" I use a different letter. It could be a "b" or a "d" or whatever. Or you can assign each letter of the alphabet a number. And send a number message. Every 2 is a "b" and so forth."

"Sounds really complicated." Peggy pulled a chair beside the desk. "So can you solve this message from Joe means?"

Johnny studied the paper and was quiet for a few minutes. He wrote several words down on the sheet of paper and then scratched them out. Finally, he said, "I'm a bit rusty on this. It's been years since I've had to translate something like this into sensible words. I have to try different ideas. He might have changed the words around backwards."

Peggy noticed her watch. "I had better get going. Sarah said she wanted to leave early tonight. She was supposed to have had a meeting with a buyer last night but she got held up with her friend."

Johnny stood and stretched. He walked to the door with Peggy. "Why don't you call me when you close? Maybe, I'll know something by then."

"When are you going to have Joe's service in Reno?"

"Ugh, I was due at the funeral home at one today." He looked at the time. It was almost one. "I completely forgot what with everything that was going on."

"Will you let me know when you decide?"

"I'll call the funeral home and tell them that I will be running late. Clausen is supposed to let me know when Joe's body is picked up by the funeral home."

Peggy tilted backward and wilted against the wall. "You mean the police haven't released his body yet?"

Her eyes were wide and her mouth was open. She took a deep breath. "Isn't that rather unusual?"

"I don't know. I find everything about this case unusual. I'm not sure what the norm is in Reno."

Peggy curled her lips in disapproval and turned. As she walked toward the elevator, she turned and smiled. "I'll be in touch later today."

Johnny stood and admired her natural hip motion, her sensuous sway she walked. He didn't know if Joe had been interested in her, but if he had been, Johnny could certainly understand why. She was provocative in her own way. He remembered he was married with a family at home, and blanked out his thoughts.

CHAPTER TWENTY-FIVE

Johnny walked to his room thinking about the note that Joe had left for him. Once again, he sat down at the desk and started through the ciphering process.

The phone rang and he leaned across the desk toward the nightstand. "Yes," he uttered, still thinking about the paper in front of him.

"John, is that you?" the voice asked.

Johnny blinked, clinched the phone, and then looked at his watch. "Honey, how nice to hear from you. How's your day going?"

"Not too great," Margaret Collins answered. "John, I think that someone has been following me."

Johnny laughed. "Honey, in Iowa? I hardly think so."

"John, this isn't a laughing matter. I'll have you know that I'm aware when I am being followed and when I'm not," she snapped back. Her voice cracked and she sounded close to crying.

"Now, honey, tell me what happened," Johnny said. He put the pen down, staring at the window across the room. A deep frown rippled the skin on his forehead.

"I went downtown to the grocery store this morning like I do normally. When I parked the van in front of the Econofood store another car parked beside me. I didn't think anything about it and went about my business. When I came out with my groceries, there was still a man sitting in the car. When I looked toward him, he turned and looked in the opposite direction."

"Honey, that isn't unusual. Did anything else happen?" he asked.

"Well, if you would just give me a moment to take a breath and think, I'll elaborate it," she answered quickly.

"All right, honey, go on," he said. He had picked up the pen and started making notes on a blank sheet of paper.

"I got in the car and then drove over to highway 18 to the hardware store. I had to go in and get a new heavy extension cord for the edger. When I came back out that same car was parked in the parking lot and the same man was in it."

"Okay, this does seem a bit unusual. What time was this?"

"I went to the store around ten this morning and then on to the hardware store. Well, I left there and stopped at the dollar store to pick up a few things."

"Don't tell me. The car was in the parking lot of the dollar store?"

"Yes, John, the same car and the same lone driver. This time I had a chance to see the license plate and it was a Minnesota plate."

"Margaret, it might be just a coincidence. Seeing the same car three times in a town the size of Clear Lake, Iowa isn't usual. After all it is a tourist town. Maybe the driver owns a cabin there."

"Yes, maybe he does but I feel creepy about this. My instinct tells me that he was watching me. It is certainly strange that this happens the same time that you are out of town for your brother's death."

"Yes, honey, I agree it sounds a bit strange but not totally unusual." Johnny wrote several things as his wife talked and then added some comments of his own.

"Well, it is mighty weird that your brother was murdered out in Nevada and then here in Iowa someone is watching your family. I'm certain that man was watching me."

"Well, what do you suggest?"

"Oh, John, I don't really know. I guess I could alert the police but I don't want to cry wolf if it isn't anything. They would stop the man and find out he is someone looking over the town to buy some land or some such thing."

"I'm inclined to agree. Why don't you keep a watch around the house and you call me at once if anything else happens?"

Johnny could hear his wife breathing on the other side of the line, finally she asked, "John, do you have any idea when you will be back?"

"Honey, I told you last night that I don't even have any arrangements made for Joe's body yet. Hopefully, the police will release his body today and I can make arrangements for the service here in Nevada."

Margaret Collins sighed deeply. "I hope it happens soon. I'd feel a lot better if you were home."

"Honey, you were with me all over the world and these type of things didn't bother you. It isn't any different in Iowa. In fact, there in Iowa you are much safer than anywhere else in the world."

"Yea, I know. It just is a bit unnerving," she answered.

"Margaret, I have some things to do. Call me if you have any problems. I am going to be in and out all day. I am trying to find out what happened to Joe and who was responsible for his death."

"All right, you stay safe and don't worry about me. Maybe you are right and I am overreacting."

"By for now, honey, I love you."

"I love you too, John. Stay safe."

Johnny held the phone until he heard his wife hang up the receiver. He had an uneasy feeling that his wife was right and someone was watching his house. He had to have time to think about what to do next. Maybe he would have to get in touch with his office at CIA headquarters.

ASSIGNMENT: RENO, NEVADA

CHAPTER TWENTY-SIX

It was almost four when Johnny walked out of the funeral home. He stood outside of the large white house and leaned against a tall pillar wiping his forehead. The street in front of the business was completely empty.

He turned toward the parking lot where he had left his rental car. After he took a step forward, he felt shaky and leaned back against the pole. Going through the funeral service arrangements had taken more energy out of him than he had expected.

An image of Joe flashed through his mind and a tremor of grief passed over him. He pressed his lips together tightly and concentrated on regaining his composure. He needed to get back to the hotel and get something to eat. The slice of toast that he had eaten for breakfast had worn off long ago and it was way past his normal lunchtime.

By four fifteen Johnny was back in his hotel room. He had a folder including information about the service and he had finalized arrangements to send Joe's body back to Iowa. Now all he needed was for the police to release Joe's body. The funeral home director told him the body would be released later in the afternoon.

Out of a long established habit that he'd probably never forget, he looked around the room and locked his gaze on his suitcase. It was turned around from the way that he had left it earlier in the day.

"Someone has been snooping through my things," he said aloud as he walked around the room. He knew the cleaning lady had been in but she hadn't touched his suitcase and shaving items before. Now, they had all been carelessly rearranged out of his usual order on the shelf.

Opening his suitcase, he found its contents were all unfolded and in complete disarray. "Well, I'll be," He wondered aloud as he refolded several t-shirts and pairs of socks.

Shaking his head in disbelief, he sat on the bed and looked around. The plastic sack of food was still near the closet door. From the slight flour dust on the floor, it was obvious someone had opened it and looked inside.

With a thumping heart, he retrieved the sack, holding the bag of flour over the open sack while he dug his fingers through the contents. Within seconds he felt a hard item apparently protected by a small paper bag, pulled it out and shook off the flour into the plastic bag.

Taking care not to make a mess, he put the small bag in his hand and went into the bathroom to get a towel. He wiped off the outside of the paper and then went back to the dresser. Carefully, he opened the paper.

ASSIGNMENT: RENO, NEVADA

"Good heavens," Johnny exclaimed as he looked inside. "Where in the world did Joe get these?"

Taking care not to drop anything, Johnny rewrapped the packet and put it carefully in his front left jean pocket. Puzzled, he paused to think about what to do next, picking up loose change from the top of the desk.

CHAPTER TWENTY-SEVEN

The CIA complex in Langley, Virginia is a massive structure consisting of two main buildings. The two are the Original Headquarters building and the New Headquarters building. The four story new building has a joining courtyard that provides a smooth transition from the modern glass structure to the traditional architecture of the original building.

Most of the year, weather permitting, it offers guests and workers an extensive plush lawn, fishpond, flowering plants and shrubs. It is an ideal meeting place for lunch, chats or simple fresh air breaks. Throughout the year, events are planned ranging from ethnic celebrations to music concerts.

Six floors beneath the main floor of the Agency is an area that is always busy. It contains the Operation Center. Within this enormous space, men and women monitor ongoing spy operations throughout the world.

These employees keep in touch with embassies and consulates through out the world. The staff does not control operations but serve as a monitoring

ASSIGNMENT: RENO, NEVADA

department and a communications link between the field agents and the rest of the Agency.

The Operations Center is divided into several sections. Each of these divisions has a large computer projection screen showing the entire region they control. Each section has a direct supervisor and several operators who handle activities within their region.

Bill Weaver sat in one of the wooden chairs, his eyes fixed on the monitor on one of the desks. He had the receiver to the telephone sitting on the desk. A speakerphone symbol was displayed on the monitor.

An operator and another agent were also in the cubicle. The female agent stood directly behind Weaver and studied a large projection screen without looking aside. The male operator sat at a nearby desk, constantly typing on his keyboard. He moved stick figures around on the projection screen as he was monitoring an ongoing Moscow operation.

"Johnny, are you talking on a secure line?" Weaver asked.

"Yes, as secure as I can have here in Reno, Nevada. No one is near me. I am standing on a street corner and just over my head is the famous Reno sign."

"Well, what is so important?" Weaver asked with a touch of irritation in his voice.

"I need to know what is going on?"

Weaver frowned and questioned, "What do you mean, Johnny?"

"Come on, Bill. What is going down there that would involve me?"

"Johnny, I don't have the slightest idea what you mean." Weaver reached out and lightly touched the agent behind him and indicated for her to pull up a chair and listen to the conversation. "What makes you think something is going on here that involves you?"

Johnny laughed. "Let's just say, I know how you operate."

Weaver sighed. "Be more specific."

"Well, something is going on. My wife called me from Iowa this morning and said that someone is following her. Now, both you and I know that she knows what she is talking about. She has been around the block enough times to be able to spot when someone is tailing her."

Weaver reached for a pen and paper. "Give me the specifics and I'll try to find out what is going on."

For the next several minutes the two men talked. Johnny explained about his brother Joe's murder and why he was in Reno.

Finally, Johnny asked, "Anything that I should know that you aren't telling me?"

Weaver reflected to himself and wrote the name "Schmidt" on the paper and shoved it toward the agent.

"Remember you are semi-retired. I can't tell you about anything that is on going here now. Do you want to get me fired?"

Johnny snorted. "That will be the day! I know that something is happening that you aren't telling me. You know that I'm going to be more than just upset if I have to find it out on my own, so you might as well inform me now."

Weaver looked at the female agent. She nodded to him and made a sympathetic gesture. She understood the risks on both ends of the call. Her eyes were big as she looked into Weaver's face. Finally, Weaver said,

ASSIGNMENT: RENO, NEVADA

"Well, there is something that you might be interested in."

Johnny answered quickly, "I thought so. I felt you were holding something back. What is it?"

"Rumor has it that Viktor Schmidt is in the states."

Johnny jumped as though he had been stung. "That SOB. What do you mean rumor has it? Has he been seen? Is the source reliable?"

Weaver spoke softly. "There is a report that someone intercepted a message and his name was in the message. An operative thought he saw him here on the East coast. We didn't put much truth in the report because the agent said Schmidt looked so different. We tracked him but lost him and have no idea where he might be at this time."

Johnny whistled. "How do they know it is him? Last we heard he was in Moscow, on his death bed."

"The agent overheard someone talking about him and then he was tentatively identified," Weaver answered. "We have no internal confirmation however, that it was Schmidt."

"It's been years. How did they recognize him? I doubt if there are any up to date photos of him anywhere. The last ones I saw were at least fifteen years old."

"Johnny, it was one of those strange things. Someone from another agency ran across one of his fingerprints at a security crossing. I could not find anyone that had remembered seeing him, so we don't have any visual description to go on."

Johnny licked his lips. "I have had the strangest feeling since I arrived here in this city that something just hasn't been right. Do you think he could be here?"

Weaver silently shook his head sideways. "I can't imagine why. He thinks you're dead. I doubt if he would be out there unless he was going to go gambling and why would he be in Reno when he could go to all the glitz in Vegas?"

Johnny took a deep breath. "You're probably right. I can't imagine what would bring him to Reno either."

Weaver tapped his pen on the desktop and then said, "We'll get in touch with someone reliable and have him check out your wife in Iowa. When you get a chance, next time you talk to her, let her know that someone might be contacting her. I think it might make her feel better."

"I agree. Thanks," Johnny answered. "I'll get in touch if I find out anything that I think you need to know."

"Do that. Stay out of trouble."

Johnny said, "Always." He hung up the phone. It was getting late and he still wanted to get in touch with Sarah and Peggy. He needed their help in finalizing the plans for Joe's memorial service.

CHAPTER TWENTY-EIGHT

It was almost five by the time Johnny pulled into the antique mall parking lot. Two large moving vans took up most of the space. He turned his rental car around so that it wouldn't block their way when the trucks wanted to leave.

As he got out of the car, he acted as though he was checking the doors to make sure the locks worked and covertly looked over the whole parking lot. Of the other parked cars, one was a red BMW sedan and the other was a light blue Cadillac. He smiled. He knew that Peggy was in the mall because the Cadillac was hers. None of the other cars was of particular note to him, and he went on toward the door.

"Hey, how are things going?" Peggy called when Johnny opened the door.

She was standing just inside the door directing two moving men carrying a large table. She turned from Johnny and said, "Be careful guys, I don't want anything broken in those cases near you." She turned to Johnny and sadly remarked in a low voice, "You have to watch them all the time. If you don't, everything could come crashing down around us."

Johnny knowingly nodded; he had made many household moves and knew exactly what could happen. "What's going on? Are you moving?"

"No, we sold some things and had to have some things brought in from one of the warehouses. We are constantly restocking."

Johnny took several steps closer to where the men were moving several pieces of furniture. "Is all this furniture yours?"

Peggy sighed and waved her hands around. "Yes, the pieces they are moving around now are mine. Some of the pieces on the other side of the building are Sarah's. We just keep switching things around as we redecorate and restock." She stood and looked at the men and then toward Johnny. "It gets a bit tiring after a while." She bowed her head slightly and continued. "Guess I'm getting old."

Johnny walked closer to her and touched her shoulder. "I believe we all think that at least once a day when we get to be our age."

"You're just a kid. Look at you." She studied his face for a moment and then asked, "How old are you anyway? I know we said that Joe was in his early 60's, but you have to be about ten years younger than him."

Johnny smiled. "Pretty close. I'll be fifty-two in September."

"See, you're just a kid," Peggy responded. Once again, she took a step forward and called to the men. "Okay, guys. I think that is good for those pieces. Do we have everything off the trucks?"

One of the moving company men called back, "Yes, this table was the last piece." He walked toward the other man who was waiting and they talked for a few seconds. Then, both men approached Peggy and Johnny.

When they paused in front of Peggy, she said, "Thanks guys. Once again I appreciate everything that you have done for us. Be sure and turn your hours in so that you can get paid on schedule. Take the vans and park at the storage unit. We probably won't need them again until next week, and I think that Sam wants to use them before then."

The moving man nodded and answered, "Sure. We'll return them to where we picked them up. What should I do with the keys?"

Peggy answered, "Just put them in the warehouse on the key rack. When Sam goes to use the trucks, he can find the keys there. That's where he will look." She turned and walked toward the door with the two men.

Johnny stood where he was and watched the trio move away. He couldn't hear anyone else in the mall so decided to just wait where he was until Peggy returned. As he waited he turned slowly around and checked out the mall. His eyes moved to the back of the mall and the space where Joe had his booth.

He started to take a couple steps toward it when Peggy reappeared. "Where are you going?" she asked.

Johnny hesitated momentarily. "I just remembered about Joe's space. I thought now would be a good time to walk back there and try to decide what to do with Joe's things that remain in the booth."

"I'll walk with you," Peggy answered. She crossed to Johnny's side and they both moved toward the back of the building. After they stood and studied the booth for a moment, she said, "What do you think you want to do with these things that are here?"

Johnny walked over to a glass showcase and looked at the collection of knives. He recognized some from World War II and Vietnam. Finally, he said, "I guess I should look for someone to buy these. I don't want to take them back home to Iowa and I can't imagine what else I could do with them."

Peggy walked toward him and put her hand on his arm. She turned slightly and looked up into his eyes. "What say I just buy everything that is here in the booth and we can just leave things the way they are?"

Johnny patted her hand and looked around. He grimaced in thought for a moment, and then answered, "Yes, I think that would be fine. You have a better idea of the value of the items than I do."

Peggy walked toward a display of paintings hanging in the back of the booth. She pointed to them. "These are all worth about $100 each retail, so, for example, I will offer you $50 each, which would be wholesale price. They are by an old local artist and wouldn't be worth much outside of Reno. Would that be agreeable for them and in general for all the items here?"

Johnny rubbed his hands together and sighed. "Whatever you think is fair is fine with me. How do you want to handle the sale?"

"I'll take a quick inventory of things just as soon as I get a chance. When will you be leaving for Iowa?"

Johnny slapped his forehead. "I almost forgot why I came to see you today. I made arrangements for Joe's memorial service and transporting his remains back to Iowa."

"Well, that's great," exclaimed Peggy. "Come on, let's go up front and talk to Sarah. She will want to hear all about this too."

As they walked, Johnny remarked, "I thought Sarah was leaving early tonight?" He remembered what Peggy had told him before.

Peggy laughed, "She ran some errands after I got back and then decided to come back and close up with me."

As the pair continued toward the customer service desk in the mall they heard the sound of a bell. They both looked toward the door and saw two men standing in the doorway.

Peggy called, "Good afternoon, gentlemen. How are you two today?"

The men walked toward Peggy and Johnny. They stopped about ten feet from where the couple was standing.

Johnny watched the tall man approach. Something about the way he moved made Johnny feel as if he had seen him. He stayed silent just studying the newcomers.

"Thought we would stop by and see Sarah," the tall man said with his strong Texas accent. "We're fixing to go to dinner and thought we might be able to talk her into going with us this evening even if we have to rope and hog tie her."

Peggy laughed. "Lordy, you two must be the two characters she was telling me about earlier today." She walked between the two men and took each of them by the arm. "Come on," she called to Johnny and motioned with her head. "Let's all go and see what Sarah is doing."

CHAPTER TWENTY-NINE

A tall gray haired man stood up inside the Northwest plane and looked around before moving to debark. He glanced at the other standing passengers and retrieved his coat from the overhead compartment.

At Washington D.C. he was given a quick briefing on this assignment. Although he had heard a great deal about Iowa, he hadn't ever had the opportunity to set foot in the state during his thirty years of working for the CIA.

He was told to go to Clear Lake and check on Johnny Collins' family. During the briefing, he had been assured that it would be a simple, no-brainer assignment. There obviously was a special reason he was being sent to Iowa, but he never questioned what that reason was.

A baby started crying and the gray haired man stepped out of the aisle, allowing a woman with a small child pass. From years of traveling, he knew it was best to take your time exiting a plane. It also allowed time to study the other passengers.

As he walked toward the short gangway he looked at the setting sun. It was almost seven-thirty. Instinctively, he calculated the time it would take to get his rental car and drive the short trip to the motel where the agency had already reserved a room for him.

"Thanks for flying Northwest," said the attractive attendant as the man passed her.

He smiled and glanced at both the attendant and at the pilot who was standing beside the cockpit door. "Thanks for the smooth ride," he answered.

Standing at the top of the metal steps, he located the terminal building. He pulled at his sweater, shivered when the raw, fresh air hit his face and put on his coat. He moved down the steps quickly when he saw that there were no trees or buildings to block the chilling spring wind.

Walking through the terminal door, he noted the security man posted by the doorway. The mother and baby were standing with a young man in front of the baggage claim area.

The agent stopped just inside the building and took his right hand, running it through his hair. He wanted to check out everyone in the waiting area without appearing too obvious. Convinced that no one was watching him, he walked toward the rental car booths on the other side of the room.

Standing in front of the Avis window, he faced the entrance and kept his back toward the baggage claim area. He leaned forward on the counter and said, "I believe this reservation for me is for a week. Would it be alright if I turn it in earlier?"

ASSIGNMENT: RENO, NEVADA

The attendant smiled and answered, "Of course, but you get a better rate keeping it for the week. I'd have to charge you a daily rate if you turn it in early."

The man frowned and turned his head slightly. He looked at the young woman and smiled. "Ah, come on. It can't make that much difference in cost."

The young lady sighed and answered, "Well, I'll try and give you the best rate that I can when you turn the car in." She thought for a moment and then added, "Remember, I'm not promising anything but I'll try."

The man reached for the young lady's hand and patted it lightly. "That is all I can ask for. Now, what car do you have for me tonight?"

The girl turned on her heel and reached for a paper that had just finished printing. With one hand she took the paper and with the other hand she reached for a key on her desk. "I have a Ford Taurus. It is maroon. The reservation was for a dark colored sedan and that's the best I have."

The man reached for the paperwork and the key. He smiled and answered, "That's perfect." He glanced at the girl's nametag and added. "Thank you, Rose Marie. You have been most helpful. I'll ask for you when I return."

"You are very welcome," the young lady answered moving from the gray haired man to the next customer at the other end of the counter.

A loud humming noise started behind the man and caused him to abruptly whirl and look at the group of people rushing toward the baggage claim area. He walked closer to the others watching the suitcases drop off a belt. An airport employee stood beside the luggage asking to see the matching luggage claim tickets.

"Here you go," the older man said as he showed the employee his ticket and reached for his bag. The older man had waited to claim his bag until all the other passengers had cleared the terminal.

Within minutes, the older man unlocked his rental car, unlocked the driver's side only, and slid in behind the steering wheel. He turned on the overhead light and pulled a map out of his coat pocket and studied it. He ran his finger along highway 122, down 8th Street to the main street in Clear Lake. He found North Shore Drive and followed it all the way to Clark Road. Someone at Langley had drawn a large black circle between North Shore and 34th Street. He knew that was where Johnny Collins lived.

He exited the airport parking lot and drove onto highway 122. As he turned right, he realized he was the only car on the highway. Without thinking of a speed limit, he pushed the gas pedal hard and within minutes crossed under Interstate 35 arriving at the Best Western motel.

By nine, the agent was sitting at the bar in Bennigan's restaurant. First, he had checked into the motel, checked out his room and freshened up. Although he was tired, he still wanted to get the feel of the area and knew that a local bar was a good place to start.

"I'll take a Coors," the man nodded at the bartender.

"Coming right up," the bar keeper answered back quickly.

ASSIGNMENT: RENO, NEVADA

The gray haired man didn't say another word, waiting for the drink to be placed in front of him. He turned on the bar stool slightly and checked out the room. Since it was a week day evening, there were only two couples eating at one of the nearby tables and another couple having some drinks on the other side of the room.

"Rather slow?" the man asked the bartender, who was wiping off the counter in front of him.

"Yea, spring break is just over and everyone is back to school and work. Not much going on," the young attendant answered.

"So what is there to do in Clear Lake?"

The young man said, "Pretty quiet this time of year, especially during week days. On the weekend there is the comedy club and several of the bars have events going on. The Surf ballroom normally has something going for Friday and Saturday nights. Actually, there is a lot going on for such a small town."

"Oh," the older man asked. He would never have guessed.

"Yeah, in the summertime we are packed every night. Tourists and vacationers keep the town jumping from Memorial Day to Labor Day."

"Sounds like fun," said the gray haired man. "I suppose the lake brings plenty of people during the summer."

"You'd better believe it," the bartender smiled. "It is awesome."

As the bartender talked another man walked up to the bar. He was a middle aged bald man.

The gray haired man greeted the newcomer saying, "Glad to see that I'm not going to be the only guy here at the bar tonight."

The bald headed man answered, "Yeah, I normally come in for a night cap about now." He studied the stranger and asked, "So what brings you to Clear Lake?"

"I'm here on business," the gray haired man answered. He had been given a cover before he left Washington and quickly tried to recall all the details.

"Me too," the bald headed man replied. He looked around the room and hitched the bar stool closer to the bar. "What business you in?"

The gray haired man smiled and slowly answered, "I'm in agriculture. I sell supplies to the various businesses."

"Oh," the bald headed man said. "I'm in seed corn. I also work with the farmers."

The gray haired man laughed. "I guess ninety nine percent of businesses in Iowa deal with farmers." He thought for a moment and then asked, "Where are you from?"

The bald headed man ran his hand over the smooth top of his head shrugging. "I'm from Minnesota."

"Ah, not too far from home," the gray haired man said. He thought for a moment and then asked, "What's the accent I hear in your speech? Is it Czech or Scandinavian?"

The bald headed man laughed in turn. "I thought I had gotten rid of my accent. My parents came over to Minnesota from Denmark, so I guess you would say I'm Scandinavian."

"That's what I thought," the gray haired man said. "I have a good ear and can usually detect accents."

The two men sat and talked for another hour. Rising, the gray haired man said, "Well, time for bed. I have a zillion things to do tomorrow." He turned toward the bartender who was wiping off the countertop, glanced at his nametag and said, "Night now, Mark. Probably will see you again tomorrow night."

CHAPTER THIRTY

"Hey, Sarah, look who I found," Peggy called as she walked toward the customer service counter.

Sarah lifted her head and smiled. "Well, I'll be. Glad to see you all again." She turned toward Johnny and shook his hand, then moved toward Victor Smith and Chris Gannon and shook their hands.

"Hey, we missed you last night," Victor said. He held onto Sarah's hand as he talked and studied her facial expression.

Sarah leaned toward him and in a whisper answered, "Yes, sorry about that. Something came up and I didn't have a phone to get in touch with you."

Victor smiled. "Well, you are forgiven if you'll go with us tonight. We can go eat anywhere you like." He leaned toward Sarah and whispered, "Is it too late to go look at those storage units?"

Sarah shook her head and then looked at Johnny and the two men. "I'm sorry, I bet you haven't been introduced to one another." She hesitated for a moment as she looked at Victor and then continued. "Johnny Collins, I would like you to meet Victor

Smith." She looked toward Chris, "Sorry, Chris, I can't remember your last name."

"Gannon. Chris Gannon," he answered on cue.

"Yes, that's right. Johnny, I want you to meet Chris Gannon." As she talked the men shook hands.

Victor had recognized Johnny when he entered the mall. He tried hard not to show any reaction. He smiled at Johnny and said, "Nice to meet you. Are you a friend of these two fine ladies?"

"Casual," Johnny answered quickly. "How about you?"

Victor laughed and put his arm around Sarah. "Would like to be good friends but we are just starting to get acquainted."

Sarah slightly twisted her body forward and pushed Victor's arm away. "Now, behave," she said.

Victor turned toward Peggy, motioned with his hand and asked, "How about you and your friend here joining us?"

Johnny looked at Peggy and Sarah. He shrugged his shoulders and nodded. "Sure, that's fine with me if that is alright with all of you," he answered.

"Well, great," answered Victor with emphasis. He slapped his hands together as though he was very pleased. "So what do we do next?"

"Why don't you three men talk while Peggy and I finish up here. We just need to close down for the night," Sarah answered walking back to the pile of papers she had been working on.

"We won't be long," Peggy echoed. She smiled at the men and then walked around the counter and followed Sarah.

Victor felt uncomfortable. He smiled at Johnny and Chris. "What say we go over to those chairs and sit down and relax? Johnny, you can tell me a bit about yourself." Victor pointed to an area down the aisle where the moving men had earlier placed a display of table and chairs.

After they all were seated, Johnny asked, "So where are you guys from?"

Victor looked at Chris, smiled and looked back at Johnny. "I thought my accent and cowboy boots already gave me away," he answered.

Johnny said, "So where are you from in Texas?"

"From a small town of about thirty thousand people out in West Texas," Victor answered. He looked toward Chris and said, "Chris is from California."

Johnny frowned and thought for a moment and then said, "Where in West Texas? Abilene?"

Victor laughed. "A bit further South. Down in San Angelo, out in the ranch area."

"Oh, San Angelo," Johnny answered. "I've been through there on my way to San Antonio. It seemed like a nice city, don't they have a college there?"

Victor reached down, brushing a speck of dust from his boot. He looked back at Johnny and said, "Yes, we have the University of Texas there."

"Oh, I had forgotten that," Johnny answered.

While the men sat and talked about Texas and Reno, Johnny looked back toward the customer service area and said, "I forgot there is something that I need to talk to the ladies about. You both sit here, I'll be right back." Without waiting for an answer, he got up and walked away from Victor and Chris.

CHAPTER THIRTY-ONE

As Johnny walked to the customer service area, he reached into his pocket and pulled out a paper that the funeral director had given him. He scanned it and frowned.

When he got to the counter, he said, "Say, ladies, I wanted just a moment alone to ask you something about Joe's memorial service."

Both of the ladies looked up from the book they were working with. Peggy said, "So you finally made the arrangements?"

Johnny smiled and nodded. "Yes, finally got things settled." He took the paper in his hand and read it again. "The director thought the best time for the service would be at six in the evening. What do you two think of that?"

Sarah nodded. "I think that is perfect. It gives working people a chance to attend. What day are you going to hold it?"

Johnny answered, "Tomorrow evening at the Fallan Funeral Home. The director said that they would receive visiting from one in the afternoon for those that wanted to come by earlier. He will post a notice in tomorrow's paper and I was hoping that you ladies would tell anyone that you thought might be interested."

Peggy asked, "When did they release Joe's body?"

Johnny answered, "They were supposed to have done it today. The director promised he would have everything ready and there wouldn't be any problems. Evidently, from the way he talked, Joe's attorney, had already contacted him as well as the police, and all the paperwork had been completed. It was now just a matter of getting Joe's body and making the final arrangements at the funeral home."

"Oh," Sarah answered. She thought for a moment and then said, "That seems funny that his attorney, Terrance Ruddick, would make all those arrangements. I thought Joe wanted to be cremated?"

Johnny gently touched her hand. "Yes, he is going to be but not until after the service tomorrow. I will take his ashes back to Iowa when I go and have them buried there."

Peggy softly eyed Johnny. There were tears in her eyes. "That's fine. Joe would have liked that. So what can we do to help with the service? Do you need any flowers or such?"

Johnny shrugged. "I don't think that flowers will be necessary. I have ordered some from the family and the funeral director said that he had calls from local florists that were holding floral arrangements for the service. I just need you to let everyone know about the service. If any of Joe's acquaintances want to say something at the service, that would be appreciated."

ASSIGNMENT: RENO, NEVADA

Sarah looked at Peggy. "You should say something, Peggy. You knew Joe better than me. He would have liked that."

Peggy wiped a tear and smiled. "Yes, of course. I'll say a few words and I'll make phone calls later tonight to some of his buddies and tell them about the service." She turned her back to Johnny reaching for a tissue on the table behind her. When she turned back, she had managed a smile on her face.

"So," Johnny said. "I guess that is that. Are you about ready?" He looked down the aisle where Victor Smith and Chris Gannon were waiting. "Those two are probably getting hungry." He glanced at his watch. "Wow, it is almost six."

Just as he spoke, a bell rang. Johnny and the ladies looked toward the door. Lt. Clausen entered the mall and walked toward the group.

"Hey, you're open late tonight aren't you?" he said with a wide smile on his face.

Sarah frowned and shook her finger at Peggy. "I thought I told you to lock the door."

Peggy reached for her keys and scurried to lock the door before anyone else came in. She flipped over the sign to show "CLOSED" and strode back to the counter.

"So what brings you out here so late?" Peggy asked Clausen.

He shifted like his feet hurt and brushed some unseen lint off of his tweed jacket. With a shy expression on his face, he ran his fingers through his gray hair. "Have been out running down some leads on a case and was in the neighborhood and thought I would drop in and see what is going on with both of you."

"Not much," Peggy answered. "What case are you working on?"

Clausen held his hands up and made a straight face. "Hey, you know I can't tell you what cases I'm working on. That's confidential in police business."

"Yeah, right," Sarah said sarcastically. "Sounds more like monkey business to me."

Clausen tapped Sarah playfully on her shoulder. "You had better be good or I'll take you in for harassing an officer of the law."

As the couple talked, Victor Smith and Chris Gannon joined the group. Victor said, "Hey, gang, I'm getting hungry. How soon are we going to get something to eat?"

Peggy laughed. "Give me a minute to lock these books in the safe and then we will be out of here." She picked up the books and walked to an area behind the counter. "Sarah, why don't you go turn off the lights so we'll be ready to leave."

Sarah started to walk away and then turned to the group and said, "Where are we going to eat? I can't remember if we decided on anything. I know last night we were going to the Liberty Belle but tonight they are having a fish fry and I don't want fish."

Victor laughed. "I probably am the only one that remembers you talking about a place. We were going to some German restaurant not too far from some plant nursery. I think someone said that it was just North of Virginia."

"Sure, that place is fine," Sarah said. She turned toward Clausen and said, "Want to go with us?"

Clausen nodded to Sarah, turned to the men extending his right hand, "I'm Tom Clausen. I'd like to go if that is okay with everyone."

Sarah gasped. "Sorry, I should have introduced you all. Tom, this is Victor Smith and Chris Gannon. Of course, you know Johnny Collins." She turned toward Victor and Chris and pointed to Clausen. "This is Lt. Tom Clausen with the Reno Police Department. Just in case you didn't guess, he is a plain clothes policeman, hence no uniform." Turning back to Clausen she added, "Victor is from Texas and Chris is from California. They are interested in some primitive furniture that we're offering."

Peggy reached for her purse and swung it over her shoulder. "Come on," she called. "Let's go eat. Does anyone want to ride with me?"

Johnny smiled and said, "No, I have my car. I'll just follow you."

"We have our car and we also will follow," Victor said, including Chris.

Clausen looked at Sarah and said, "I have my car so I'll follow too. Don't any of you drive too fast, I'm not sure where this place is."

Sarah turned and answered, "You know the one. It's that German restaurant in that small strip mall across the street from the nursery just north of Virginia. You turn right off of Virginia by the Land Rover dealership."

"Oh, right," Clausen answered. "I know the place." He checked the wall clock. "What say I meet you there, I'm have to run an errand first. You go ahead and order me a diet coke and a schnitzel. I won't be long."

Before anyone could answer, Clausen turned and hurried out of the mall. He was leaving the parking lot before the rest of the party got to the door.

"Johnny, can you come by my car a minute?" Peggy whispered as they walked toward the door.

Johnny nodded and answered softly, "Sure, what do you need?"

"I have a box of Joe's things that I want to give to you."

Johnny stepped aside and let Victor and Chris follow Sarah out the door. He stood in the doorway while Peggy armed the alarm system. They trailed slowly allowing the other three to reach their cars ahead of them.

"You two follow Sarah," Peggy called to Victor. "I'll have Johnny follow me. That way we won't have any problems because it is still rush hour."

The men nodded and got into their Jeep.

Sarah opened her car door retrieving a bag from the back seat. She walked over to Johnny, "Joe gave me these a while back and I think you might like one this evening. It might help you to unwind."

Johnny took the sack and peered into it. Smiling, he said, "Thanks. I'm not much of a liquor person but I appreciate this."

Without another word, Sarah hurried to her car and pulled out of the parking lot in her red BMW. Victor and Chris followed in their Jeep.

Johnny stepped behind Peggy as she opened the trunk to her light blue Cadillac. "This is a box of things that Joe left with me some years ago for safe keeping. He said he didn't want any mice getting in and chewing on them and he knew that they would be safe at my house. I'm not sure they are worth much but thought you should have them. I know that there are some family pictures but he never talked about them."

She noted the bag Johnny was holding. "I see that Sarah gave you a couple bottles of Russian champagne. Joe had a couple of cases of that and he gave some to Sarah. I'm not a champagne drinker but everyone tells me that Russian champagne is good stuff. Don't have any idea where Joe got it, he definitely wasn't the champagne type."

Johnny reached inside the trunk, put the bottles inside of the box and lifted the box out. "Thanks. I'll go through these things and see if any of it is worth keeping. As for the champagne, I like a glass or two occasionally."

He went to his rental car and put the box in the trunk. As he put down the trunk lid, he called back to Peggy, "Don't drive too fast so I can follow you. I have no idea where we are going."

CHAPTER THIRTY-TWO

It was almost seven by the time Johnny parked his rental car in the lot behind Peggy's Cadillac. Stepping out, he looked around at the strip mall. In front of him was a sprawling building with a large sign. He smiled. He had been in Germany many times and enjoyed seeing the Bavarian decorations on the building.

He ran to catch up with Peggy and held the door as she entered "The Bavarian Haus". The smell of fresh baked bread made his mouth water.

"Wow, am I hungry," he said leaning toward Peggy.

She laughed. "Yea, I think they use some kind of a spray to create that aroma. I have been here all hours of the day and I can't believe that they are baking bread all the time."

"Whatever they are doing, it surely works," Johnny answered following her past a row of tables toward the back room. He could see that Sarah and the two buyers were already seated.

Sarah looked up and said, "Everything on the menu is good and fresh. It is all authentic German."

ASSIGNMENT: RENO, NEVADA

The group ordered drinks study their menus. After several minutes, Victor Smith said, "Sarah, when can we get together and see about the furniture that I am interested in?"

Sarah reached for his hand and held it tight. "My dear, we can do it tomorrow. The warehouses are far too poor illuminated to enter at night." She turned away and spoke in a soft voice, "Now, let's concentrate on eating and visiting. Victor, why don't you start by telling us a bit about Texas? I've been there several times and it is still one of the states that has always intrigued me."

Victor sighed and pressed Sarah's hand. "Yes, it is an intriguing state. It has mountains, desert, lush green sections and water. There is something for everyone. If you travel from El Paso to the Louisiana border, it takes you over a day of steady driving. We have large cities and small towns. We have horses, cattle, goats, pigs and farming of all types." He looked around the table and added, "I bet no one of you can say that about your home state?"

Peggy answered, "I'm a native Nevadan. We too have desert, mountains, green areas and various livestock. It also takes almost a day to drive from the Utah border to the California border across the breadth of Nevada, and from Las Vegas to Reno is a long trip. However, I would agree that Texas is much larger in area than Nevada."

Johnny added, "It takes a bit over six hours driving from the most south eastern part of Iowa down by Davenport to the far northwestern corner of Iowa. However, we don't have desert, just lush green farmland. It's the corn belt state."

Johnny studied the two men sitting across the table from him, then he said, "Chris, tell us about your home state."

Chris shrugged and avoided looking directly at Johnny. "I live in California now but I was also born in Nevada and I can't add much more to what Peggy said." He picked up his glass and took a long drink of brew to terminate his answer.

Sarah said, "Well, I'm from Nevada too." She looked around the room and pointed to Peggy and Chris. "I guess we Nevada people outnumber the rest of you tonight. So does everyone know what they are going to order?"

Everyone nodded in unison and Sarah motioned toward a passing server. For the next several minutes the group was busy ordering their meals.

Johnny spent the remainder of the evening listening to the others. He couldn't quite put to rest the singularly tantalizing feeling that he had met Victor Smith before. Victor didn't talk as if he had ever been on the East coast or traveled outside of the United States.

It was almost ten by the time the group gathered to say their good byes in the parking lot. Lt. Tom Clausen had rejoined the group just in time to eat his schnitzel.

"Don't forget to tell everyone about Joe's service tomorrow," Joe called to Sarah and Peggy.

Clausen asked, "Oh, you are having a service tomorrow?"

"Yes," Johnny answered. "It will be at the funeral home at six tomorrow evening. There will be viewing after one o'clock tomorrow afternoon. Please stop by if you have the opportunity."

Sarah took Clausen's arm and looked up into his face, "Tom, you surely can arrange to stop by at six tomorrow evening. Also, please tell everyone that you know at the station or even post it. Johnny said there will be a notice in the paper but you know how some people don't get around to reading the paper until later in the evening."

Clausen answered, "Yes, of course, I'll tell everyone." He looked down at Sarah and said, "May I follow you home?"

Sarah nodded.

Johnny watched the two and wondered about their relationship. Before he could say anything to Peggy he saw that she had gotten into her car and was leaving the parking lot.

CHAPTER THIRTY-THREE

Located off of Interstate 35, almost halfway between Minneapolis and Des Moines is the small town named Clear Lake, Iowa. The town partially circles its namesake lake making an ideal spot for tourism.

There is year around fishing, numerous antique shops, quaint shops filled with clothing, art, furniture and everyday living items. The city hosts a variety of excellent restaurants, bowling and nightspots. The famous Surf Ballroom offers dancing and a wide music selection with live bands.

Because of its location, it is the preferred summer vacation area for people from nearby larger cities. The lakefront is dotted with homes from elegant three floor structures to small lakeside cabins.

It was almost ten in the evening by the time the tall gray haired CIA agent stopped his car on Clark Road on the west side of Clear Lake. He had left his room at the Best Western motel about noon and had spent the greater part of the day exploring the town and surrounding area.

ASSIGNMENT: RENO, NEVADA

After studying the rental agency map, he drove several times past Johnny Collins' corner home on North Shore Drive. He finally parked down the street near a public fishing dock and began walking around the area, imitating several of the other residents.

Whenever a fishing party would leave, and the dock was empty he would walk out on it and sit on the lone bench, looking at the lake. When other fishermen arrived, he would walk back to his car, pretend to be changing shoes, then, once again he would take a long walk down North Shore Drive and pass Johnny's home.

On one of his earlier walks he watched Johnny's son arrive home on the Ventura school bus. Although at times he felt as if he were being watched, he never was able to spot anyone else watching the Collins house.

When it was dark, the agent took his time casually sauntering through the shadows in the neighborhood near the Collins house. He stopped several times, listing to the sounds about him. His night vision goggles hung around his neck. Occasionally he reached up to use them, making sure not to bump into bushes or jar any other obstacles as he passed.

As he moved out of the shadows on North Shore Drive and began walking past Collins' house on Thirty-Fourth Street he heard the slight snap of a twig behind him. He paused, turning slowly just as a heavy set man pressed the cold muzzle barrel of a handgun against his head.

"Stand easy, hang loose," said a chilling, menacing voice.

The CIA agent flinched as the stranger pulled one of his dangling arms behind his back. The loud click of a handcuff locking filled the night air as his wrist was fastened. Then, the other arm was pulled back and was secured beside the first.

The stranger whispered, "Why are you interested in this house?"

The gray haired man grunted cleared his throat as though preparing to reply. He tried to turn his head, but the pressure of stranger's gun prevented any movement. It reminded the agent who was in control.

The captured agent answered in a soft voice, "I have no idea what you mean. I'm simply out for a nightly stroll."

The stranger chuckled softly and said, "Yeah, right. I saw you walk past here at least a dozen times today." He pulled at the handcuffs and asked again, "What are you looking for?"

The gray haired man tried to laugh to ease his tension. "Wait, you have this all wrong. Unhook my arms. I'm simply walking in the area, getting some exercise. I have no specific interest in anything."

"Yes, you do," the stranger answered. "You are interested in the Collins house. Why?" He slapped the gun barrel roughly against the agent's temple and waited for an answer.

The gray haired man recoiled. He had trouble thinking. He could feel blood running down his cheek. Desperately, he tried to move his arms but they were secure bound securely. He tried to move his body around to face the stranger. He said, "I insist that you undo my hands and we can talk. I can't think clearly like this."

"Yes, you can and you will if you know what is good for you," the stranger answered quickly and sharply. He kicked at the gray haired man's legs. "I will ask you once more, what do you want with the Collins family?"

The gray haired man could feel the bile from his stomach rise in his mouth. He spit and answered, "I am simply out for a nightly stroll and just happen to be walking through this neighborhood. Who are these Collins people you are talking about?"

The stranger patted his prisoner down then roughly reached into the captive man's jacket pocket. He pulled out a wallet, stepped into the streetlight and held it up to the light. His lips moved as he read the identification card.

"Ah, you are CIA. Anyway, that is what your identification card says." He closed the wallet and stuck it back in the agent's pocket. He turned the gray haired man around and studied him.

With his hand secure on the gun, he asked, "Once again, I ask what you are doing here?"

"I told you before I have no idea what you mean," the agent answered quite sharply. He stepped backward trying his best to get out of the stranger's range.

The stranger pulled the gray haired man forward and stared directly into his eyes. He adjusted the gun slightly but held it steady against the gray haired man.

"You!" the stranger said louder. "I am tired of playing this game. What are you doing here?"

He waited for a few seconds and continued, "That is enough. We are getting nowhere." He shook his finger angrily several times pointing at the man.

ELIZABETH JUNG

Finally, he pulled the gun a couple inches from the gray haired man's temple, leaned backward and squeezed the trigger. A sharp pop snapped through the still, crisp night.

CHAPTER THIRTY-FOUR

It was after ten by the time that Johnny returned to his motel room. On the drive back, all he could think about was his brother and the memorial service the next day.

He felt like a total stranger in Reno. He realized that he had no idea how he had just driven back to the motel.

On the bed in front of him was the box of things that Peggy had given him. He couldn't remember even taking them out of the trunk of his car and carrying them up to his room.

He considered the box several minutes, debating whether to look through it now or wait until sometime over the weekend. Just as he reached to open the lid, the telephone rang. As if in a daze, he wondered "what next," and let it ring as though it was someone else's phone.

When the ringing finally stopped, a tiny red light on the side of the phone blinked. Shaking his head a couple times to wake up, Johnny finally realized what he was doing.

He brought himself to alertness and realized he now needed to quickly read the instructions for retrieving a message. He did so, and pushed the "0" button and spoke into the mouthpiece, "You have a message for me?"

A brisk voice answered, "Yes, Mr. Collins. Your wife called and asked that you call home."

Johnny knew it was after midnight in Iowa. "Thanks," he said automatically.

He held the phone for several seconds and then put it down. Unbuttoning his shirt, he stood and walked to the bathroom, took his shirt and slacks off, doused his face with cold water and slipped on a pair of sweatpants and a sweatshirt.

Glancing at his watch, he picked up his cell phone from the nightstand. He smiled as he heard the phone ring. He could envision his wife lying in bed waiting for his call. Suddenly, he shuddered as if a cold wind had blown into his motel room.

"Yes, honey. You called?" he asked as he sat on the edge of the bed.

"Johnny, are you alright?" she asked. "You sound as if something is wrong."

Johnny laughed. He was never able to keep anything from his wife. "I'm just tired," he finally answered. "It's been rough couple of days." He thought for a moment and then continued, "Why did you call? Is everything alright?"

His wife, Margaret, answered, "I'm just feeling a bit spooked. I'm sure that it isn't anything but I thought I'd feel better if I just talked to you."

Johnny frowned and got up and walked to the window. "Do you still feel as if someone is watching you?"

Margaret chuckled softly. "Yes, I know I'm being paranoid but I can't help it. I had to run to Fareway for groceries tonight and I was sure that I was being followed but when I came out of the grocery store I couldn't find anything out of place." She was silent for a moment and then added, "I just wish you were back home."

"I'll be there sometime next week." He thought for a moment and wanted to tell her that maybe Weaver had sent someone to Clear Lake to watch his house but he was afraid that it would only scare her further. Softly, he said, "Honey, I'm sure it is nothing, and you know I have always said that it is better to be safe than sorry. Have you seen any unfamiliar faces around the area during the daytime?"

She asked, "How can I tell? There are so many people that rent their homes to strangers. I see people that I don't know all the time. Remember, this is a tourist destination."

"Yes, I know, honey. But, is there anyone in around the house that is a newcomer or someone that just doesn't seem to fit into the scene? Remember the training that we were given before we went to Europe? Look for the out-of-place person or thing. Then follow your instincts."

Margaret replied with a hum. Finally, she said, "I'll really check closer tomorrow. I think I may have seen two men this evening out near the light pole by the docks. Before drawing the curtains, I looked out the den window about ten and though they were standing in the shadows, I could see them very clearly. At the time, I thought that they were strangers, even to each other. I'll watch to see if they come back tomorrow."

Johnny felt a chill and took a deep breath. He knew that something wasn't right but he didn't want to alarm his wife.

With a smile in his voice that he didn't feel, he answered, "Honey, you do that. It could simply be someone out walking dogs or people just taking a late night stroll. You know in that community people are always walking around the lake. But, be very careful, nevertheless."

Margaret sighed. "Yes, I know. Well, I feel better now just having talked to you. Are you having the memorial service tomorrow?"

"Yes," Johnny answered. "I'm not looking forward to it but I think that Joe would have liked it. He apparently had many good friends here."

"Well, stay safe, honey," Margaret said. "I'm going to try and get some sleep. Morning will be here before you know it."

"I love you," Johnny said. "Have pleasant dreams."

Margaret replied softly, "I love you too, Johnny. You be careful."

CHAPTER THIRTY-FIVE

Johnny walked around the room and looked down at the bed. The sheets were in a wad at the bottom of the bed and his blankets were on the floor. He smiled and stretched his legs. It was just six a.m.

Standing in the middle of the room he glanced over at the box that he had received from Peggy. He hadn't taken the time to look through it last night and definitely didn't feel like doing it now.

He had spent a restless night worrying about his wife Margaret and thinking about Joe's death. Viewing himself in the mirror on the other side of the room revolted him. His dark hair was standing straight up and he had bag-like dark circles under his eyes.

He glared at the image in the mirror and then giggled at his image. He was pathetic looking. In short order, he took a shower, dressed and spent a few minutes straightening up things in the room. He didn't know why but he didn't want the cleaning ladies to see his bed in such a mess. Maybe it was the old military training in him.

It was nearly seven when he got out of the elevator and entered the small coffee shop on the street level. Turning slightly, he noticed the casino. He could hear the slot machines ringing and wondered if the players ever slept.

After ordering coffee and a large breakfast, he took the notebook from his pocket and started making a list of things that he still had to do before he returned to Iowa. Several minutes later, he put down the pen and reread the list.

The first thing on the list was a call to CIA headquarters. He wanted to know if Weaver had sent someone to Iowa to watch his family.

As he signaled for another cup of coffee, he noticed a courtesy copy of the Reno Gazette on the empty table next to him. He reached over, taking the paper and began to read.

After browsing the headlines with indifferent interest, he dropped his gaze to below the front page fold. In grateful amazement, he found an article about his brother Joe filling the bottom right hand corner. As he read he fought back tears.

The article gave some details about Joe as well as information about the coming memorial service. The article mentioned the murder of Joe's family and briefly mentioned his working for the government.

Johnny took the newspaper, and picking up his notebook he left money on the table. He walked back to the elevator, then wheeled and made a beeline to the bank of pay telephones in the lobby.

No one paid any attention to him that he could notice as he put the newspaper on the phone ledge and dug through his pockets for a quarter. Absently minded, he dialed the toll free number that he knew would connect him to Weaver at CIA Headquarters. It was just seven-thirty.

"Anything you want to tell me?" he questioned when Weaver came to the phone.

Weaver said something, but Johnny couldn't understand what he was saying.

"I think I have a bad connection. Can you repeat that again?" he asked.

Weaver spoke more distinctly, "Yes, I have a couple things to tell you. Are you at a place where we can talk?"

Johnny surveyed around the area. No one was near him. He could still hear the clicking and ringing of the slot machines in the casino area near him. "No one here but me. What's up?" he questioned.

"I have some bad news to report. Have you talked to your wife lately?"

Johnny stiffened. He didn't like the tone of Weaver's words. He flexed his shoulders and rolled his head back and forth. The lack of sleep was making his neck sore. "I talked to her late last night. Why, what's happened?"

"Remember we talked about Iowa in our previous conversation?"

Johnny frowned. "Yes, of course. What's the matter? Did something happen to my wife or family?"

Weaver sighed. "No, nothing to them." He paused for a moment and then continued, "But the man I sent out to check on your family was killed sometime late last night."

"What in the hell do you mean?"

"Just that. He was killed. Murdered. I was notified early this morning. Clear Lake police called the notification number in his wallet around six this morning, Iowa time. I was contacted at once."

"What the devil is going on?" Johnny asked in disbelief.

"I, we have no idea. We were just told that he was shot and the Iowa police are investigating. I am going to send someone else out. He is at the airport now."

"Don't you have anymore information than that?" Johnny asked. "Nothing," Weaver said. "All I know is what I have said. I should know something more about noon. My guy's plane is due to land in Mason City around noon. He is going to rent a car and then dig into the details."

"I'm going to call Margaret and find out if she knows anything," Johnny said.

"Johnny, don't get her all excited," Weaver answered. "I'll let you know what is going on as soon as I find out something." He paused for a moment and then continued, "Can you call me back about noon, your time? I should know more then."

Johnny agreed, "Yes, I'll call then. I have to go to the funeral home. They are holding the memorial service for Joe this afternoon. I told the Director that I would be at the home shortly after lunch time, but I'll call no matter what."

"Johnny, be careful. We have no idea how deep this killing goes. It could easily be related to your brother's death. Do you want me to send someone out to help you in Reno?"

Johnny thought for a moment and then answered, "No, I'll be fine. I have to run now, I'll call you back around noon."

Johnny hung up the phone before Weaver could respond. The last thing that he wanted was someone from any of the government agencies in Reno with him. He wanted to find out what happened to Joe and he was sure that in time he would.

ELIZABETH JUNG

CHAPTER THIRTY-SIX

Director Korovkin pulled at the shoulder of his black wool sweater and then yanked the bottom down below his waist. He hated this time of the year. As in all of Eastern Europe when it was spring it was still cold. As was usual for the regimes, the heat had been turned off too early.

He reached across his wide antique wooden desk and pressed a black button above the telephone.

"Did you find that space heater yet?" he barked. He remembered seeing a small electric space heater in one of the office closets over the winter. Now he needed it. He knew it would only heat up a small portion of this large office preferably in the foot space under his desk that at least it would help take the chill out of his aging body.

His secretary had told him earlier in the day that she had seen a new Phillips space heater at the Gumpf's Department Store. She said that it was a multi-system one. That was just what he needed.

Since the fall of the Iron Curtain he loved the opportunity to buy consumer products from the West.

ASSIGNMENT: RENO, NEVADA

They were always more modern, efficient and stylish than the domestic Russia made ones. He made up his mind that if his secretary couldn't find a space heater in the closet, he would go to Gumpf's himself and buy a new one. He would do it even if he had to pay for it himself.

He walked to the window and looked down on Red Square. The sky was cloudy and he could tell the wind was blowing strong from the way the people in the square below had their coats pulled tight around their bodies.

After he tapped his feet to the floor several times, he felt a bit warmer and decided that he would have to go on with his work, cold or not.

Sitting down in the wooden, swivel desk chair, he looked across the room to the series of appropriately set time-zone clocks above the door. He frowned as he located the time in Reno, Nevada.

Smiling, he leaned on the desk and turned his right wrist upward. He activated on a button on his watch and grinned. He knew that signals would flow to a relay transmitter and within seconds the watch on Victor Smith's arm would begin vibrating. Then, within minutes Victor Smith would be calling to report on what he was doing in Reno.

Korovkin sighed and leaned back in his chair. His meeting with the other members of the committee wasn't for a couple days. He hoped he had good news to report by then.

The committee was waiting for the final go-ahead to expand on Project Replacement and Project Eve. Both Projects were Korovkin's pet projects that he had inherited from his old boss. It was time to go twenty-first century with his ideas, but first he needed funds. These funds would only be forthcoming if Smith located and retrieved the items that were lost or simply misplaced in Reno, Nevada.

Korovkin mulled over the turn of events. He was totally disgusted that his future and the future of his projects hinged on events so far away. He hated not having full control.

Waiting, his thoughts drifted to past events. He remembered how things eventually come back to haunt you. Vividly, he remembered receiving the orders to eliminate Joe Collins' family. That was so many years ago. In those days, he was climbing the ladder within the KGB.

At that time in his career, he never questioned what he was told to do. He just followed orders. It was ironic that after all these years Joe Collins was also killed by Russians. A cold tremor pulsed through his body when he thought it scarcely seemed possible that the years had run a full cycle.

CHAPTER THIRTY-SEVEN

Victor Smith sprung awake. He touched his arm and cursed. For a few seconds he wondered what was happening. Then, he realized that his watch had interrupted his sleep.

He shook the remains of sleep from his head and wondered about his health and hardening of the arteries as he crawled out of bed and skidded on the linoleum floor with bare feet. As he slipped off his watch before getting into the shower, he saw that it was just seven a.m.

As fast as he could, he dressed and descended in the elevator. He hurried toward the lobby of the motel where he was staying. He thought about calling from the telephone there but decided it would be better to be safe than sorry. He changed direction and walked to the door and out into the morning air.

Searching up and down the street, his eyes stopped on the Embers restaurant across the street. He studied the outside of the building and saw three pay telephones just to the right of the entrance. Out of habit, he waited for a few more seconds to see if anyone was paying any attention to the area or him.

When he was sure that the coast was clear, he walked across the street, took his cell phone out of his jacket pocket and removed the plastic transmitting piece. He pressed it against the box of the pay phone as he had done before.

He smiled, marveling at this modern equipment. When he heard a buzz, he picked up the receiver and said, "Yes, Smith here."

Korovkin answered, "That was pretty quick. Were you waiting for my call?"

"Hardly," Smith retorted. "It is only seven here and I was still asleep in bed."

"In bed," Korovkin barked. "I would have thought that you would have been up and out trying to find my missing merchandise. What do you mean sleeping? You have things to do, you can sleep after the recovery."

Smith ignored the Director's comment and looked up and down the street. He was used to Korovkin' bark so just waited until he calmed down. Finally, he said, "I have an appointment this morning with Sarah Cummings, the antique mall owner. She is going to take us to all of Charlie McGuire's storage sheds. She still thinks that we are only interested in buying all of his old furniture."

"Well, then, buy it," the old man snapped quickly. "Buy whatever you have to. Rent a truck and load everything into it and then you can go through it later. That way at least you might have a chance of finding the missing items. If you go from place to place you might miss them. After all they are not so big."

ASSIGNMENT: RENO, NEVADA

Smith gently replied in a subdued manner, "Yes, I remember what we are looking for. I saw Sarah hand Johnny Collins a bag last evening that I am sure contained a bottle of Russian champagne."

"All the more reason to buy everything," the old Russian barked.

Smith felt he was getting what he wanted. He had already planned out the day in his mind. He answered, "If you want to approve the purchase of all of his items, that would be the way to go. It'll be expensive, but I might be able to resell it somewhere."

Korovkin sighed, "Yes, buy anything that looks as if it were part of the shipment, but, don't go wild on the price. Keep your cover solid and buy it as cheap as you can. Remember we are working on a budget and resale may not be reasonable if you have to dismantle things."

"Yes, I realize that," Smith answered. "I'll see if it is necessary. I will only buy from the sheds that look as if they have some of the old primitive furniture in them. It wouldn't be probable that he would have put our merchandise in with something that he has owned for had months or years."

"Who knows with Americans?" Korovkin responded. "It might be best to buy everything. You can take it to California and they can quickly dispose of the unwanted items at a flea market once you have gone through all the boxes. You don't want to miss a thing."

"Alright then, that is what I will do. I'll make the arrangements this morning. We should have some idea of what we will be taking to California in a day or so."

Korovkin sighed. "So what else is going on in Reno? How is the "Biggest Little City in the World?"

Smith laughed. "I haven't had a chance to explore much of it. We went out to eat last night with Johnny Collins, though."

"Oh?" Korovkin questioned. The tone of his voice became concerned. "I don't want you attracting attention to yourself."

Smith smiled with satisfaction with himself at his own undercover skill and answered, "I am sure he has no idea who I am."

"You make damn sure that he doesn't," Korovkin snapped back. There was silence for a moment and then he continued, "Your next job is too important to have your cover blown over this assignment. Try and stay away from him as much as you can. You just might say something that would trigger his memory. That is the last thing that you want to do."

Smith answered, "Actually, it is more fun this way. This way it is like playing cat and mouse."

Korovkin choked out, "Yes, but remember you are the cat not the mouse. Remember what the cat does to the mouse? You just make sure that he doesn't become the cat. We can't afford bravado, and, anyway it's not professional. Bravado gets people killed."

"I'll be careful," Smith answered. "I'll call you just as soon as I hear something."

"That's fine. I'll be waiting to hear from you. Remember my committee is meeting in two days. I want to be able to report that we will have the funding to go on with my projects," Korovkin answered. "I will wait for your call."

Smith put the receiver back on the cradle and unhooked his secure connection. He put the phone back in his jacket pocket and looked around. As he turned to walk away back to the motel, a customer came out of the restaurant releasing the smell of bacon frying.

Smiling, he turned and walked into the restaurant deciding to have breakfast before he and Chris left to meet Sarah at the Antique mall.

CHAPTER THIRTY-EIGHT

Johnny Collins stepped off the elevator carrying a large Starbuck's Styrofoam coffee cup. He casually glimpsed the people that he passed and didn't really pay any special attention to them. His mind was on the activities of the day ahead. Just as he passed outside his motel room to insert the card key into the slot, the room telephone rang.

He rushed to the phone almost slopping the coffee out. "Yes," he said breathlessly.

"Johnny, is that you?" his wife asked.

"Hi, honey. It's me. Sorry, I sound so out of breath but the phone caught me in the hall and I rushed to pick it up." He fidgeted with the coffee cup and then put the cup on the edge of the desk and pulled the chair out with his foot to lean against. "What's up?"

"Johnny, the police just left our house."

Johnny knew what was coming and he sighed deeply. "The police? What did they want?" He tried not to reveal too much concern in the tone of his voice.

Sounding really frightened, Margaret answered quickly, "They wanted to know if I knew anything about a man that was found dead just across the street from our front lawn last night."

Johnny licked his lips a couple times and then said calmly, "Honey, take your time. Start at the beginning. Tell me exactly what happened."

After a couple moments of silence, she stated, "The Clear Lake police, a detective by the name of Stein, was here. He asked me several questions about a dead man. I told him I had no idea who the poor man was nor why he was found near our door."

Johnny looked around his motel room and paced nervously as far as the phone cord would allow him. His neck began to ache. He wondered if he should tell Margaret about his earlier talk with Weaver but didn't want to concern her more than necessary. Yet he wanted to be cautious, finally, he said, "Honey, that's alright. Did he show you a picture of the dead man or give you a description?"

"No, Johnny, the detective didn't show me a picture but he did give a rather general description. He was a tall man in his mid fifties with gray hair. I told the detective that I didn't know a person with that general of a description. But, Johnny, I thought I saw him walking on North Shore in front of the house earlier yesterday."

Johnny wondered exactly what Margaret knew. From experience, he knew that something she might recall might be very helpful. Also, he knew that if she talked about the situation it would make her feel better. "When was that, Margaret?"

"Yesterday afternoon. I was busy in the family room and I just happened to look out the window and I think I saw a man like the police described walk past.

But, you know how busy this part of North Shore Drive is. There are always people out there walking. I don't think that it was my imagination either. I think it might have been him. He was wearing a jogging suit so I didn't pay a lot of attention. I see men with jogging suits pass by here every day."

Johnny didn't know what to do. He was in Reno and couldn't be of any help now. He kicked around a pair of shoes that were on the floor. He thought for a moment and then answered, "You're right, honey. North Shore is a busy area for pedestrians. Did the detective say anything else? Did he mention any speculation about who the man might be?"

Margaret reflected on Johnny's question before answering. "You are sure full of questions. No, Honey, no one said." She paused for a moment more and then continued, "I feel better just talking to you. How is everything going there in Reno?"

Johnny knew his wife had a way of dealing with issues and making problems diminish. "I'm fine. I'm going to get ready to go to the funeral home in a few minutes. Now, let's get back to the dead guy. Did they tell you how he died?"

Margaret answered, "No, I am not sure if he had a heart attack, fell into the lake or if a car might have hit him. The detective didn't say."

Johnny took a deep breath. He was glad that the detective hadn't told his wife that it was a CIA man that had been murdered. "Margaret, you go on with whatever your plans were for today. I'll make a couple of phone calls and see if I can find out anything else about the dead man."

ASSIGNMENT: RENO, NEVADA

"Thanks, Johnny. I appreciate it. I'm going to be gone most of the day, I have to take Chris to a golfing tournament and we probably won't be home until late this evening. If you hear anything just leave a message on the answering machine. I'll call you later tonight when I get home."

"Margaret, that's fine. You have a safe day and wish Chris the best of luck for me."

"Honey, you have a good day too. I know that it is going to be a long and difficult one," his wife answered.

"I will. Margaret, don't worry about that man. I am sure that his death near the house was accidental, but, nevertheless, you stay extra alert and on guard. I don't believe in coincidences especially with Joe and I both having CIA connections. You drive careful."

When Johnny hung up the phone he leaned over the desk and cradled his throbbing head in his hands. He wondered if the police had talked to Margaret before they had talked to Weaver. For now, he had no intention of calling the Clear Lake Police Department because he didn't want to focus any undue attention to the dead man.

He especially didn't want to attract attention to the CIA. He was aware that the police department knew that he had worked for the CIA, but they thought he was fully retired. The last thing he wanted to do was draw attention to him and his family and make the police department aware of his semi-retired status with the agency.

243

CHAPTER THIRTY-NINE

It was almost noon by the time Johnny arrived at the Fallan Funeral Home. He opened the front door and slowly walked up the steps. The eerie silence of the building sent qualms through him and spooked him. Respectfully, he slipped off his brown leather jacket and carried it over his arm.

"Good afternoon, Mr. Collins," a corpse of a man whispered as he walked out of an office and greeted him.

Getting the creeps, Johnny regained his composure, solemnly nodded and answered, "Good afternoon. I hope you don't mind if I'm here early?"

The emaciated man brushed his hair with his hand, adjusting his black rim glasses, he answered, "Not at all." He took Johnny's arm and guided the way toward a room at the side of a long entrance hall. "We have everything ready. You are more than welcome to go into this room or if you would like to spend some time in our chapel you may do so." He turned and pointed in the opposite direction to a door on the other side of the hallway.

ASSIGNMENT: RENO, NEVADA

Johnny remembered how helpful the man had been when he had made the arrangements. Johnny just nodded. "I'd like to see my brother now, if you don't mind?"

"Of course, just follow me." Ceremoniously, he opened the door in front of them with a theatrical flourish. He stepped back slightly and spread his arms out, "This is a lovely room and we have arranged chairs for about one hundred people."

Once Johnny entered the room, the thin man followed him into the room, turned slightly to Johnny and said, "I have no idea how many people will come for the service this afternoon, but we hope to be prepared. Please look around the room. Several flower arrangements have already arrived. As I explained yesterday, you'll need to instruct me on what you would like to do with the flowers since the body will be cremated and taken back to Iowa. There are several nursing homes and churches in the area that deeply appreciate such lovely arrangements, and we'd be happy to deliver them as a service."

Johnny viewed the arrangements and then looked at the tall man. "I'd be happy for you to distribute the flowers wherever you feel they would be appreciated. I only ask that some are sent to Catholic churches in the area. My family is Catholic and we would appreciate that." He turned and looked at the arrangements again, and then added, "You will make sure that I get all the cards from them so I can send thank you notes, won't you?"

The tall man nodded. "As you wish. I will take care of everything. With church services tomorrow and then on Sunday, there are several churches that would be very grateful." He stood quietly for just a moment as if he wanted to say something else but then he added, "I'll leave you alone. Please come by the office and talk to me when you have a spare moment. There is something that I'd like to discuss with you before you leave this afternoon."

Johnny nodded his head in agreement and then turned and walked toward the casket on the opposite side of the room. He was glad that he had time to visit with his brother now without anyone else around.

He walked to the casket and looked down at Joe. This was the first time that he had seen him in almost fifteen years.

He felt as if he were looking down at his father rather than at his brother. After what seemed to be several minutes of silent prayer, Johnny walked around the room and read the notes on the arrangements. There were about fifteen of them strategically placed throughout the room. He was surprised to see so many.

Johnny turned quickly and stared toward the source of an intruding noise behind him. For an instant he had forgotten where he was.

"It is time to open for the viewing," the funeral director said, as he pushed the large oak doors open.

Johnny looked at his watch. He had been in the room for the past hour and half praying and remembering. He was amazed how fast the time had flown.

"I need to get a sandwich or something and freshen up. Is there a place nearby that I can run to?"

The director smiled and pointed to a back door. "Yes, there is a Subway shop about a half-block out that door. I go over there often when I am busy." He reminded Johnny of the schedule. "You have about thirty minutes before the after-work crowd come."

"Thanks," Johnny answered and hurried out the back door.

By the time Johnny returned to the funeral home he was surprised how many cars were parked in the lot. He had walked around to the front of the building and up the front steps. As he passed through the front door, he saw the director talking to a distinguished looking gray-haired man on the other side of the room. They both stopped talking when Johnny entered and looked toward him. Johnny saw the director nod as he walked near.

"Johnny, this is Terrance Ruddick. He tells me that he has spoken to you on the phone but never met you in person."

Johnny smiled and said, "That's right. Good afternoon, Mr. Ruddick."

"Please, just call me, Terry," the older man quipped. "If you say Mr. Ruddick, I feel as if you are talking to my dad." He turned back to the director and said, "Please, excuse us. I need to talk to Johnny for a few minutes."

Johnny and the attorney moved to an empty space on the opposite side of the lobby. Then Mr. Ruddick said, "I have several papers that I need you to sign later today and I'd like to schedule when we can get together."

Johnny sighed, "Today? How about tomorrow morning? Would you want to meet at your office or near my hotel someplace?"

Ruddick answered, "Your hotel room is fine. I hate to have you drive all over town trying to find my place. I also think we should inspect Joe's acreage, if we meet first at your hotel then we can easily drive out there together."

Johnny shrugged. "That's fine. How about nine in the morning? That will work fine for me."

"So nine it is then," the lawyer answered. He shook hands with Johnny. "Now, let's go meet these people."

As the two men walked out the door, Sarah Cummings and Lt. Clausen were waiting for Johnny. Sarah walked up to the men and said, "Nice seeing you together. Good to see you again, Terry." She extended her hand to each.

Johnny said, "Nice of both of you to come."

Sarah said, "I wanted to catch you before the service started and I'm glad that I caught you together." She reached into her purse and pulled out an envelope and handed it to Johnny. "Joe provided this to me some time ago and I thought it best to wait until now to give it to you. It is a copy of a signed sale agreement to his property." She looked at both men with a smile and then continued. "I thought I would take ownership on Monday, if that is alright with the two of you?"

Johnny's face blanched as he opened the envelope and read the paper. His hands were shaking. "Why did you wait until now to tell me about this?"

Sarah smiled and looked at the policeman standing beside her. "I thought it was best. I am sure that you will see that the document is perfectly legal. For years

Joe had been after me to buy his land and about six months ago I told him that I would."

Ruddick adjusted his wire-framed glasses and glanced at Sarah and then at Lt. Clausen. He made a face and questioned, "Has this document been filed at the court house?"

Sarah laughed. "No, I'm going to do that on Monday when I take over the property. I thought I would get the key from Johnny before he flew back to Iowa."

Johnny looked at the lawyer, and back at the woman with the policeman. Bewildered, he just shook his head. This was so sudden. Finally, he took the document and handed it to the lawyer. "Terry, you keep this. Let's go into the viewing room now. We can talk about this matter later."

CHAPTER FORTY

Victor Smith and Chris Gannon spent the morning checking out all the storage unit facilities listed in the Reno yellow pages. Oscar had heard a rumor that Charlie McGuire and Joe Collins had rental spaces in the same units.

During the afternoon, the two men drove out of the city on Interstate 80 towards Lake Tahoe. They stopped at several small units, finding nothing.

They returned to Reno after four and drove by the Fallan Funeral Home on their way to the Antique Mall.

Smith pointed to the funeral home and asked, "Shall we stop and go in and pay our last respects to Joe Collins?"

Gannon's face drew a sour mouth. He looked at Smith and then at the funeral home parking lot. He shook his head sideways, "Uh-uh. The place will be crawling with cops. Look there are a couple police cars already in the lot."

Smith turned and viewed the cars. "Yes, the irony of that would be to validate the fictional statement that the killer always returns to the scene of the crime."

After driving around for some time, Gannon finally drove to the parking lot at the mall. With everyone's busy schedules and because of a late Friday night closing time, Sarah had agreed to meet at the Mall.

She said she had some powerful flashlights. Then, they could drive to the storage units that McGuire and Collins had. She told Victor that she had a stack of keys and was willing to bring them along just in case they would open any of the units.

"Hey, nice to see you both again," Peggy called from the other side of the room when the two men entered.

Chris nodded and Victor asked, "Is Sarah back from the funeral home yet?" She had told him earlier that she wanted to attend Joe Collins' service.

Peggy nodded and answered, "Yes, we both got back a little while ago. She's in the back checking the doors for the evening. She'll be up front in a few minutes." She motioned for the two men to come closer to the counter. "So what have you two been up to today? Did you do anything interesting?"

Chris opened his mouth to speak but Victor spoke first. "No, we just did some sightseeing around town. I wanted to get better acquainted with the area."

"That's great," Peggy answered. "There is a lot to see in town. If you get a chance you should go visit our car museum. It is one of the best in the world."

Victor glanced toward the back, then walked over to a straight back chair and sat down. He looked around the office area and commented, "Yes, we drove by it today. It is quite impressive from the outside. It must be very popular, there were many cars in the parking lot."

Before Peggy could answer, Sarah came rushing down one of the long display aisles. "Sorry I'm late fellows," she said, wiping her hands on a bright red smock that she was wearing.

Victor stood as Sarah approached. "Nice to see you again, Miss Sarah," he said with a smile. "Are you about ready to go with us?"

Sarah wiped her hands again and then extended her hand to each man. "Yes, I am," she answered with a curtsy. "You big Texans always make me feel like such a lady." She looked toward Peggy and asked, "Is it alright with you if I leave now? The rear doors are all secure and the money is in the safe."

Peggy answered, "Yes, you best be going before it gets much darker." She reached under the counter and pulled out three big long flashlights. "Here don't forget to take these. It's hard to see in those sheds when it gets too dark."

"Thanks," Sarah answered, taking the lights. She turned toward the two men and said, "Well, that's that! Let's go." She waited until they were beside her, linked her arms through theirs and said, "Let's go see what we can find."

When they got to the door, Victor held the door opened and asked, "What do you want to do with your car?"

"I'll leave it here and you all can bring me back later when we've finished." Sarah checked her watch and added, "I've another appointment later tonight and I don't want to miss it." She looked up at both. "This is going to be a very profitable evening for me, I can feel it in my bones."

CHAPTER FORTY-ONE

It was almost six by the time Johnny bid farewell to the last person leaving the funeral home. He turned to Joe's attorney, Terrance Ruddick and asked, "Is it too late to go to the court house?"

Ruddick wrinkled his nose and answered, "No, I called over and someone is going to be there until six thirty working on a project. If we hurry we can make it. It is about a ten minute walk from here."

Johnny walked quickly to the funeral director who was standing in the entrance hall. "I'll be back tomorrow morning, if that is alright with you. Then, I'll take care of anything else that you might have."

The director shook Johnny's hand. "That's fine. Even though it is Saturday, I'll be here about nine in the morning. You can come any time after that."

Ruddick stood beside Johnny and nudged him with his arm. Johnny said, "Thanks", following Ruddick out the door.

As they rushed down the street toward the courthouse, Johnny asked, "Did you have a chance to look at the document that Sarah gave me?"

Ruddick sighed and took a deep breath. "Yes, it appears to be legal. But, before we do anything I want to see how Joe's land is listed in the records." He caught his breath and added, "There's the courthouse, right up there. Now, we can slow down a bit. I'm not as young as I use to be."

Johnny laughed. "I can sure relate to that." He looked up and saw that most of the building was dark but there were a few rooms with lights on. He walked to the door and found that it was locked. "How will we get in?" he asked as he stepped back and strained to see which rooms had lights in them.

Ruddick patted his coat pocket and said, "The marvels of the cell phone." He pulled out a phone and dialed a number. Within seconds an elderly man appeared at the front door.

"Good evening, Terrance," the old gent said as he let the two men into the building. "Just wait a moment, I have to be sure to lock this again. We don't want anyone else trying to get into the building tonight."

Ruddick quickly introduced Johnny and all three men went to an office on the second floor as indicated by his friend. After they entered the office, the elderly man said, "I had some idea what you are looking for, so I pulled some of the records." He turned toward Terrance and smiled. "There are all the records that I could find on Joseph Collins." He put three manila colored files in front of the two men.

Johnny looked doubtfully at Ruddick. "I thought the only property that Joe owned was his house and land out by the river?"

ASSIGNMENT: RENO, NEVADA

Terrance nodded. "Yes, that's right. All the land is out by his house, but he bought additional acreages over the years as they became available. Altogether, he bought land at three different times, hence, the three files."

Johnny fingered the files and then looked at Ruddick. He said, "Please take that envelope Sarah gave me and see what the description is on the land that she is supposed to have purchased."

As the two men studied the documents and compared notes, they both just shook their heads. Finally, Ruddick said, "She certainly has done her homework. In this one agreement, she has accurately described all the land that Joe owned."

Johnny looked at Sarah's sales agreement and said, "Where does it say what she paid for the land?"

Ruddick held the paper up to the light and pointed to a place on the paper. "Right here. It states that she paid twenty thousand dollars for everything."

"Is that all?"

Ruddick reread the document and answered, "Yes, that is what it says. It also says "other considerations" but no other monetary amount. Just the twenty thousand."

Johnny frowned and stared at the attorney. "That doesn't seem to be fair money for that amount of land. Do you think so?"

Ruddick agreed. "No, that would only buy about a tenth of an acre according to my calculations." He looked at the elderly man, "Do you have any idea what the city was offering Joe for his land?"

The elderly man walked to a book on the other side of the room and scanned through several pages, finally, he said, "Oh, here it is. The last offer was almost two million for the entire property."

Johnny whistled, "Wow, that much?"

"Yes," the older man said. "The city had been after Collins for some time to buy his land. They want to develop it into a park. About three years ago the city was given a cash donation of two million dollars to develop a park in that area."

"I didn't know that of course," Johnny said. His eyes were wide.

"No," Ruddick answered. "I doubt that Joe told many people about it. He used to get letters from the city regarding the purchase and he would stack them up on his windowsill."

Johnny nodded and answered, "I saw those letters. I only briefly looked at one of them and took the pile back to my hotel room. I don't remember them mentioning anything about a park or any specific amount of money."

Ruddick laughed. "You probably read one of the early letters. As time went by, the letters became more specific. Joe didn't want to sell the land so he ignored the letters."

Johnny thought and then asked the two men, "Would Sarah know about the city wanting this land?"

Ruddick looked at the older man, shrugged his shoulders and answered, "Sure, it's all a matter of public record. Also, Joe might have mentioned something to her about it. I would say since she gave you this sales agreement, she knew exactly what the land was worth."

By the time Johnny and Ruddick walked back to the funeral home to get their cars, Johnny's had a fierce headache. As he put his key in the car door, he turned to Ruddick and said, "Well, I don't think that there is much that we can do tonight. It's too late to go out to Joe's place. Will you think over our options tonight and decide what to do? I'm not too familiar with Joe's handwriting, but I definitely want to have the signature on Sarah's document checked for forgery before we go any further. She appears to be a bit too greedy for my liking."

Ruddick looked around the empty parking lot and then answered with a whisper, "Yes, I agree. I think we should have several things checked first thing Monday morning. I'll go home and see what kind of legal hocus-pocus we can do to stall her and prevent her from taking over the property on Monday. Do you want to go out to Joe's tomorrow sometime?"

Johnny said, "Thanks, tomorrow is perfect. I'm really mentally and physically exhausted now and can barely think clearly. I have to stop here at the funeral home in the morning around nine, but how about one or so in the afternoon? That gives us time to think things out. Now, I'm going to the hotel and then get something to eat and do something about this headache."

Ruddick jiggled his car keys. "I'm going home, get a bite, take my shoes off, pour a beer and mediate on this whole matter. It's been a long week. I'll be at your hotel about one tomorrow afternoon."

Johnny sat in his rental car and watched Joe's attorney pull his vehicle out of the parking lot. He was very much troubled how involved Joe's death had become.

CHAPTER FORTY-TWO

It was almost eight by the time Johnny walked to his hotel room door. He slid the card through the key slot totally unaware of anything around him, then, he flicked on the light.

"Holy cow," he exclaimed. The room was in complete shambles. The blankets and pillows from the bed were on the floor and the mattress had several deep cuts in it. Its stuffing was hanging out and several pieces were spread around the room.

Johnny saw his suitcase near the closet. "Damn," he exclaimed when he saw that it had deep slash marks and the lining had been torn completely loose.

He walked to the room phone, extended his hand and then stopped. Suddenly, he thought of fingerprints. Carefully, he stepped around the mess on the floor and walked back out of the room.

Within five minutes, two large men dressed in dark blue suits came rushing down the hall toward Johnny. He had called the front desk from a courtesy phone in the hallway.

"What seems to be the matter," the tallest silver haired man asked.

He looks like a line backer from the Vikings, Johnny thought. His broad shoulders strained the suit coat seams. Johnny watched the man walk and was amazed at his agility.

"My room has been ransacked," Johnny said, pushing the door open with his elbow. "I haven't touched anything. I thought you might want to take fingerprints."

The shorter of the two guards discouragingly remarked, "In these rooms you would probably find enough fingerprints to start your own company." He looked around the room and walked carefully into the middle. "Someone sure made a mess of this. Do you know if anything is missing?"

Johnny looked around and said, "I haven't had a chance to check, but since you aren't going to fingerprint the area, I can check now. Just give me a little time."

The two men faced each other in the middle of the room and talked softly to one another. Johnny gave them a pausing reference as he went around the room and took a mental inventory of his clothing and personal items. After several minutes, he said, "The only thing that I find missing is a bottle of Russian champagne that a friend gave me last night. It was in the bag on the floor."

He picked up the bag and as he handed the bag to the tall guard, a small receipt fluttered out. Johnny reached down and picked it up put it in his pocket.

The two guards moved around the room and the shorter one pulled a small camera out of his suit pocket. As he took pictures, the older guard walked toward Johnny.

"So who do you think did this?" the guard asked.

"How would I know?" uttered Johnny. "I am a visitor here. I've only been here a couple days and I certainly haven't made any enemies in that short of time."

The guard turned his head slightly and peered intensely at Johnny. "Well, some one sure as hell didn't like you. Why are you here in Reno? Are you here for a reunion?"

"No," Johnny answered. He pushed the door shut with his foot. "I'm here because my brother was murdered. I am here to settle his matters."

"Murdered?" the taller man questioned with a loud voice. He took a notebook out of his pocket and began making notes. "Whom are you dealing with at the police station?"

Johnny thought for a moment and then answered, "A tall red headed guy by the name of Larson. He was my contact." He waited to see if the name made any impression on the men and then added, "I'm just returning from the funeral home. We held a memorial service this afternoon for my brother."

The older man continued to make notes and then asked, "What was your brother's name?"

Johnny licked his lips and then replied, "Collins. Joe Collins."

Neither of the men showed any recognition when hearing the mention of Joe's name. Johnny asked, "Neither of you knew my brother, did you?"

ASSIGNMENT: RENO, NEVADA

The big man answered, "No, can't say that I did." He looked at his partner and asked, "How about you, Clem, did you know his brother?"

The shorter man stopped taking pictures long enough to shake his head. "Nope, doesn't mean anything to me," he answered.

Johnny went over to the closet and began picking up his clothes. They were on the floor in a pile. He checked each piece as he hung it back on the hanger. Silently, he wondered if his insurance company would pay for any of the damages.

Finally, the two guards walked to the door. The older man said, "There isn't anything further that we can do here. We will report this to the Reno police but I have to tell you this is fairly common here in Reno. People often have their rooms ransacked."

He turned and again looked closely at Johnny and asked, "Are you sure there isn't something else that you need to tell us? Did you bring a woman back here to the room and she got upset and did this to you?"

Johnny snorted. "Hardly," he replied with a shake of his head. "I told you, I have been at the funeral home most of the day and then I was at the courthouse just before I came here."

The shorter man looked at his watch and asked, "What do you mean? It is after eight in the evening. The courthouse closes at five."

"Oh, that's no problem to explain. I was with my brother's attorney and he had made special arrangements," Johnny answered. "After I left the courthouse I stopped downstairs and got a sandwich. You can check it out." He reached in his pocket and pulled out a receipt from the Barker's restaurant and handed to the men. "See, it is stamped 7:55 p.m. It clearly states where I was."

"We'll check everything out," the older man said. "We have security cameras all over the hotel and lobby areas. We will pull them up and watch them. That way we may get some idea what went on." He started walking away and then turned back to Johnny and asked, "Would you be free to review the tapes in the morning. Say about nine or so?"

"I have to be at the funeral home about then but I could come down at eight and take a look at them. Maybe I'll recognize someone."

The older man made another note in his notebook and said, "Yes, that will be fine. Eight is all right. Just come to the front desk and ask for Clem and Charlie. They will buzz us."

"Thanks," Johnny said. "Say, can you get someone up here to get me a new mattress and clean up this mess?"

The shorter man answered as he put his notebook back in his coat pocket, "Just call room service and tell them that we are done here. They will send someone up to help you."

"Thanks again," Johnny called as he watched the men walk down the hallway. He turned and stepped into his room.

CHAPTER FORTY-THREE

It was seven in the morning when Victor Smith walked across the street from his hotel to the Embers Restaurant. He checked to make sure that no one was paying attention when he took out his cell phone and hooked up his secure telephone line.

"Yes, Victor," the deep voice answered almost immediately. "How is everything in Nevada today?"

Once again, Victor looked around the area, then leaned closer to the receiver and said, "It is so, so. We were able to find ten of the missing bottles and some of the missing paintings. There are still three bottles missing."

Korovkin sighed. "Well, thank heaven. That is better than nothing. Have you checked the bottles to see if the merchandise is there?"

Victor glanced again around the area and then answered, "Yes, all the bottles have merchandise embedded in them. What do you want me to do with them?"

The Russian chuckled softly and answered, "Get the bottles and the art pieces to our agent in

Sacramento, California. I will notify him that you will be in touch. He already has the connections to convert and extract the merchandise."

Victor thought for a moment and asked, "Do you want me to hand-carry the merchandise or should I send it with Chris and Oscar?"

"I think that they can handle getting them to California." Static filled the line, after a pause in the line to clear, Korovkin said, "Do you think there is any possibility of getting the other three bottles?"

Smith grimaced his lips and stretched them across his teeth, paused, and replied. "I rather doubt it."

Korovkin asked, "Does it seem as if someone else has discovered my secret?"

"I haven't found anything that points that way," Smith answered. "Can you put the word out and see if there is any rumors along that line?"

Korovkin answered, "Yes, I will instruct California to keep their ears open. Maybe they can pick something up." He thought for a moment and then continued, "But it is so hard these days because of all the drug money that is floating around."

Smith asked, "What should I do?"

"Why don't you spend the weekend in Reno, keep your ears open and maybe head out on Monday or Tuesday for Washington, D.C. Your next assignment is ready to begin." The long distance line buzzed for a second and then once again became clear. "Is that alright with you?"

"Sorry, you faded in and out for a moment there," Victor said. "Am I to go with the men or back to Washington?"

"To Washington. You can spend the weekend in Reno but be in Washington, D.C. by Tuesday night at the latest. That will give you a couple days for R & R. I am sure that you need a bit of down time."

"You have that right," Victor answered. "I'd like to spend a couple days here anyway, it'll give me a chance to see some of the shows and try my luck."

"Did you run into any problems in recovering the merchandise?" the Russian asked.

Victor thought for a moment and then said, "Nothing that I couldn't handle. Everything is fine now. All loose ends are tied up."

Victor looked around the street as he talked; watching watched two young ladies parade back and forth in front of him. For a moment he thought they wanted to use his telephone and then he realized that they were professional ladies looking for a customer.

"Ah, that is fine," the Russian replied. "Do we have any disposable parts lying around?"

Victor thought and then answered, "Yes, there was one but all tracks are covered."

The old Russian sighed. "That's great. Now I can recall my man in Iowa that was watching Collins' house." He was quiet for a moment and then continued, "He ran into a problem in Iowa and it is best I get him away from there."

"Oh," Victor said. "What kind of a problem?"

"Let's just say that he finished off another cup of alphabet soup."

Victor frowned and contemplated whether that would create any complications for him. "Oh, was it that Virginia recipe?"

The old man answered quickly, "Yes, pure Virginia."

"When did that happen?" Victor asked.

"Yesterday. But, it is all right. You know how I hate loose ends."

"Yes, I know," Victor answered automatically.

"Remember if you spend a couple more days in Reno you are not to be in touch with Johnny Collins," the old man said. "I don't want anything to happen to you that could jeopardize your next assignment. Do you understand?"

"Yes, of course, I understand. Shall I contact you when I get to D.C.?"

"No need to do that. Just report to the Embassy. They will be expecting you. Once you are settled in, I will be in touch with you with all the details." For a moment, the Russian was quiet, then, he said, "Victor, thank you for finding the merchandise. Without it our projects would have been terminated."

Victor rubbed his finger along his hairline, smiled and answered, "I am happy that I could be of service."

CHAPTER FORTY-FOUR

Johnny had just walked out of the security office in the hotel and was still confused. He had studied the videotapes for almost an hour and didn't see any one enter or leave his hotel room other than the cleaning ladies. His stomach growled as he neared the restaurant.

"Just one, please," he told the waitress as he stood in line for a booth. He turned back toward the door and saw an upright coin-operated dispenser of Reno Gazette newspapers. Without thinking, he went over, put a quarter into the container on the side of the rack and took one of the papers.

As he waited for coffee and his breakfast of pancakes and sausage, he glanced at the front page of the paper. His eyes slowly went over the local news and he read the article about the new Homeland Security Department. He hoped that the CIA would never be a part of it.

Just as the waitress poured his coffee, his eyes moved to a small article in the bottom left hand corner of the front page. He unintentionally gasped as he read that Sarah Cummings, local antique mall owner, was found dead sometime during the night, in her car in the antique mall parking lot.

"Good heavens," he exclaimed, throwing his arms sideways to snap the newspaper sheet flatter. His sudden movement startled the waitress and she spilled coffee all over the top of the table.

"I am so sorry," Johnny said, as he reached for some napkins to help clean up the hot fluid.

"That's alright," the waitress answered. "I should have been more careful. What in the world did you find in the paper that startled you so?"

Johnny pushed a wad of wet napkins into the center of the table and answered, "I just read about a friend that was found dead late last night."

"Oh, who was that?" the waitress asked as she leaned over Johnny to get a look at the paper.

"Sarah Cummings. She owns a local antique mall here in Reno."

"Yes, I know her. She comes in here often."

"She does?" Johnny questioned. His voice was like shrill like to his ears. He thought for a moment and then asked, "She didn't happen to have been here last night, was she?"

The waitress stood up straight and brushed her hand against her long brown hair. She wrinkled her nose and answered, "I worked until ten last night and I'm not sure that she was here. She comes in often with one of the plain clothes policemen." She thought for a moment and then added, "But, then, she also comes in with other people. She loves our Spanish omelets. She orders one every time she's here."

ASSIGNMENT: RENO, NEVADA

Johnny finished handing the waitress the wet napkins and said, "Well, if you can remember the last time that she was in here, just let me know. I'll be back. I saw her yesterday afternoon myself."

"I will," the waitress answered as she hurried off to get a cloth to finish cleaning up the mess on Johnny's table.

Johnny took a sip of coffee, rereading the article about Sarah Cummings. The article simply stated that she had been found dead. Nothing was said about how she died. After the waitress brought Johnny his breakfast, he quickly ate it and headed for the door. He walked to a pay phone in the lobby, took out his wallet and found Lt. Larson's business card.

"May I speak to Larson," Johnny responded when the phone was answered.

"I'm sorry but Lt. Larson is out of the office. May I take a message?" the young voice asked.

Johnny glanced at his watch. "Do you have any idea when he will be returning to the office?"

The lady replied, "No, he is out on a call. It could be hours."

"Oh," Johnny replied. He thought for a moment and then asked, "He doesn't happen to be over at the antique mall where Sarah Cummings was found, does he?"

The lady stuttered and then whispered, "Yes, but I didn't tell you." She hung up with a loud clicking noise.

"Alright!" Johnny answered hanging up the phone. He looked out the window and slipped into his leather jackct.

As soon as he got into his rental car, he went directly toward the funeral home. He knew that stopping by the funeral home would only take a few minutes. He knew he would have time to drive by the antique mall and still make it back to his hotel room before one o'clock when Ruddick was scheduled to arrive.

After leaving the funeral home, Johnny drove straight to the antique mall. He was still undecided if he was going to tell Lt. Larson about the sales agreement that Sarah had given him.

He felt it was probably still too early to tell, but he wanted to know if Larson had any idea how or why Sarah had died. She certainly had looked the perfect picture of health when she left the funeral home after Joe's service.

When Johnny pulled up to the stop sign by the mall parking lot, he saw that the police had hung yellow crime scene tape around the entire parking lot.

He circled the area once and then found a parking place behind the mall building. He was sure that the rear door to the mall would be locked, so he started walking around the building in order to enter through the front door. As he approached the mall, a huge policeman swinging a long black nightstick by a cord stopped him.

"You can't go in there, this is a crime scene," the policeman said. "Step back, please."

Johnny edged past several on lookers and said, "I'd like to see Lt. Larson." He looked around as he talked trying to see if Larson was in the area.

The policeman looked around and then said, "The Lt. is over there by the railing in the parking lot. You stay here and I'll go see if he wants to talk to you."

Before the policeman could take any action, Johnny looked toward the area where the policeman indicated, saw Larson and gestured to him. Larson saw Johnny and waved for him to come to him.

"He's seen me and he's motioned for me," Johnny explained as he stepped over the yellow plastic. He hurried toward the Lt. before the policeman could intercept him.

"What are you doing here, Collins?" Lt. Larson asked, as Johnny walked up to him.

"I wanted to see what you know about this case. I was just with Sarah yesterday and wondered if you had any idea how she died so suddenly."

Larson took a deep breath and studied Johnny's face. Finally, he said, "I just got a call from the coroner. It took them a while to find it, but preliminary tests show that she was killed with a sharp knife or ice pick."

Johnny recoiled. "You mean she was murdered!"

"Looks that way. The sharp object was forced into her left ear and through her brain. She died almost instantly. It appears that she had the window down on the driver's side and the assailant leaned in and killed her."

Johnny thought for a moment and then asked, "Then she must have known the killer?"

"Evidently or it was someone that was asking directions or something. My inclination without further knowledge would be that she knew the killer." Larson's eyes searched the area for the two plainclothes, homicide detectives that emerged from behind a car and began walking toward him. "I have to go. We have more things to do and I have to go over to the mall and talk to Peggy."

He took out his notebook and asked, "You don't happen to know her last name do you? All it says here is that her name is Peggy."

Johnny turned and began walking in step with the three men. "She answers to the name Blue Jean Peggy. I don't think that I heard anyone ever call her by any other name." He shrugged and added, "She must have some type of a family name."

"Well, I'll need it," Larson answered. He turned back to the men and in a crisp voice gave them some specific instructions regarding Sarah's car that was being lifted onto a flat bed truck.

Johnny stood at the entrance of the mall and waited for Larson. Before opening the door, Johnny said, "There is something that I need to tell you about Sarah."

Larson stood back. He glanced out of the corner of his eye and asked, "What?"

"Well, yesterday at my brother's memorial service she came up to me and gave me a copy of a sales agreement that she said my brother had signed."

Larson grunted. "So?"

"Well, Terrance Ruddick was there with me and he has the document now, but we both were questioning whether the document was authentic."

Larson squinted, confused. "And, what does this have to do with the fact that Sarah Cummings was murdered last night?"

"I really don't know," Johnny answered quickly. "But, it might have something to do with it."

Larson opened the door and turned back to Johnny. "Get me a copy of the document. Are you going to have someone compare signatures to make sure that the paper is authentic?"

Johnny reached for the door. "Yes, where would I find someone that could do that?"

Larson took a small step inside the building. "You get me a copy of something that shows your brother's handwriting and give me the document and I'll have my people check it out. We could know if it was the real thing or not in an hour or so."

Johnny hesitated and checked his watch. "I'm going to meet Ruddick in an hour. Can I drop the documents off for you at the station?"

Larson took another step inside the building while Johnny held the door open. He said, "Yes, leave it in an envelope with my name on it. Make sure that you leave information where I can get back to you. I'll have it done later today."

Johnny glanced at his watch again and questioned, "But it's Saturday. Can you do it today?"

"Crime works 24/7 here in Reno. We always need someone either working or on call. It shouldn't be any problem. Later, it would take a genuine handwriting analysis that would stand up in court. However, for now, a superficial review might be helpful."

CHAPTER FORTY-FIVE

It was exactly one p.m. when Terrance Ruddick arrived at Johnny's hotel room. He knocked on the door waiting patiently for Johnny to answer. He recognized a voice behind him and turned around.

"I saw you step into the elevator," Johnny said. "It took me a while to get up here, some kid was on the elevator and had pressed every button. His parents thought it was cute when we had to stop at every floor."

Ruddick laughed. "That has happened to me, too. There have been times when I would have liked to give the kid a swat on the bottom." He looked at Johnny and continued, "Are you ready to go?"

Johnny was carrying his leather jacket over his arm. "Yes, I'm ready. Where to first?"

"I think that we should go back to Joe's house and make a list of what is there so we can plan disposal of it. Is that all right with you?"

Johnny thought for a moment and then said, "Yes, that's fine. We might as well go there while the sun is shining. I've been there in the evening and it was really dark."

On the way out to the house, Johnny told Ruddick everything that he had done during the morning. He told him about Sarah Cummings death, his talk with Lt. Larson and the plan to have the sales agreement authenticated. By the time they arrived at the house, Ruddick was well up to date.

"Since the house is so small, I don't think that it is going to take us very long," Ruddick said. "Let's just start on one side of the main room." He reached into the trunk of his car and brought out a roll of green plastic garbage bags and several folded boxes. "I thought what you wanted to get rid of either via the trash or Goodwill Industries can go into one of these green plastic bags, and what you want to take back to Iowa can be placed in these boxes as needed. We can always get more of either if we need them."

Johnny smiled. "There seems to be plenty here. Let me help you. I'll unlock the door and we can get busy."

It was almost four by the time the two men had thoroughly gone over every inch of Joe's home. Ruddick had gone to the back of the house to get a broom and Johnny knelt down on the floor to remove an oriental rug that was nailed to the floor in spots.

"Are you going to take that up?" Ruddick asked as Johnny tried to pull up some nails with a screwdriver that he had found in one of the kitchen drawers.

"I'm going to try. It looks like a nice rug and I thought that maybe if it were cleaned it might make a nice rug for the entrance hall in my house. It's a good size for that area."

For the next several minutes, Johnny worked to get the rug loose. When it was loose, he began to roll it up. Suddenly, he whistled at Terrance. "Hey, look at this!"

Ruddick was standing by the front door holding a dustpan. He hurried to the center of the room. "What's the matter?" he answered.

"There's a trap door here," Johnny said. He took the screwdriver and began to pry up one of the corners of the door. It swung up easily.

Ruddick looked through the open trap door and into an area below the floor and both of tem simultaneously saw a case. "What do you suppose could be in that?" he asked.

Johnny reached for the case and pulled it up to the main floor of the house and flipped the lid off. "It's Russian champagne! There are three bottles of it. It is just like the bottle that Sarah gave me and was stolen out of my room at the hotel."

Ruddick reached for a bottle and brushed off a film of dirt. "It looks just like any other bottle of champagne to me. Do you see anything special about it? I can't imagine what Joe was saving it for and putting it down here. What else is down there?"

Johnny took out a bottle and walked to the open door way, held up the bottle and looked at it in the sunlight. "It looks like a normal bottle to me too."

He turned it around in his hand and then walked back into the room and placed it in the box with the other two bottles.

He leaned over the open hole in the floor and reached below the floor as far as he could. "Can you hand me that flashlight by the stove? I could use some light here."

Ruddick did as requested, got the light and held it for Johnny. As Johnny motioned, Ruddick moved it around for Johnny to see the area. Johnny pulled out a portfolio, a small metal file box and an old shoebox. He placed everything on the floor beside him.

After putting his arm back into the hole, he took the flashlight from Terrance and moved it around so he could see the area better. Finally, he stood up and said, "I believe, nothing else is down here, just these three bottles in the case, a portfolio, a metal box and an old shoebox. That's it."

Ruddick picked up the portfolio and opened it. He took out several small-framed paintings and put them around the room. "What is so special about these?"

Johnny looked at the paintings, running the light up and down and across the front and back. "I have no idea," he said finally. "They look like some of these that Joe had in his booth at the mall." He put the paintings back in the portfolio and set it along side of the desk.

Next, Johnny the metal box and placed it on the table. He turned off the flashlight, swung the door over the hole and placed the shoebox on the table. Both men pulled chairs up to the table.

"Well, let's see what's here," Johnny said. "These things must have meant something to Joe for him to have secreted them as well as he did.

ELIZABETH JUNG

CHAPTER FORTY-SIX

It was midmorning when Victor Smith stood on the corner of Virginia & Third Street and peered at the large sign hanging directly over his head. The sign read "The Biggest Little City in The World". He smiled as he remembered reading stories about Reno and the wild, Wild West. He felt disappointed. People rushing in and out of casinos were not his idea of what the old west should be.

A feeling of loneliness swept over him because he had just told Chris Gannon and Oscar good by. The two men were going to run some personal errands and then head for California.

They had the bottles of Russian champagne and the Hans Meyer-Kassel paintings carefully packed and stored securely in their vehicle. Knowing how important the items where, he hoped everything arrived safely.

Turning the corner, by habit of training he looked through the motel coffee shop window in order to be fully aware of his surroundings. Johnny Collins was sitting in a window booth, reading a paper.

Smith saw the waitress spill the coffee. He continued to covertly watch as the two conversed and read an article in the newspaper. Smith wondered what was so important. He turned and began moving away. He continued until he found a newspaper vending machine.

As he stood examining the various machines, he scanned the front pages to see if anything unusual caught his eye. When he didn't see anything specific, he decided to get a copy of all three papers. It might take him a while but he would discover what had made Johnny Collins so nervous.

With the three papers under his arm, he decided to walk back towards the restaurant where he had seen Collins. He ducked his head when he saw Collins walking toward the exit.

Holding one of the papers in front of his face, he walked around the corner and waited until Collins passed. Once Collins was safely out of sight, Victor walked into the restaurant and took Johnny's old booth.

He ordered coffee and sat and read the front pages of all three newspapers. On the last paper, he saw the article about Sarah Cummings' death. With a smile on his face, he took his pocketknife out of his pocket and caressed it. He was grinning from ear to ear.

CHAPTER FORTY-SEVEN

By late Sunday afternoon, Johnny finally had time to reflect and collect his thoughts. He had spent most of the morning with Lt. Larson. He knew he had about an hour before his meeting with Joe's lawyer, Terrance Ruddick.

He sat on the edge of his hotel bed. All around him was his brother Joe's personal effects. He had the box of things that Peggy had given him. On the other side was the pillowcase full of things that he had retrieved from one of the earlier trips to Joe's house. In another bag were the items that he had picked up from the coroner's office.

On the floor in front of him was the bag of flour that he had taken out of the refrigerator when he was at the house with Lt. Clausen. He had already disposed of all of the food that he had taken out of the refrigerator.

Also, in front of him was a box of things that he brought from his last trip with Ruddick. In his pocket was the small packet he had retrieved from the flour. He also had the envelope that Sarah Cummings had given him regarding the suspicious sale of Joe's property.

He paused to consider a course of action, and began methodically looking through each collection, item by item. He handled and inspected every item closely. As he finished each one, he divided it in one of two piles. One pile he would send back to Iowa and the other he would give to the cleaning ladies in the hotel to dispose of as they deemed fit.

He narrowed down the items to be sent back to Iowa to just a few. After mentally sizing up his suitcase, he thought he could probably squeeze those items in. Positive that he didn't want the other pile, he pushed it away from the bed with his foot.

He bent over and picked up the items from the coroner's office. The first thing that he took out of the bag was Joe's wallet. Tears involuntarily welled up and his throat ached.

He pulled out an old, faded picture of Joe with his wife and two children. For a time he softly viewed the picture and then carefully ran his finger over each person remembering how they had once been.

He pulled out another picture. It was taken when Joe and he were youngsters. They were standing beside an obviously new shiny Radio Flyer wagon. Johnny remembered the Christmas they had gotten the wagon and reached for a tissue on the nightstand. He read the back of the picture. It was dated 1946.

Digging through another compartment, Johnny found a receipt to a car repair shop. It was located in Sparks. Johnny put it on the nightstand and decided to call the business the next day when it should be open.

Shaking the wallet upside down, a small slip of paper fell out. He carefully unfolded it and saw the words "unscrew the bottom of bottles and take apart the frames". This was the same message he had uncovered in the cipher paper that he had taken from the freezer earlier in the week.

Johnny thought about the words, knowing they had to mean something special, but he had no idea what. Then it stuck him. He understood the message. He eagerly leapt to the open box that had the three champagne bottles in it. He gingerly lifted one of the bottles and unscrewed the bottom of it.

The bottom twisted off in Johnny's hand. "Wow!" he exclaimed, as several sparkling diamonds fell into his hand and on the floor.

"So that is where the diamonds came from," Johnny said to himself as he reached into his pocket and carefully took out the small packet that he had found in the flour.

He quickly cleared off the top of the desk and spread a towel over the surface. On his hands and knees, he carefully gathered up the diamonds that were on the floor. Taking the diamonds from the three bottles and the packet from the flour, he worked with a certain precision, placing them carefully on the towel.

"So this is why people were killed," Johnny mused aloud.

Next, he took a painting and carefully studied the frame. With his pocketknife, he pulled one of the ends loose. The frame was hollow. He shook it over the towel and several more diamonds fell out. Within minutes, he had removed all the diamonds from the frames.

He was admiring the gems when he heard a knock on his door. He answered loudly, "Just a minute. I have to finish dressing."

He looked around the room, wondering what to do with the diamonds. He remembered that leaving things in plain sight is often the best place to hide something. He casually placed a shirt over the top of the diamonds and quickly screwed the bottoms onto the bottles and returned them to the box. He carefully put the paintings back in the portfolio.

Leaving everything else spread out all over the room, he walked to the door and opened it.

"Nice to see you again," he said, as Terrance Ruddick entered the room.

Ruddick was dressed in a dark three-piece suit and looked as if he had just come from church. He carried a large black leather briefcase. "I am hoping that we can get this finished today so you can get back to your family," Ruddick said.

Collins brushed a pair of Joe's trousers from a chair and pointed to it. "Have a seat. Sorry about the mess. I've been going through Joe's things."

Ruddick peered over his dark horn rimmed glasses before he spoke. "That's all right. I can imagine that here is as suitable place as any place to check things out."

He sat down and placed the briefcase on his lap. "I have drawn up papers for you to sign. First is the agreement with the city to sell Joe's land to them for the park." He pulled out a long document and handed it to Johnny to read. It was mostly standard form with only the legal description and the contract amount listed.

"Yes, I think this is fine now that Larson has verified that the signature on Sarah's document wasn't Joe's. Do you think that we will have any problems with her estate regarding the document?"

The attorney shook his head. "No, I doubt that we will hear about it from anyone." He indicated his briefcase. "I stopped by the police station earlier today and got a paper from them stating that it wasn't Joe's signature. I have their document here in my briefcase and I intend to keep it just in case."

The attorney handed Johnny a pen. "Just sign it on the bottom dotted line. I will make sure that payment for the land is sent to you in Iowa."

Johnny did as he was told without giving the matter another thought. He hadn't told his wife about the value of the land and wondered what she and the children would say when they found out that after taxes and expenses the sale of Joe's land would net over a million dollars.

The attorney glanced sideways at Johnny and asked, "You do realize that you will have to pay taxes and my fees, which will be well within the norm for this area, from the sale of the property? There might also be some transfer costs involved."

Johnny nodded, signed the paper and handed it back to Ruddick. "Yes, I completely understand, if Joe trusted you, then I can too," he said. "This is business."

"When I was with Larson earlier today, I showed him this receipt," Johnny said. He pulled out the receipt that fell out of the bag that Sarah Cummings had given him with the champagne bottle in it. "This is a receipt for a standard sales agreement form from Staples. It is dated about a week ago."

Ruddick chuckled softly. "What did Larson say?"

Johnny answered, "He advised me to give the receipt to you for safe keeping. He said it was just a further collaborating piece of evidence that the Property Sales Agreement couldn't have been signed by Joe."

Ruddick took the receipt and paper-clipped it to the agreement that Johnny had just signed. He reached into his briefcase and brought out another document. "This is a copy of Joe's life insurance policy. It is for a million dollars. He named you as the beneficiary."

Johnny gasped. "I didn't know that Joe had this."

Ruddick chuckled again and handed a paper to Johnny. "I love this job," he said. "Just sign here and I'll have it processed."

Johnny signed the paper but his hand was shaking. He felt weak. He remembered the diamonds and walked to the desk and took the shirt carefully off of them. "I want you to look at these," he said to Ruddick.

Without talking, Ruddick put down his briefcase and walked to the desk. He frowned and then asked, "Where did these come from?"

Johnny walked over and took a champagne bottle and unscrewed the bottom of it. Then, he took a painting out of the portfolio and shook the frame. He said, "I found them in these bottles and the hollow frames."

It was Ruddick' turn to gasp. "Wow, this is probably the reason that Joe was killed. How did you find them?" He picked up a couple diamonds and held them up to the light. He just shook his head in disbelief.

By late in the afternoon, Ruddick and Johnny finished all of the legal paperwork and together walked down stairs to the lobby. Ruddick patted his briefcase several times as they walked.

"I'll make sure that everything I have in here is taken care of tomorrow. You make sure that you talk to Larson about those items you have upstairs." He started to walk away, then turned and walked back to Johnny. He gave him a fatherly hug and said, "It has been great meeting and working with you. Now, you take care of yourself and stay safe."

Without looking back, the old man turned and walked through the lobby and out the door.

CHAPTER FORTY-EIGHT

It was just after nine when Johnny walked into the Reno Police Department. He stopped in front of the policeman at the desk and asked, "May I speak to Lt. Larson?"

The policeman recognized Johnny and nodded. "I think that he is expecting you. You did call earlier this morning, didn't you?"

Johnny ambled casually along the narrow hallway to Lt. Larson's small office. As he neared the office, he could hear Larson in a loud voice apparently making heated remarks to someone either in person or on the phone. Johnny strained to hear what was being said but couldn't make out any words.

He hesitated, then approached the open door, rapped his knuckles on the frame and stuck his head in. "The man at the front desk sent me down," he said. "I hope that I'm not here at the wrong time."

Lt. Larson's face was beet red and he definitely was not talking on the phone. It was obvious to Johnny that the other man, Tom Clausen, was the target of Larson's tirade. Larson glanced at Johnny, then turned to Clausen and reached for a phone. He asked for someone to come to his office immediately.

Johnny stepped aside as two policemen rapidly came through the hall and into Larson's office. He could hear Larson say, "Take this man out of her and read him his rights like anyone else. Then, place him under arrest. I'll charge him later." Larson called, "Collins, come in here."

Johnny walked into the already crowded room. He stared at Clausen and the two policemen.

Larson looked at the two policemen and said, "Let's show some respect for the uniform. You don't need to handcuff him. Just escort him to the interrogation room and give him a chance to call a lawyer."

"Yes, sir," the men answered in unison. Each man walked around Clausen and stood beside him, one on each side.

Clausen glared at Larson and then at Collins but didn't say a word. Silently, he walked out of Larson's office between the two policemen.

Once the three men left Larson motioned for Johnny to close his door. He sat down behind his desk and motioned for Johnny to take a seat.

"I suppose you wonder what this is all about, don't you?" he asked looking candidly at Johnny.

Johnny leaned back in his chair and ran his hands up and down his jeans. "Yes, I would like to know."

Larson shifted in his chair and turned it sideways. He gazed at the wall for a few seconds and then shifted his eyes to Johnny's face. "I suspect Clausen is a killer. I believe he deliberately killed Terry Granger, an old man." He rubbed his forehead a couple times and added, "And, all the evidence points to a conclusion that he killed Sarah Cummings."

Johnny was stunned. He croaked out, "I can hardly believe that. Why would he kill them?"

Larson leaned his arms on his desktop and simply answered, "Greed."

"Do you think that he killed my brother Joe?" Johnny asked.

"No, I think Joe and Charlie McGuire were both killed by a man from California but we haven't been able to locate him. We suspect that they were both killed because of an antique deal that went bad."

Johnny reached into his pocket and pulled out a zip lock bag. He handed it to Larson.

"What is this," Larson asked. He took the bag and looked at it. "That looks like diamonds."

"Yes, I believe they are. I am no expert but from my untrained eye I would say they were very good ones."

Larson held the bag up to the light, examined them closer, frowned and asked, "And, my friend, where did you get them?"

Johnny reached down and took out a champagne bottle and small painting from the bag that he was carrying. He didn't answer but carefully unscrewed the bottom of the bottle and opened the hollow frame. "I found them inside these," he indicated. He put the two items on top of Larson's desk.

Larson studied the items carefully. "This is ingenious," he muttered as he connected them. "Where did you get these?"

Johnny leaned back in his chair and folded the bag into a small square and stuck it in his pocket. "These were in a furniture shipment that Charlie McGuire bought. I found these under the floorboards at Joe's house."

"Under the floor boards," Larson exclaimed. "I had my men check that house and they didn't find anything."

"It was under a trap door that was hidden by an oriental rug that had been nailed securely to the floor. Your men probably thought that the rug was so secured down all that they didn't check it closer."

Larson sighed. "Wouldn't you know it? I guess the next time I'll have to tell them to check such things." He played with the zip lock bag in his hand. "So these were in the bottles and frames? Evidently the items were never intended to be in the furniture shipment." He thought for a moment and then asked, "I wonder who they were intended for?"

Johnny answered, "Hard telling. They perhaps were going to be used to buy drugs, guns or almost any contraband. Maybe even sell them for hard currency. I'm not sure that we will ever know."

Larson mulled Johnny's remarks over. "We will find out someday, but it might take some time." He raised the bag in the air and questioned, "You do know that I will have to keep these? You didn't think that you were going to be able to keep them, did you?"

Johnny laughed. "I can only dream. But, I knew that once I told you about them that you would inventory and keep them for evidence." He thought for a moment and then asked, "What will happen to them eventually?"

Larson shrugged. "Probably become state or city property and be sold for hard cash, which in turn would be used to keep the city or state government running."

"Well, that's what I thought," Johnny answered. "May I ask why Clausen kill Granger? Granger seemed like such a helpless old man."

Larson thought for a moment and then answered, "Clausen admitted to the hit but claimed that Granger walked out into the street in front of him. However, we have a witness that saw Granger talking to Sarah Cummings earlier in the week at a storage unit near the airport. They were overheard talking about your brother Joe's land and the fact that the city wanted to buy it. We know that Clausen and Sarah cooked up the plot to get Joe's property with the phony sales agreement. He admitted that this morning. He was also the last person who was seen with Sarah Cummings the night she was killed. Everything else fell into place."

Johnny stood up and took a step toward the door. He asked, "What about finding the man that killed Joe, do you think that you will find him?"

Larson ran his fingers through his hair. "It may take time but eventually we will find someone that can give us a good description. We know Joe was killed at the end of his driveway. We found a discarded flashlight in the driveway with his fingerprints on it. We also found traces of Joe's blood there. We believe someone tried to force him into a car."

"I guess I didn't ask before, but where was Joe's body found?"

"In the river outside of his front door. Two young boys found him. They were trying to catch a turtle for a science project."

Johnny glanced at his watch and then at Lt. Larson. He took another step toward the door and said, "I'm going to have to go. I have to return my rental car and I have a flight in about four hours. With all the security at the airports these days I don't want to be delayed."

Larson stood up and shook Johnny's hand. Then he said, "There is something else that I just found out this morning. Your brother was dying. He had radiation poisoning."

"What? How would that be?"

"We ran some tests and believe it was from some of the furniture that he had. We have a crew over at the Antique Mall now. They are confiscating all of that primitive furniture. We suspect it came from Chernobyl in Russia. With all of these parts going together, everything is falling into place."

Johnny nodded. "You may well be right. I believe the agency discovered something similar about a year ago."

Larson used his hand to motion for Johnny to walk before him as the two began to leave the office. "I'm sure there is a Russian connection to all of this. I have my men checking the hotels in the area to see if any Russians are visiting or have been here in the past couple weeks."

Johnny laughed, "You will never find them. They would not come in and register as Russians. They would be as American as you or I."

"You are probably right," Larson said as he followed Johnny out of his office.

ASSIGNMENT: RENO, NEVADA

CHAPTER FORTY-NINE

It was almost two when Johnny Collins walked into the Reno-Tahoe International Airport Terminal. He had returned his rental car and checked his luggage for Mason City via Minneapolis at the airport curb.

He had just called his wife and told her when to expect him. His stomach growled. It had been several hours since he had eaten. He knew he had time to grab a sandwich before boarding his flight.

After checking out of the hotel, he had stopped by the funeral home and signed all the necessary papers to have his brother's body shipped back to Iowa. Earlier he had thought he would have his brother cremated but he decided to have Joe's body flown back instead.

The funeral director didn't know exactly when the body would arrive but assured Johnny it would be within a day or so. That gave him time to finalize the burial arrangements in Iowa.

Terrance Ruddick had also contacted Johnny before he left his hotel room. The attorney had already been to the city offices and filed the necessary papers to sell Joe's property. He was making arrangements to have Joe's house emptied.

Johnny had told Ruddick about Joe's 1942 Ford pickup that was being restored in Sparks. He asked Ruddick to make arrangements to have it shipped to Iowa when all the restoration was complete.

As he left the Subway shop, Johnny wondered about Joe's desk and chair. He was sure Lt. Larson would arrange to have all the pieces confiscated and destroyed. He had also called Larson and left a message regarding the furniture.

The terminal entrance was crowded. Several lines had formed for various procedures. Johnny read the overhead instructions and began walking towards the security line that would allow him to pass through to the gates.

He stepped around a lady with two small children in a stroller and headed toward the line that allowed those with tickets to proceed. As he stepped into line, he felt a nudge.

"Well, Mr. Collins, you are leaving Reno today?" Victor Smith asked as the two men stood face to face.

Johnny nodded, smiled and glanced around. "Where is your friend Gannon?"

"Oh, he is off doing something else. I am headed back to Texas. You know business calls," Smith answered casually.

"Oh, yes, how well I know," answered Johnny. He shifted the carry-on bag to his other shoulder. It was filled with souvenirs he had gotten for his wife and children.

"Are you going back to Iowa?" Smith asked stepping back so that an attractive flight attendant could pass. His eyes followed her as she turned toward her gate and out of his eyesight.

Johnny took a step forward and said, "Yes, time to get back to the family."

"That's nice," Smith said. He looked at Johnny for a moment and then asked, "Did you get all of your brother's affairs settled?"

"Yes, I think so," Johnny answered. He didn't feel like telling the man anything else about his personal matters.

The security attendant motioned for Johnny to walk through the metal detector. Johnny nodded and placed his carry-on bag on the moving belt and walked through. By the time he picked up his bag on the other side, Smith was through and standing beside him.

Smith extended his hand and Collins took it. "Have a safe flight," Smith said.

Collins automatically responded, "You too."

Smith stopped to listen to an announcement that was being broadcast over the loud speaker. "That's my flight," Smith called as he moved away and headed quickly toward his gate. He looked back at Collins and mouthed something.

Collins watched Smith and frowned. He wasn't able to hear Smith's last words but it looked as if Smith had said, "See you in Washington."

Johnny stood still for several moments, studying Smith's movements until he vanished from his sight.

"What is it about that man that is so familiar? I know I've met him somewhere before," Collins muttered to himself as he turned and walked slowly to his gate. Just as the gate attendant called Johnny's flight something flashed through his mind.

ELIZABETH JUNG

"San Angelo, Texas doesn't have a state university," he muttered aloud. "It's Angelo State University." Automatically, he handed the boarding pass to the agent and began walking down the enclosed walkway to the plane. He stopped in mid step and said, "Damn, that was Viktor Schmidt. I knew that I had seen that walk."

####

ABOUT THE AUTHOR

Elizabeth Jung was born and raised on a farm near Danbury, in Western Iowa, one of seven children. After graduating from Danbury Catholic, she received her AA degree at Mt. Mercy, in Cedar Rapids, Iowa. After her children graduated, she returned to college and received her Bachelor of Arts degree in Business Administration.

She has lived and traveled extensively in the United States and Europe. In her writing, she draws on this knowledge and real life experiences to create in-depth realistic stories.

Ms. Jung has written three previous intrigue novels, *The Budapest Connection*, *Game Between Spies* and *Project Eve*. Her latest novel, *Assignment: Reno, Nevada* combines local and international color. She is presently working on her fifth novel, *Iowa's Double Agent*.

Her books may be obtained through any major bookstore in the world and from most internet on-line book stores. All books are available both in paperback and hardcover.

She spends her time writing, reading, antiquing and gardening at her lakeside home in Clear Lake, Iowa. She has three grown children, two sons and one daughter and two grandchildren, one boy and one girl.

Printed in the United States
24817LVS00001B/370-378